To Dee

Love

Peta

Knight

HEAVEN PROMISES NO FAVOURS

PART I

Peta Knight

authorHOUSE®

AuthorHouse™ UK Ltd.
500 Avebury Boulevard
Central Milton Keynes, MK9 2BE
www.authorhouse.co.uk
Phone: 08001974150

© 2012 Peta Knight. All rights reserved.

No part of this book may be reproduced, stored in a retrieval system, or transmitted by any means without the written permission of the author.

First published by AuthorHouse 3/21/2012

ISBN: 978-1-4567-8742-4 (sc)
ISBN: 978-1-4567-8761-5 (e)

Any people depicted in stock imagery provided by Thinkstock are models, and such images are being used for illustrative purposes only. Certain stock imagery © Thinkstock.

This book is printed on acid-free paper.

Because of the dynamic nature of the Internet, any web addresses or links contained in this book may have changed since publication and may no longer be valid. The views expressed in this work are solely those of the author and do not necessarily reflect the views of the publisher, and the publisher hereby disclaims any responsibility for them.

All characters appearing in this work are fictitious. Any resemblance to real persons, living or dead, is purely coincidental.

Preface

At the tender age of 12 years Gregoire Vasilov Fellini witnessed the brutal beating of his Italian father at the hands of Russian guards whilst he and a small group of fellow artists attempted to flee from the harsh regime imposed by the occupying forces during the Hungarian uprising, having innocently fallen foul of the authorities.

When his beautiful Russian mother ran to plead for her husband they shot him and the rest of the group, threw her to the ground and raped her.

The boy courageously tried to intervene pounding the burly guards to no avail. With raucous laughter they picked him up and tossed him from one to the other, then rode off leaving him kneeling beside his dead father and dying mother. His thin body convulsed with sobs as he watched her die.

He dragged each of the bodies to a deep crevice in the snow, buried them with his bare hands, then lay between the two mounds and wept, the freshly falling snow serving as a blanket protecting him a little from the elements.

After a while he stood up. Horrified at the carnage around him, he brushed the tears and the snow from his face. His eyes transfixed on the deep red stains spreading around the bodies of his peers. He was the only one left alive and for the rest of his days he never understood why they had not killed him with the rest of the group.

Half crazy with grief and fear he persevered on his perilous journey alone and terrified, hatred and revenge in his heart.

Unsure of the way forward he plodded on, half crawling when his boots sank into the deep snow. A small lonely figure he learned to lie, steal and beg in his efforts to stay alive.

When a straggling band of disorganised renegades captured him at gunpoint he was terrified, but almost relieved at the sight of other human beings. He pleaded and grovelled with then and with calculated cunning, persuaded them to help him.

For reasons best known to themselves they took him with them to a disused camp, where exhausted and half frozen the boy passed out.

They revived him and fed him and although he was weak they made him slave for them.

He became adept at keeping a low profile. He amused them with his quick wit and bouts of charm which often saved him from a beating.

They tormented him and abused him in turn but they kept him alive, sharing with him their meagre rations.

Even so Gregoire was terrified of them and he hated them.

After weeks, traipsing from one camp to the next he managed to escape, when a brawl broke out between them and another contingent of soldiers.

When, with a few stolen roubles by the grace of god and a superhuman effort to survive he finally reached his paternal grandparents in Italy, he was little more than a savage.

It took them all their strength and understanding to tame this angry man child.

They cared for him, shed tears for him and did their utmost to love him, but he was like a frightened animal, unable to respond to their love.

For three years they nurtured him, educated him, encouraged him to trust and eventually to love them, so that by the age of 15 they had moulded him into a reasonably law abiding citizen.

Then when his elderly grandfather died followed two years later by his grandmother Gregoire cried his last tears, sold the farm he had inherited and with the generous legacy left to him by his grandparents, packed his few belongings and left.

He travelled across the continent to France performing menial tasks, washing greasy dishes in bistros and restaurants, cleaning, labouring etc until he was fortunate enough - to join up with a small travelling theatre group.

He learned his craft the hard way, working enthusiastically day and night learning the trade from every angle.

He took dance classes and language classes. He already had a vast knowledge of music and played several instruments.

He worked solidly, almost frantically until he had grasped every aspect of the workings of the theatre, from sweeping the stage, to preparing props. From call boy to directing and producing. He seemed too good to be true but his determination to succeed was phenomenal.

He excelled as an actor and was hilarious in comedy.

He had natural charisma and became a favourite with provincial audiences. He kept himself aloof, talked to no-one. In his spare moments and late into the night he studied hard to perfect his French and improve his English. He was a loner, took life seriously, seldom smiled. He had no time for frivolity, anger still churning inside of him. He was 18 years of age when Jacques le Roux, scouring the provinces for talent noticed him.

Fascinated with this intense young performer he studied him over the weeks and at the end of the season offered him work in Paris and later London.

He took him under his wing, unofficially adopted him, introduced him to the ballet and Gregoire knew instantly that this was where his future lay.

Le Roux realised his great potential not only as an accomplished performer but the unusual beauty of this young man. He was tall, his countenance, passionate and intense, bore the premature lines of pain, struggle and hardship, but it was the haunted look in his beautiful flecked grey eyes. Majestic, penetrating and cold as steel, shaded by dense black lashes which fascinated Le Roux.

After many months working closely together Jacques La Roux with careful strategy persuaded the young man to talk about the horrors of his childhood, releasing gradually some of his pent up anger and heartache. He clasped the youth in his arms, soothing him with wise compassionate words.

"Let it go boy" he said "revenge is a cancer, do not let it destroy you".

"I can never forgive, I can never forget" Gregoire declared with forceful passion.

"Of course not" Jacques agreed. "But you must let go of the past. You are alive, you have survived the horrors. You have a great future. Let the past go boy – think to the future."

Le Roux taught him the rudiments of the ballet as well as introducing him to the pleasantries of living, tried to instil into him the quality of life. Gregoire and Jacques worked together for 4 years.

The youth's style and technique were unbelievable as he danced much of the anger out of his system, delighting audiences wherever they went. Le Roux was proud and delighted with his protégée.

They travelled the continent and parts of America, eventually captivating audiences in London. It was one of the happiest periods in Gregoire's life, but he became restless and insular and Jacques realised he was ready to move on.

He helped him to acquire a small theatre in a provincial town in the North of England, where the youth expressed a wish to remain. He liked England, felt comfortable and safe. Here he became aquainted with Justin Costello, a few years his junior and although their personalities were completely different, they gathered a collection of out of work artists and got to work forming a company.

Though they worked well together in harmony and mostly in silence, Gregoire still reserved to a degree of hostility.

They produced and took part in all of their productions until later, again with the help and advice of Jacques Le Roux he rented and eventually bought the Little Daly, a failing theatre in London.

He was only 24 and Justin 21 years of age when they wrote and produced their own full length ballet together.

Now 20 years later he had established himself as an accomplished master of the ballet, not only conducting his own shows but with the help and cooperation of his partner Justin, training his own dancers.

He was a genius, a maker of stars and eventually became known throughout Europe. He lived quietly and comfortably, if not ostentatiously in a large, old house in the heart of his adopted city London, with his housekeeper and friend Maddie, and although on his way to becoming a multi millionaire, he was generous with his wealth, sponsoring and taking an interest in new young talent.

He had escorted many beautiful women over the years, but had never married. He was always impeccably dressed although on the eccentric side, and although he had mellowed since Jacques Le Roux had befriended him, he was sometimes still a formidable figure to be reckoned with.

His values were high and he sustained this quality throughout his life.

Chapter 1

Gregoire Fellini ran his company with a rod of iron. He was ruthless with his dancers; stood no nonsense. Ballet was his field and if you did not share his enthusiasm, you had better not be there. He could raise the hopes of the students with one word of praise, only to dash their spirits the next day with angry criticisms.

Many young hopefuls floundered after only a few weeks of training, some were turned away. He demanded perfection, was hard and strict, but he always obtained results. His technique and expertise were second to none. Students came from far and wide to audition in the hope of working and studying with him. He made no charge for his services. Serious minded and dedicated he drove himself and his students to the limit. He chose each one carefully, spelling out the pros and cons of becoming one of his dancers. He was seldom wrong in his judgement and if some failed to aspire to his high standards, there were many who thrived under his method of teaching. At this moment he found himself about to break the rules of a lifetime.

He paused before going through to the studio to instruct his class of first year students. Scrutinising each one of the 20 youngsters, his eye alighted on the new recruit. He had agreed with some misgiving to take Trudi's little au pair. It was against his principles to accept or to mete out favours, but Trudi, his secretary, had pleaded with him to at least see her. He recalled the conversation he had with her last week.

'I promised I would ask you', she said. 'She is so keen to dance. She is quite delightful, Greg. She is graceful and so beautiful.'

'Beauty is no guarantee', Greg was dubious. 'Why don't you enrol her in a local dance school?'

'She is shy, innocent. I am responsible for her. Her parents were very reluctant for her to leave France and I can be sure she would come to no harm with you.'

'Hmmm.' Greg was not impressed.

'She is so young, not yet seventeen, and I believe you will agree with me, she is different Greg'.

'Different! I see. What do her parents do?'

'They are farmers, very strict apparently.'

'Oh, all right Trudi. You know I cannot treat her any differently from other contenders. If she is not good material, she will have to leave. Are you prepared for that? Will she be?'

'Of course'.

'I hope so. Send her along on Saturday. I will take a look at her'.

The diversity from his usual strict procedure bothered Greg. He had to doubt in his mind that this was just another frustrated stage-struck youngster and he was not relishing the idea of having to disappoint her and Trudi. He had arranged for Justin, his partner, to sit in on the class with him. His assessment would probably be less stringent than his own. Now they stood looking at her. Greg beckoned her to come forward, to the front of the class.

He recognised Nicole's potential the moment she walked across the stage. Both he and Justin were stunned by her childlike beauty. They watched her closely. Greg was impressed with the way she was able to follow most of the steps with the rest of the class. She was a natural, her movements graceful and strong.

'What do you think, Justin', Greg asked.

'She's damned good, I would have no hesitation in taking her on. Who is she?'

'She is Trudi's au pair, Nicole Perrin, and I agree, she is a treasure.'

When the class was over, Greg motioned for her to stay.

'Sit down Nicole', he said. 'I am Dr Fellini, this is my partner Justin Portello. I understand you are interested in becoming a dancer, is that so?'

'Oui Monsieur'.

'Very well.' He proceeded to warn her of the rigorous commitments she would be expected to undertake. Justin interrupted, sensing that the girl did not understand a lot of what Greg was saying. She was becoming nervous.

'How old are you, Nicole?' he asked.

'Next week I am seventeen', she said.

'Well', he turned to Greg, 'I think we could give her a trial, don't you'.

'Very well.' Greg looked at her. 'Go with Justin, he will acquaint you with the rules etc. I will telephone Trudi. You will attend here at 8.30 sharp next Saturday. Justin will be looking after you.'

'Oui Monsieur, merci'.

Justin took Nicole's arm and led her into the tiny office adjacent to the stage.

'Have you attended any other dance school, Nicole?' he asked.

'Non Monsieur. I dance by myself at home. In France we go to the ballet sometimes, Monsieur.'

'Justin, you may call me Justin. You will be in my class for a little while and then I am sure you will progress very quickly into Dr Fellini's class.'

'Oui Monsieur.'

'Justin', he prompted. 'I daresay you are thirsty. I will get you a drink.... orange, coke, tea, coffee...?'

'Orange Monsieur, merci. Oui, I am a little thirsty'.

Justin talked to her, putting her at ease, then let her go. 'Until Saturday then Nicole'.

Greg telephoned his secretary. 'Your little au pair is very promising Trudi. I was surprised and gratified that I have not had to disappoint you. I will see you tomorrow when you can fill me in regarding her background. She will study first with Justin each Saturday morning. Make sure she is on time.'

Justin was amazed with her alacrity to learn. She made few mistakes and her graceful movements were a joy to watch. He would have liked to keep her in his class, but he knew she would soon be ready for more advanced work, which meant that Greg would be instructing her.

Within a few weeks, she had lost most of her shyness due to Justin's gentle handling and he wondered how she would react to Greg's strict, unbending method. He made a point of talking to him.

'You remember Nicole Perrin,' he asked him.

'Of course. Trudi's little au pair. How is she getting on?'

'Why don't you drop in and see for yourself.'

'And that means?' Greg said.

'It mans that she is extremely good, probably ready for your class.'
'I'll look in on Saturday.'
'Greg, she is gentle, innocent, vulnerable.'
'What are you trying to say to me, Justin?'
'Go easy on her. She is not a toughy.'
'Oh dear Justin, sometimes I despair of your expressions. A 'toughy', what does that mean?'
'You know exactly what I mean, Greg. Perhaps she should stay with me for a few more months until she gets used to the routine here. She has been very sheltered – a little timid, like a child.'
'I am afraid she must take her chances. I will look in on Saturday.'

The following week Greg joined Justin. He sat back and lit a cigarette. Justin's look of disapproval did not escape Greg.
'Do you wish to instruct the class then?' he asked.
'No Justin, they will work better with you, they will not yet be used to my methods.'
'I would rather you refrained from smoking during my class, Greg.'

Greg took a few more drags from the cigarette, then obliged. He watched for half an hour then asked Justin to meet him outside after the class. They sat at the desk in the office. Greg poured Justin and himself a whisky.
'All right Justin, I agree, you have done well with her'.
'She takes direction extremely well, Greg. I hardly ever have to correct her. I would rather you did not push her too much at first'.
'All right Justin. I see you have taken quite a shine to her'.
'It's not that, it is just that she is very sensitive'.
'You know, my friend, we cannot keep her wrapped in cotton wool – that would do no good at all.'
'Just take it slowly with her, I beg you.'
Greg was becoming irritated and changed the subject.
'I noticed' he said 'there are one or two others almost ready to progress to my class,'
'Greg! Nicole! She really is quite timid'.
'Just tell her, Justin, what to expect in my sessions. I will expect to see her next Saturday at 9am.'

Chapter 2

Justin was well aware that Greg would do exactly as he saw fit with Nicole. However, he hoped he had at least made it clear how unworldly the child was. She needed understanding and patience, especially as she did not always comprehend the language and for the first few weeks, Greg took little notice of her apart from a correction here and there, taking Justin's advice and letting her get acquainted with his method of teaching. He watched and encouraged her with patience.

After a while, however, he began to work her as hard as the others. When she faltered, his vitriolic tongue lashed her unmercifully, many times reducing her to tears. He praised and criticised her in turn, becoming angry when she misunderstood his instructions.

'You obviously have a language problem. Would you like me to present you with a dictionary? Please listen to what I tell you.'

Once, after a particularly gruelling session, she broke down, collapsed exhausted in front of him. He strode purposefully towards her and with the long staff he always carried, he prodded her.

'Get up', he commanded.

She was so terrified she did as he commanded. He stared at her, the tears running down her cheeks. He dismissed the rest of the class, ordered her to stay. Walking to the side of the room he picked up a box of tissues and handed them to her.

'Do you wish to stay with us, Nicole?'

'Oui Monsieur.'

'Right, go through the exercise I have just taught you.'

She dried her tears and did as he instructed. He made her repeat the exercise twice more.

'Good' he said, 'why did you not do this in class?'
She began to weep again.
'For God sake girl, don't start that again.'
She quickly composed herself.

'Listen to me,' he said. He took hold of her shoulders. God how frail she was. He shook her slightly.

'Listen to me', he repeated. 'You have the making of an excellent dancer, but if you wish to continue with this company, you must learn that there will be no time for tears or tantrums. These emotions are of no use to me, no matter how good you are. There is only time for dance and hard work. Do not expect an easy ride with me, Nicole. You will work until you are perfect and then continue to work harder. Come now, dry your tears, go home, rest and you will return on Monday at 9. I am transferring you to the theatre class. You will find the work hard, strenuous, but I am sure you will manage. For the theatre class we use the stage above the studio. Justin will instruct you sometimes, but it will be mostly me. I will have a word with Trudi later. She will need to replace you.'

'Merci Monsieur.'
'Go along now. Remember you will attend here every morning at 9.'
Greg watched her leave… 'and do not ever be late for your classes' he threw at her.

He sighed, lit a cigarette, then turned as he heard a familiar rustle from the wings. He banged his staff on the boards, his irritation rising.

'What the hell are you doing here again?' he yelled. 'I told you yesterday to stop bothering me. Go home boy.'

'I only wanted to watch', Jed faltered.

'What for? It will do you no good. Go home before I lose my temper.'

Twelve year old Jed Paxton hurried away determined to return as often as he could. He bumped into Nicole at the stage door.

'Hello Nicki, I'm Jed' he introduced himself.

'I know, I see you hiding in the wings sometimes. I do not know how you are not afraid of monsieur, he always gets so angry'.

'May I walk home with you?' he asked shyly.

She nodded. 'Why do you keep coming? He always sends you away. Aren't you afraid when he gets so cross?'

'A bit maybe – I love watching him. And you, Nicki – I want to join his company when I leave school if he will let me.'

'You are crazy, you are just a boy.'

'I'm nearly thirteen' he protested. 'It's what I want. You are really good, Nicki. He knows you are good.'

'He was angry with me. I do not like when he is angry' she told him.

'Why do you stay then? As far as I can see, he is always in a bad temper.'

'Like you, I hope one day he will take me into his company. And I love to dance.'

Jed gazed admiringly at her. 'You are lucky' he said to her. 'He has picked you out. He will make you a star. I like watching you, Nicki, you are better than all the others!'

'Thank you Jed, but I do not think that is true'.

'Yes it is. You are so beautiful, Nicki'.

'Well'…she looked around nervously…'if he comes out and finds us here, he will be angry again.'

'Don't be silly, anyway he never comes this way.'

'You seem to know everything.'

'I have been coming here after school and in the holidays for over a year. He doesn't often catch me.'

They walked a little way together then went their separate ways.

At the end of two months Greg took Nicole from the morning class and transferred her to the corps de ballet.

'This does not mean, Nicole, that your sessions with me are over. You will still attend the class for a while and then we shall see how you progress. Now go to the office and Justin will instruct you regarding rehearsal times etc. Also, you will be on the payroll – I assume you have a permit to work here?'

'Oui Monsieur, Trudi was very kind, she helped me and she…'

'Yes, yes. Well, the money will not be much, but I'm sure you will make use of it.'

'Merci Monsieur', she smiled up at him. 'Merci.'

'Do not forget you will attend the morning class. Be here on time please.'

Jed meanwhile watched avidly every move and instruction Greg rasped out to the students, but he kept out of sight. Mick, the stage door keeper, let him in, sometimes selecting a secluded spot in the auditorium so that he could occasionally watch a performance.

'Keep out of his way boy or you will get me the sack', he warned.

Every spare moment he could muster after school, during every holiday,

Jed crept into one or other of his hiding places so that he could observe the master. When he returned home he would practise everything he had learned. Quite often, he managed to walk home with his idol. They talked – she told him of her life in France.

'My maman does not know that I am dancing', she confided. 'She would not like it, you see. She believes I am here to do some helping as an au pair for Madame Trudi, Monsieur Fellini's secretary, to look after her little girl. She helps me to get a permit for the working. She was very nice. She let me audition for monsieur. I have always wanted to dance. I feel very guilty because Trudi has to find another au pair and I must find another place to live. She says there is not a hurry, but I must do it soon. Why are you smiling at me like that?'

'I love listening to you talk, Nicole.'

'My English is bad it is true.'

'Your English is perfect, it is just the way you say the words.'

'You will teach me to say them properly, Jed?'

'You say them perfectly, Nicki.'

'That is not true. My papa is clever – he tried to teach me every day.'

'Nicole', Jed was suddenly quite excited. 'Come and stay with us. My Gran is lovely – she won't mind. We have a great big house and there is only my sister, Gran and Granddad and me. There is plenty of room. Please say you will come.'

'Are you sure they would not mind?' Nicole was a little apprehensive. 'I could pay a little now that I am working.'

'Of course they won't mind. You'll love my Gran. Why don't you come home with me now and meet them. You could have lunch with us.

'Oh no, I could not do that. It would be impolite.'

'Don't be silly – come on!'

'You had better ask first.'

'Oh, come on, it will be okay'.

Amy Paxton met them at the door.

'Hello Gran'. Jed threw his arm around his grandmother. 'This is Nicki – she is a ballerina from the theatre'.

'Hello my dear', Amy greeted her. 'So! You are one of the victims my grandson pesters every spare moment he gets.'

'Oh no, Madame, I am not a ballerina, I have only just started dancing.'

'But you will be Nicki, you will be.'

'Gran', Jed turned back to his grandmother, 'Nicki is looking for somewhere to stay. I told her to come here, she can can't she?'

'Well of course darling.' Amy looked concerned. 'But what about your parents, my dear? You are very young to be on your own.'

'My parents live in France, madame, and I shall be seventeen soon.' Nicole explained about Trudi. 'You see, now that monsieur Fellini says he will take me to dance in the ballet, Trudi must find another au pair.'

'I see. Well…seventeen, my goodness. You don't look any older than Jed here. Would you like to join us for lunch?'

'Merci Madame, you are very kind.'

So Nicole moved in with Jed's grandparents and he was over the moon with joy.

'You are my very good friend', Nicole told him, 'and your grand-mère is very kind.'

Chapter 3

Jed continued his clandestine visits to the theatre and afterwards walked home with Nicole.

'You must be very careful Jed,' Nicole warned. 'Monsieur will be very angry if he finds you hiding in the theatre.'

'Don't worry, he won't. I am very careful.'

He made himself useful to the theatre staff. They had become used to seeing him around. But over the next few weeks he was often careless about keeping out of sight of Greg, especially with the desire to watch Nicole's private sessions with the master. He hid behind the scenery or props, anywhere he could find, sometimes venturing nearer to the stage than was wise. Crouched in the wings where he could see them more clearly, waiting for the sessions to end, when he was able to slip out unnoticed and walk home with Nicole.

Greg sometimes kept her for over half an hour, correcting and perfecting her movements. She was often exhausted when he finally let her go. One such time she felt so tired, nervous, she paused as she brushed her hand across her face, then stumbled.

Greg looked at his watch, then glanced at Nicole, 'What is wrong with you girl, have you tired of the ballet already.

Nicole looked apologetically at him, 'I am a little tired Monsieur,' she dared to admit.

'What!' Greg bellowed. 'I am giving my time and you tell me you are tired. What is wrong with you? You are young you should relish the exercise!

'I am sorry Monsieur, I am alright now.'

Greg studied her and softened a little. She was tiny, so frail looking, perhaps this was too much for her and he could see she was struggling with her emotions. Then quite suddenly she burst into tears.

'All right Nicole,' he said kindly, 'get changed, go home and rest. Do not be late for this evening's performance.'

She stood still, eyes downcast.

'That is it now,' he said with slight exasperation.

'Nothing Monsieur'.

He walked over to her, lifted her chin so that she was looking up at him. 'What is it Nicole? Come dry your tears.'

He reached for some tissues and wiped her face, then placed a kiss on her forehead trying to reassure her and in so doing caused her heart to miss a beat.

'Off you go now,' he said.

He watched her leave the stage, his own peace of mind disturbed.

He felt protective towards this beautiful child – she would make an outstanding dancer given the confidence. There was something there, indefinable at the moment. He paced the boards slowly, contemplating, marvelling at her grace and overwhelming beauty. She had a rare talent.

Jed, wedged amongst the props off stage had unwittingly witnessed this unusually tender gesture and waited with baited breath for the master to leave, but Greg sat down on a box at the side, lit a cigarette and leaned back, deep in thought.

Jed was uncomfortable, his legs ached, he was holding a metal pole – his hands were becoming numb. His foot moved slightly, knocking a small round object which rolled across the boards in front of Greg, who turned, waited a few seconds then yelled.

'Alright boy, get out here at once!'

Jed froze. Maybe if he was quiet and still Greg would think he had been mistaken, when the metal pole slipped from his grasp crashing to the floor.

Greg waited, then, 'I am not in the habit of repeating myself boy. So if you know what is good for you, you will do as I say.'

Jed slowly, reluctantly appeared and stood at the back of the stage.

'Come here, where I can see you.'

Jed moved slightly forward.

'What is your problem boy, has your bravado vanished. Come here.'

Jed moved closer.

'Now, what is it you want from me? Have you nothing better to do with your time than to hang around here, making a nuisance of yourself.'

'I am sorry sir,' Jed found a little courage. 'I want to be a dancer.'
'Enrol in a dance school, there are plenty around.'
'I want you sir.'

'Do you indeed. Do you imagine I have nothing better to do with my time than to accommodate stage struck school boys?'

Jed said nothing – just stood looking at Greg.

Greg stood up and walked nearer to the boy, 'Do you know anything about dance?'

'No sir.'

'You have been spying and pestering me for the past six months and you have learned nothing.'

'Yes sir – I mean I have learned a lot, quite a lot really… I watch. I want you to teach me.' Jed was fast losing his courage.

Greg's eyes were like steel.

'So!' He said. 'What makes you think I have the time or inclination to train you?'

Although Jed was tall for his age, Greg towered above him. Jed remained silent, wishing that he could escape.

'Have you lost your power of speech boy?'

Jed swallowed hard. 'Please Dr. Fellini.'

'How old are you boy?'

'Nearly thirteen sir.'

'And you have been getting under my feet for the past six months.'

'Longer sir.'

'What!!'

'During the holidays sir, I watch you.'

'How did you get in here?'

Not wishing to implicate Mick, Jed replied, 'I sneaked in sir.'

'Did you indeed.' Greg sighed, lit another cigarette glanced at the boy with a grudging admiration.

'What about school,' he said.

'I don't know about school. I hadn't thought about school.'

'So! You think you would like to be a dancer, and you have the audacity to expect me to train you.'

Jed lowered his eyes and his spirits sank.

'Alright boy,' Greg walked around him then stood facing him, 'If you are so keen, report here on Saturday morning before my classes begin – I presume you have no school then – We shall see what you have learned, what you are made of. You have observed my methods for long enough, albeit without my permission, so you should have grasped at least some of the routine. If there is anything to warrant you joining my classes, I might perhaps think about it. That is of course in the future.'

Jed could not believe his luck. 'Yes sir,' he said, 'and thank you, I'll be here.' He allowed himself a smile, then turned to go.

'Wait,' Greg yelled. 'I have not yet dismissed you, and before you run off, you had better curb your exuberance. If I decide you are worth training you will be expected from the very beginning to work hard, to obey without question. If you have the stamina to endure the frustration and pain and I assure you there will be plenty of both, you will never complain. Do you understand?'

'Yes sir.'

'Go home boy, think seriously about what I have said, and if you still wish to attend here on Saturday – we shall see.'

'Yes sir, thank you, thank you very much.'

When Jed finally made his way outside, he leapt in the air, letting out a great whoop of delight as he rushed home to tell his Gran and Nicole his good news. The whole of the week Nicole imparted as much knowledge as she could to her friend.

'You are very good Jed,' she encouraged. 'As good as the rest of us. I am sure Monsieur will be impressed.'

They stopped practising – Jed looked wistfully at Nicole. 'He kissed you Nicki, and then stayed for ages – I couldn't hold the pole. He was so angry.'

'Still he is going to teach you.'

'Do you really think he will?'

'I'm sure of it.'

'He kissed you Nicki,' Jed repeated. 'He likes you.'

Nicole was silent, remembering the strange and wonderful feeling his kiss had caused her. She lowered her eyes thinking about it.

'Do you like him?'

'I would die for him,' she replied. 'He makes my heart jump.'

'But he makes you cry.'

'Yes'

'You are crazy, come on let's practice some more. Tomorrow is Saturday. I have to make him want to teach me. You don't mind helping me Nicki?'

Of course not, but I think Monsieur will be surprised.

'I am terrified,' Jed confessed.

Chapter 4

Greg drove Jed almost beyond his limit that Saturday morning, but he was impressed with the natural movement of the boy. He was tall with a pleasing personality. His expressive brown eyes alert and compelling. He perspired with fear as Greg rasped out his commands for over half an hour. Greg liked his style and admired his courage given the fact that he criticised, yelled and purposefully demoralised him. In fact Jed came perilously near to tears toward the conclusion of Greg's gruelling instruction.

Justin, watching from the auditorium marvelled at Jed's self control – silently he willed Greg to bring the session to a close, before the boy broke down.

But Greg was astute, he knew how terrifying he could appear, especially to the younger students and he knew when to stop.

Suddenly he banged his staff on the boards causing Jed to jump with fear.

'That's enough boy, go and change then return to me here.'

Jed allowed himself a few tears before he changed. With shaking hands he splashed his face with cold water before making his way back to the stage.

He came slowly, nervously and stood in front of the master.

'Alright boy. I have decided to give you a trial. You may join Justin's class every Saturday for one term. The rest depends on you. We shall see how you shape up.'

As an afterthought he said with half a smile, 'you did very well, I think you might make a dancer in time providing you obey the rules.' He patted Jed's shoulder, 'Well done boy.'

It was the only praise Jed would receive from Greg for many months.

'And,' Greg continued, 'we will have no more of these cloak and dagger tactics. Oh yes I have been aware of your defiance in creeping about the theatre against my wishes. If you wish to observe my methods you may sit in the auditorium or at the back of the stage during rehearsals in a civilised manner. If you wish to see a performance Justin will allocate you a seat somewhere. Is that clear?'

'Yes sir.' Jed started to move away.

Greg banged his staff. 'Come back here. What did I tell you? You do not leave without my permission. Remember that at all times.'

'Yes sir.'

Justin closed his eyes in despair, 'for god sake did he have to be so damned autocratic.'

However, the next moment Greg relaxed held out his hand and grasped Jed's. 'Congratulations. Jed isn't it?'

'Yes sir. Jed Paxton'

'Well Jed. I will see you on Saturday next 8.30 sharp. Justin here will be instructing you. I hope you will not disappoint either of us.'

Justin was introduced to Jed.

'You may go,' Greg said curtly.

Jed could not get away quickly enough. He was shaking when he collected his things from the dressing room where Nicole was waiting for him.

'You were wonderful Jed. I am so proud of you. He was pleased I could tell.'

'Well, he absolutely terrified me,' Jed said.

'Never mind, it is over and he is going to teach you. It is what you wanted isn't it Jed?'

'Yes, it is, but I didn't think I had a chance. He was so, so. I don't know but he sounded as though I was no good at all.'

'Well, you are going to be in Justin's class. You will like Justin. He's nice, you'll like working with Justin.'

'Come on Nicki. I want to forget if for now. Let's go for a coke. I'm so thirsty. Look I'm still shaking.'

Nicole laughed, 'Okay, then we will tell your grand-mère and grand-père and afterward you and I can go skating. Yes. You will teach me to skate Jed.

'Of course. Let's go.'

Chapter 5

Greg turned to Justin. 'I must be slipping,' he said. 'I was prepared for him to have a splattering of know how, but I was not expecting such sheer and utter potential as that lad has. What do you think, Justin?'

Justin's anger with Greg was still rife.

'What do I think,' he replied. 'I think you are a complete bastard, you almost destroyed that kid.'

'Nonsense, he is a survivor. I needed to test his metal.'

'You did that alright, you absolutely terrified him. It's a miracle he made it to the end.'

'If he had not I would never have entertained taking him on,'

'I repeat, you are a bastard. He is bloody good.'

'He is Justin, I agree, but he is only thirteen years old, we must wait. He may not be quite so keen when he realises how long and hard he has to study, and he is still at school.'

'He does not seem to be a quitter,' Justin said.

'We shall see.'

'Besides you agree he has potential. We could use him, we have had kids before. I reckon with a few months training he could perform.'

'You must not get too carried away Justin. Come – if your disapproval of me has subsided perhaps we can lunch together.'

Justin found Jed a good hardworking student. He had observed Greg's methods well. So well that Justin had occasionally to curb his enthusiasm.

He was also popular with the girl students, all of them three or four years older than he. They tended to pet him, indulge him, protect him. He responded, enjoyed their motherly instincts, flattered by their attention he rewarded them with quick flashes of wit and humour. Justin allowed this to continue for a few lessons, then put his foot down. He was not so strict as Greg, however, this time he banged on the table with a wooden baton.

'Alright kids, you have had long enough to get to know our new recruit and certainly long enough to know that if Dr. Fellini walked in at this moment you would all be in deep trouble. Jed most of all.

'Jed is not a puppy, nor is he here for your entertainment. So from now on you will refrain from this ridiculous behaviour and grow up. Keep your mind on your work. You have much to learn and Jed, you will save your witty remarks and bursts of humour for outside the classes. Remember you are on trial as far as Dr. Fellini is concerned. I'd like a word with you after the class please. Now perhaps if you don't mind we can get back to work.'

Unused to any serious reprimands from Justin the class quickly responded and in seconds they were in their correct positions anxious to please, and the lesson continued. Justin dismissed the class a little earlier than usual.

'Don't forget Jed I'd like a word,' he called. 'Wait for me here, I won't be long.'

When he disappeared, some of the students crowded around Jed. 'Don't worry,' they assured him, 'Justin's okay, he won't tell you off that much. Justin's really nice,' before they scattered off home.

Even so Jed was a little nervous. Justin returned within 10 minutes.

'Sorry to have kept you Jed,' 'that call was important.'

'Justin,' Jed ventured, 'I'm sorry about this morning.'

'What! Oh that, forget it. That is not what I wanted to talk to you about. He pushed a wooden box towards the boy. Sit down. Jed listen, do you think you can cope with Dr. Fellini sitting in on the class next week.'

Jed's stomach lurched. 'Oh God,' he said.

Justin looked at him, 'It has to happen sometime Jed and soon. I half expected him to insist on today but he was busy until lunchtime.'

'Is it me he wants to look at?'

'I'm afraid this time yes it is. He usually sits in about once a month. This is an extra.'

Jed said nothing.

'You are okay Jed, as good as the rest of them. You are doing fine.'

'Will he yell at me?'

Justin smiled, 'probably, you just have to rise above it. It's the way he works.'

Jed sighed nervously.

'Look Jed, you have to learn not to be so nervous. He won't kill you. He may not even say a word.'

'He will yell at me for sure.'

'If he does, keep calm, the others will be just as nervous as you. Just do your best and for god sake don't cross him or argue with him.'

'I wouldn't dare' Jed retorted.

'Well, some have done in the past, the results of which were not very pleasant for them.'

'Right. Thanks for warning me. I wish it was already over.'

'Well, just remember, your work is as good as most of them. Don't worry. Cheers kid, I'll see you next week. '

Jed confided in Nicole, 'Do you think he will chuck me out?'

'Of course not. Monsieur knows how good you are.'

'I bet he will yell at me.'

'If he does it will be because he is trying to make you better.'

They practised a little, Nicole trying to improve his movements.

'I'm not very good at the pirouettes,' Jed confessed.

'You'll get it in the end. It is just a knack and needs lots of practice. It's difficult to teach. I can only show you. He knows it is difficult. He has been a dancer you know. He will understand.' Nicole consoled him.

'I'm fed up with practising, let's go out.' Jed pulled Nicole up and towards the door, 'It's nice and sunny.'

'If she was not working, they either went swimming or to the ice rink. She was not at all proficient at this sport and Jed took great pleasure in teaching her. All too soon Saturday loomed and Jed became more nervous as the minutes progressed.

'Will you come with me Nicki? I'll feel better if I know you are there.'

'Of course I will. Don't worry Jed. I know you will be okay.'

'He will make me nervous just by being there.'

'Pretend he is not there,' Nicole advised.

'I'll try.'

Jed was temporarily relieved when he arrived for the lesson and Greg was not there.

'Good morning,' Justin called to the class, 'all of you try to do exactly as Dr. Fellini or I tell you this morning. Dr. Fellini might call in during the session so no talking or clowning. Is that clear?'

The class was silent.

'Is that clear,' Justin repeated.

'Yes, Justin.'

'Right, we shall start with the arabesques. Jed you are a bit weak here. Then we shall proceed to the barre. After that we shall carry on with the dance.'

They were at the barre when Greg silently appeared.

Justin, correcting their footwork ignored him. When he came to Jed he bent to adjust his foot, then tapped him on the shoulder.

'You are doing fine kid,' he told him and strode towards Greg.

Three of the students froze. Greg watched for a few minutes, then took over from Justin. He banged his staff on the floor and instructed them to gather in the middle. One by one they left the barre, slowly and nervously graduating towards the centre.

'Are you all asleep,' Greg bellowed. 'Move. Come along now. I do not have all day. The girl at the side there, Janine is it, what are you doing? Are you glued to the barre?'

He hissed to Justin, 'What are they doing? What sort of routine?'

'I have choreographed a short sketch. I thought it would break the routine, give them a little encouragement.'

'Right.' He turned to the students then back to Justin. 'Let us see this dance.'

Jed began to relax. Greg had not yelled at him or anyone apart from Janine and he knew he was good in the dance, and was unlikely to make any mistakes. Greg sat back observing without comment. When it was finished he stood up.

'They are a sorry lot Justin, sloppy, no spark.'

'Be fair Greg. They are just kids, beginners. They have worked so hard. I think they did well.'

'They are performing like a group of geriatrics,' Greg retorted.

He began to put them through their paces rasping out commands, then dismissing them one by one to the barre. 'And don't just stand there, work, the barre is not a resting place.'

He carried on relentlessly, criticising a bent leg, a sagging back, a stiff movement. When he came to Jed he criticised everything he did, 'You will have to do better boy,' he said.

Justin was furious. Jed had performed as well if not better than some but he remained silent as he watched Jed move deflated towards the barre with the others.

'Did I tell you to go boy, no I did not, stay where you are. I have not finished with you yet,' he called out more instructions which Jed obeyed reasonably well, faltering on the pirouettes. He was made to repeat these several times.

Justin could no longer keep silent. 'He has not quite mastered the art,' he told Greg.

'Then it is time he had.'

Jed, after the last reprimand, terrified to move, stood waiting to be dismissed.

'Well,' Greg glared at him, 'What are you waiting for? Get over to the barre.'

Jed's terror turned to anger and for a split second he stayed glaring back at Greg before he turned and did as he was told.

Greg stayed lecturing each one in turn, then turned to Justin. 'Carry on'

'Greg, I'd like a word outside please.' Justin said.

Still furious he faced Greg across the desk in the office. 'What are you trying to do to them,' he said, 'of course they are not perfect you expect too much. You gave not one word of praise Greg. Your attitude is unacceptable.'

'Now now Justin.'

'Listen Greg. I am sick of you coming into my classes, terrifying the students. You undermine my authority and I am left to calm them.'

'They are sloppy, undisciplined.'

'No they are not.'

'You are not tough enough my boy.'

'They are doing fine and you know it. I am supposed to be a partner and you treat me like the office boy.'

'Nonsense Justin, you are invaluable to me.'

'Am I? Well Greg I would ask you not to look in on my classes in future unless you can be more constructive. You know Greg those kids are terrified of you.'

'That is how it should be,' Greg retorted. 'It is no good being soft with them Justin – as I said, you are not tough enough.'

'I work differently from you – I do not find pleasure in yelling at them for no valid reason – and what about Jed – you had no justification in yelling at him.

'Ah, Jed.' Greg's eyes lit up, 'Jed is coming along nicely, you are doing well with Jed, Justin. He is catching up fast.'

'Then why the hell didn't you tell him.'

'Too soon for praise.'

'You have no compassion.'

Greg smiled. 'You will learn my boy. Jed will not falter. He will thrive on my criticism.'

'He would thrive on praise just as well.'

'No Justin. Mark my words – did you not see? Jed was angry with me. He will strive harder, not to please me but to spite me. He will strive for the impossible.'

'What rubbish you talk Greg. Do you care if the students hate you?'

'But they do not hate me Justin, they fear me. – there is a difference.' He looked at his watch. 'I must be off and you have a class to run.'

Justin watched Greg leave wondering why he stayed working with this man. Then his fury subsided, and shaking his head indulgently, he lit a cigarette leaned against the wall, giving his students a little leeway to talk amongst themselves about Greg and his unreasonable attitude, and no matter how frustrating it all was, he knew that there would be no question of leaving Greg He was fond of the autocratic old sod. He was a genius. He made stars and he could be as generous hearted and benevolent as he was harsh. Greg was one of the greats, was known and respected throughout the continent. He commanded and got whatever he wanted especially for his dancers. No, he would never abandon Greg. He sometimes needed as much protection as the students. Of course he was right. They did not hate him, they feared him, but they also worshipped him.

Chapter 6

Jed got used to Greg calling in on the class and even though it infuriated him when he yelled at him often for no reason, he curbed his temper.

'He always criticises me,' he complained to Justin. 'I'd like to know from you if he is justified Justin.'

'What do you expect me to say Jed. Dr. Fellini has his reasons. He is a perfectionist.'

'It doesn't matter how hard I try, he still always finds some fault. '

'You are not the only one. I am afraid Jed that you are going to have to learn to take criticism, however underserved you consider it to be.'

'I'm glad I'm not in his class.'

'Are you really?'

'Yes, I am.'

'Then you are a fool.'

Jed shrugged.

'You'd better be off unless you want him to order you to stay for his class, which he is quite likely to do.'

Jed stayed with Justin for six months by which time he was proficient and ready to move on. Justin asked him to stay behind after the lesson, to tell him that Greg had decided to take him and two of the girls into his lessons.

'Listen Jed, Greg will give you hell to start with, can you take it, because if you can't you had better quit now.'

'Will it just be me he yells at?'

'Of course not, but one or two of the students have left to join other companies, Greg did nothing to stop them, but they were fools. I don't want you to make that mistake.'

Jed was dreading his first morning with Greg but the hour passed with only constructive criticism and Jed enjoyed the lesson. As the weeks continued he realised how lucky he was to be in this school of dance. He came to respect Greg's method of teaching and for a few months had no cause for complaint. However as time went on it was not all plain sailing for him. On occasions Greg criticised and belittled him, became angry when he failed to aspire to Greg's high standard. But although Jed's quick temper was often aroused he kept cool if not terribly calm, never argued or complained, so gaining Greg's respect.

Just before Nicole's 18th birthday, Greg removed her from the Corps de Ballet and started grooming her for the role of Coppelia. She had been training for almost one year. She was very graceful, her beauty captivating. Greg was obsessed with her. Still he pushed her to her limit.

Her parents were still under the illusion that she was working and living with Trudi as au pair. She collected her letters from Trudi's house. Now she wrote to them explaining the situation, telling them of her good fortune, about the ballet. She assured them that she was well looked after by Jed's grandparents and that she was happy.

They were both devastated. First, that their daughter had deceived them and secondly that she was earning money working as a dancer. Belle, her mother was incensed. She did not want her daughter dancing in a theatre, living in corrupt London.

'I thought you were helping as au pair Nicole,' she wrote back. 'Your father and I insist you return home. We were under the impression you were living with a respectable family. We will send you your air ticket. You must return.'

Jed found her at the breakfast table her eyes red with crying.

'What's the matter Nicki?' he asked. 'Why are you crying? You should be on top of the world, you are almost a ballerina. Please don't cry.'

She read him the letter.

'Don't worry Nicole, you are eighteen soon, they can't make you go back. It isn't as though you have nowhere to live – you may stay with us as long as you like, and you have some money haven't you.'

'You don't understand,' she cried. 'They will make me go home. If I refuse they will come here for me.'

'Nicole, it's your career, you are good. It would be a waste to go back to France. Your parents will understand surely.'

'No, they will not, they say I can dance in France but it will not be the same will it. I cannot go against them.'

'Nicki, take the letter to Greg. He will know what to do, he always knows.'

'Perhaps, I will see, but I love my parents Jed, I don't want to go against them.'

'Explain to them. Tell them to come to see the ballet. They will be proud of you.'

'I hope so.'

Nicole was disturbed all the same and her performance suffered in rehearsal. Greg suffered her lack of concentration for a while, then strode angrily towards her.

'Alright Nicole, what is wrong. What the hell are you doing? This is a serious rehearsal and you are wasting my time. He stood in front of her waiting for an answer.

'I am sorry Monsieur. I will try harder.'

'You certainly will,' he retorted.

He dismissed the rest of the dancers instructing her to stay.

'Now,' he rasped, 'Start from the beginning.'

Jed was waiting in the stalls.

'Come along now girl, put some effort into it for goodness sake. You are performing like a child at her first lesson.'

He railed at her relentlessly, until the tears were rolling down her cheeks. Greg stood exasperated. He walked across to her. 'Nicole, do you not want this chance I am giving you? Have I made a mistake putting my faith in you?'

Nicole said nothing.

Greg sighed. He was tired. 'Alright Nicole, go home now, we shall try again tomorrow. Perhaps you will be in better form then.'

Jed scampered through to the dressing room and found her, 'why didn't you tell him Nicki, why didn't you show him the letter?'

'It will make no difference,' she said flatly.

'It will, I'm sure it will. Then he will understand why you are not working perfectly. He'll know what to do.'

She shook her head. 'I think I must obey my parents.'

'Oh no, you mustn't give up so easily. Please tell Dr. Fellini.'

She smiled warmly, 'You are a very nice boy Jed. You and your grandparents have been so kind to me. But I must obey my parents.'

'Come on, let's get some ice cream. I am sure everything will come right. Come on Nicki.'

The next morning Jed went to the theatre and knocked on the office door.

'Yes, what is it.'

Jed opened the door. He was still very much in awe of Greg. 'May I speak to you sir.'

Greg looked up, 'Well, what is it you want, I am extremely busy.'

'It's about Nicole.'

'I hope she is prepared to work properly today.'

'That's just it sir, it's because of her parents.'

'Well, get on with it boy. What have her parents to do with anything?'

'They have written to her, they are angry. They have told her she has to return to France.'

'What,' Greg swung his chair round. 'That's out of the question.'

'I told her you would know what to do. She says she has to obey.'

'Alright, I will deal with this.'

Nicole was not much better at rehearsal, but Greg did not reprimand her. Instead, when the class was over, he took her aside.

'Now,' he said. 'What is this nonsense I hear about you returning to France?'

'My parents say I must go back Monsieur.'

'I see, and what about me?'

'Nicole, I have spent a great deal of my time training you, grooming you for Coppelia. You have an extraordinary talent. If you leave now, you will not only betray me, but also yourself. You have a great career before you. Now tell me about your parents. I am sure something can be worked out.'

'They allowed me to come here to improve my English. Trudi was recommended by friends of my parents – I was supposed to return three months ago.'

'Why have they suddenly decided to call you back? Why not before?'

'I did not tell them I had left Trudi until last week. I thought they would not understand.'

'You deceived them. That was very foolish child. Why did you not tell them you were dancing?'

'I don't know Monsieur. I suppose I was afraid they would not approve.'

'And you thought that perhaps now that you are established here they might have changed their minds.'

'I suppose so Monsieur. I do not know why I did not tell them. My maman is very angry. She says I must go home now.' Nicole started to weep at the thought, 'They do not want me to perform on the stage. They want me to go home.'

'What do you want Nicole?'

'I want to dance of course, but....'

'No buts.' He puts his arms around her shoulders, 'We will write to them, persuade them, invite them to the ballet. They could not fail to be proud of their little daughter.'

He turned her face towards him and smiled reassuringly, 'And now Nicole you are going to work extra hard – are you not? You will be a credit to me and to yourself, and there will be no more talk of returning to France, unless I say so.'

'Oui Monsieur.'

'Good. And Nicole if you have any more problems, likely to impair your dancing, you will either talk to me or Justin. That's an order.'

'Now what!!' He said as Nicole burst into tears.

He took her, folded his arms around her frail shoulders. 'Oh Nicki, Nicki, please do not cry. I know I work you too hard. You are tired. I am sorry.'

'No Monsieur, I am not tired.'

'No! Well lets us dry those tears. He took his pocket handkerchief and dried her face. That is better. You are a very beautiful girl Nicole and those eyes should not be spoiled by so many tears.'

He looked down at the stalls. 'Alright Jed, I know you are there. You had better come up here and take your friend home.'

He watched them leave, lingered for a while, thinking about this slip of a girl. She was perfect, exquisite and he knew beyond any shadow of doubt that he was falling in love with her. He certainly could not bear the thought of her leaving. She was only eighteen years old 'and I am forty-three,' he reminded himself. He squared his shoulder and left the stage. 'It would not do.'

Nicole wrote again to her parents, begging them to let her stay in England, explaining why she did not wish to return to France. Greg also wrote in perfect French inviting them to the ballet later in which their daughter was to make her debut. He enclosed information about the history of his theatre, explained that he picked and trained all his own dancers. Their Nicole would be well looked after, protected.

'She will come to no harm,' he wrote. 'We hope to see you both in the near future. I am certain you will be very proud of your daughter.'

* * *

Pierre, her father was willing to be persuaded. Nicole's future lay with the ballet, 'She was always desperate to dance Belle, even as a tiny little thing.'
'It is not dignified,' Belle protested.
'Oh, come now Belle, the ballet is a very respectable profession these days. We should let her have her chance Belle. She is a good girl.'
'I don't like it,' Belle said. 'The deceit. Why did she keep all this from us? She deceived us Pierre – I don't like it. We shall never see her, she will never come back, if we do not insist now.'
'Even so Belle, surely you wish her to be happy?'
'She will be happy here. She can dance here. She will soon forget this foolishness. She is still a child.'
'Nevertheless Belle. We shall accept Dr. Fellini's invitation, and Belle you will be pleasant and remember we shall be his guests.'
'I do not like it,' Belle protested.
Pierre wrote back accepting Greg's invitation to visit London. In spite of Belle's protests Greg received their acceptance and immediately summoned Nicole.
'Now Nicole, we have another month before your parents arrive. You have nothing more to worry about and so, you will work hard so that you are perfect. Is that clear?'
'Oui Monsieur.'
'Very well, I presume you also have received correspondence?'
'Oui Monsieur. My Maman is not pleased, but my Papa is only concerned for my happiness.'
'Good they have accepted my invitation, now it will be up to you to convince them where your future lies.'
Nicole hovered nervously.
'What is it Nicole?' Greg asked.

'Monsieur. I…I… thank you for helping me. I am so grateful to you. They would not have agreed if you had not written to them.'

'I do not wish you to be grateful Nicole. I wish you to be professional and to work hard and remember if you are troubled in any way, you will confide in Justin or me. Do you understand?'

Nicole nodded, 'Oui Monsieur.'

Chapter 7

The rest of the month of June was sheer heaven for Jed and both he and Nicole blossomed under Greg's instruction. From an early age he had taught himself to play the guitar, composing simple songs often singing along whilst recording them. His voice was surprisingly mature although as he admitted his lyrics were not the best.

Without even thinking about it he began to compose melodies with Nicole in mind, and whenever she was available he played them back to her. They danced together, enjoying the atmosphere, expressed in the music, lost in a world of their own.

'I have written something special for you Nicki,' he said.

'Really?'

'The lyrics are awful. I kept re-writing them so they weren't too sloppy.'

'Put it on Jed.'

Jed inserted the tape and Nicole listened. She sat back on her heels and looked at Jed.

'It is beautiful Jed,' she said. 'The melody is fantastic.'

'What about the lyrics?'

'The lyrics don't matter.'

'Yes the lyrics matter. It's what I feel'

'Well, they are okay as well,' she said. 'But Jed, the melody is beautiful.'

'I wrote it for you.'

'Thank you Jed. I am very flattered.'

'Could you write some lyrics?' he pleaded.

'Honestly Jed, the music does not need lyrics. Shall I dance and show you, I'd love that.'

He watched fascinated. 'God you are perfect, you will be a star soon.'

She laughed, 'I do not think monsieur would agree with you.'

'Bet he would.'

'Come and dance with me Jed,' she said holding out her hands.

He was taller than she, had a mature outlook and she was young enough to enjoy his enthusiasm. They spent as much time as was possible together and Jed missed her when Greg started rehearsals for Coppelia.

During Jed's school holidays, apart from listening to music, they went to the skating rink, swam at the local baths and in the warmer weather in the lake. Occasionally they hired a boat and rowed on the river.

Jed adored her and revelled in her beauty. He took great pleasure in taking control although always her gallant protector.

Rehearsals for Coppelia were slightly erratic because Justin and Greg were busy attempting to rearrange the choreography to improve the production and so on a Sunday morning towards the end of Summer Jed hired a boat to row down the river.

'There won't be many more decent days,' Jed said, 'and soon you will be rehearsing all the time.'

Nicole was more than willing. They rowed quite a distance down the river and on the way back Jed let an oar slip away. It took them some while to retrieve it and only with the help of another couple rowing in the same vicinity.

Nicole looked at her watch, suddenly remembering she had a rehearsal. She panicked, 'Jed, I have a rehearsal this morning. I forgot – we have to get back.'

'What time?' Jed asked her.

'I can't remember exactly but please hurry. I can't believe I forgot, Monsieur will be furious.'

'It's okay Nicole, we will be back. It's only 11.'

When they reached the theatre, she quickly changed and hurried breathless onto the stage.

'I am sorry Monsieur. We had a little accident,' she ventured.

Greg glared at her, 'You should have been here 20 minutes ago. You have disrupted the whole rehearsal and wasted my time.'

'Dr. Fellini,' Jed emerged from behind Nicole, 'It wasn't her fault.'

Greg turned sharply to face Jed, 'Get off the stage boy, go.'

They stayed glaring at each other until Jed left.

'Get into your position,' he told Nicole. 'You have wasted enough of my time. I will talk to you later.'

Nicole obeyed on the verge of tears as he pounded her with his rasping tongue and when the rehearsal was over the dancers began to disperse.

'Not you,' Greg threw at her.

He went through to the office, leaving her standing alone. She walked slowly to the side of the stage, sat down on one of the props and massaged her legs. She waited, it seemed for hours. When he eventually returned she stood up.

Greg studied her. 'This company Nicole is not a social club, where you come and go at will. I told you right from the start never to be late for a class, or a rehearsal. A rehearsal Nicole is as important as a performance. I do not expect to have to remind my dancers of this.'

'I am very sorry Monsieur, we were on the river and we had a little accident, we lost our oar and then we…'

'I am not in the least interested in your outside activities Nicole – if there was the slightest possibility that you might miss a rehearsal, you should not have been there. I assume this was one of young Jed's escapades.'

'But it was not his fault Monsieur.'

'No, of course it was not. He is only a thirteen-year-old boy. How old are you Nicole?'

'I am eighteen Monsieur.'

'Exactly. Old enough to make your own decisions.'

'As it was Sunday you see I forgot I had a rehearsal.'

'That is no excuse. This will not happen again. Do you understand?'

'Oui Monsieur.'

'You may go, be here at 10 sharp tomorrow morning.'

Jed was waiting outside. 'I am so sorry Nicki.'

'It wasn't your fault. But I must never be late again. Monsieur was really angry. Still, we had an exciting time didn't we Jed?'

'He hasn't put you off then,' Jed said.

'Of course not – he was right though, I should have remembered. He is making me rehearse tomorrow morning.'

'Shall we go to the cinema this evening?' Jed took her hand as they walked home.

'I'd like to but I must work this afternoon, I have to try to please him tomorrow.' She went straight to her room to practice and left Jed with his grandmother.

He sat down with his guitar and thought about Nicole. He felt years older than her – she must have been very sheltered in France and she was so tiny and incredibly beautiful. He wanted to protect her from the world. Her large expressive smoky grey eyes were so trusting and he desperately wished he was older.

She came downstairs just before dinner. 'My feet ache,' she complained. 'Monsieur Gregory says I should never be tired.'

'I will rub them for you after dinner,' Jed offered.

Amy brought a dish of steak and kidney pie to the table.

'I love this,' Nicole said to Amy. 'You cook such lovely meals.'

'Thank you my dear. This is an old fashioned dish but very nourishing.'

'We are going to the cinema this evening Gran,' Jed said.

'Well, don't keep Nicole out too late. You should rest my dear so that you are fresh in the morning.'

The next day Nicole tried her best to please Greg but he criticised everything she did. 'You are wasting my time again, Nicole.' 'You are not working properly.' He waved Yanni off 'You may go home,' he said. 'There is no point in being here until Nicole is ready to work. Be back here at 10 sharp tomorrow morning. Hopefully she will be awake by then.'

'Now.' Greg pulled her round to face him. 'What is the matter with you?'

'Monsieur?' The unfairness was too much. She had worked hard, had done her best, she burst into tears.

'Oh for goodness sake girl, this is becoming a habit. Stop this instant.' He lifted her chin as she continued to sob. 'Nicole, there is no need for this, tell me what in God's name is wrong with you.'

'Nothing.'

'You are making all this fuss for nothing?'

'I thought I was working well, I try so hard to please you Monsieur.' She looked up at him. 'I try.'

Unable to control his feelings he pulled her head on to his shoulder, stroked her hair. He stayed thus, feeling the closeness of her.

After a few seconds he held her away from him, he brushed his lips across her forehead. She looked up at him, her eyes penetrating his, intense, trusting, revealing her adoration of him. Before he could check himself his lips were pressing down on hers. He wrenched himself away, guiltily. 'Oh Nicole, Nicole, what am I doing. This is not right. I am so sorry my dear. Forgive me.'

'Monsieur?' Nicole was confused. He had kissed her, shown his love for her; surely he knew that she would die for him. She looked at him, her eyes again pleading. 'I try so hard to please you Monsieur, I cannot bear it when you are so angry with me. I love you Monsieur.'

'Oh no, you have your whole life before you, just beginning and you are very beautiful. You will be a star – you will go far. There will be many chances for you and many wonderful young men falling in love with you.'

'I love you Monsieur. I do not want the other young men.'

Her eyes reached out to him. He kissed her forehead again – she looked so crestfallen.

'Come Nicole, get changed. I will take you for luncheon and we will discuss the ballet.' She turned dejectedly and did as he said.

Greg gazed at this beautiful child across the table – he smiled at her and she immediately responded – he could not take his eyes off her.

'What would you like Nicole?' he asked.

'I do not know Monsieur, please will you order for me?'

'Very well, first would you like an aperitif or just wine?'

'Wine Monsieur.'

She related some of her experiences when she was living at home in France. She told him how she had always loved to dance and thanked him for allowing her to join his company. As she talked her eyes danced with enthusiasm. He listened enthralled at her chatter, loving the way she paused to find the correct English, often misplacing her words, getting her sentences the wrong way round. He loved the way she always addressed him as monsieur.

He broke into her chatter, 'Would you like a dessert Nicole?'

She chose a mixture of ice cream, topped with fruit, nuts and chocolate sauce. It came in a tall glass.

'Ha!' she exclaimed. 'C'est très grande. I cannot reach, the glass is so tall.'

She stood up and proceeded to spoon the mixture from the glass. 'Mmmm! that was delicious,' she said as she scooped the last remaining morsel from the bottom of the glass. She sat back, a look of satisfaction on her face.

'Would you care for another?'

'Ah baum – I will burst,' she cried. 'But it was so good.'

Suddenly she became wistful – she put her hand across the table.

'Monsieur, you are not cross with me now?'

'Of course not,' he assured her, 'but you must try to concentrate – you are perhaps finding the work difficult?'

'A little, but I will try harder.'

He put his hand over hers. 'You know my dear, I do not mean to make you cry, come do not look so solemn, I know I work you too hard.'

'I do not mind to work hard Monsieur – it is only when you are cross, I forget the steps.'

'You must not take my corrections to heart. It is just that I want you perfect and you will be soon – I will make you a star Nicole.'

She looked across at him, her eyes wistful. 'I do love you Monsieur.'

She lowered her eyes, 'I love you very much.'

He took her small hand in his large one. 'Now, now Nicole, it is natural for a student to think that she is in love with her teacher.'

She closed her eyes.

'Nicole my dear, you will find that in a little while you will have forgotten your infatuation for an old man like me. The world is your oyster my dear, soon everyone will be in love with the beautiful ballerina from Coppelia.'

'You do not love me then. I thought when you kissed me, I thought...............'

'Oh Nicole, you cannot imagine how much we have all grown to love you. But you are only eighteen years of age – as for my loving you well, I am forty-three. It will not do – you are a mere child.'

'No Monsieur, I am not a child. I am a woman, and I wish to live all my life with you and you are not old.'

Greg sat watching her silently. He could see she was disturbed. She was so utterly beautiful, innocent. Oh yes, he loved her. She had aroused feelings in him which had lain dormant since he was a boy. But to take her, to marry her, it would be sacrilege. She was still a child in so many ways.

'Nicole' he ventured 'I................' She interrupted him.

'I will never want to be with anyone else Monsieur.'

'Let us get back Nicole.' He pushed back his chair.

She stood up embarrassed, realising her mistake.

'Excuse Monsieur, I must go to the cloakroom.'

Greg took out a cigarette and waited for her to return.

She nervously touched his arm 'I am sorry Monsieur, I should not have been so, so………I do not know the word.'

'Come, my dear.' He took her elbow, 'we will drive back. I have to be at the theatre this afternoon. I will take you home.'

He left her at the house 'I will see you later my dear,' he said.

She watched the car until it disappeared from sight, then walked slowly into the house. Jed was strumming on his guitar; he looked up at her, 'You okay Nicole?'

'Yes, of course,' she replied.

But Jed found her quiet and uncommunicative. 'Has he been making you cry again?' 'No! He was nice,' she said.

'What then?'

'Nothing.'

'I've had lunch,' he informed her, 'and it is still quite early. Think we can catch a film before you go to the theatre this evening?'

'Why not – we'd have plenty of time.'

Nicole perked up a little, and soon regained her effervescence. As they sat together in the cinema Jed took her hand, and she did not draw away.

On the way home he said, 'Nicole, I know I'm still a kid, I wish I was older.'

'Don't be silly Jed, you will grow up fast enough. Anyway I love you the way you are. It is always fun when we are together, yes.'

'But I'll never catch up with you Nicki and I love you.'

Nicole turned to face him, 'You are a very handsome boy Jed, and so tall – you will find someone to love soon I think.'

'I love you Nicki.'

She kissed his cheeks, 'You are my very good friend Jed and I love you too, but you and I have a lot of time to grow up. Let us always be very special friends.'

'Do you love Dr. Fellini?'

'What a question.'

'I think he loves you.'

'Nonsense.' She felt herself becoming hot with embarrassment.

'The way he looks at you, even when he is angry, and the other day he kissed you.'

'That does not mean anything. He was not very nice yesterday.'

'I'd never make you cry Nicole. I'll always love you. I'll always be your friend.'

'Thank you Jed. Did you enjoy the film?'

'Especially as we were together, yes I did. Have we time for a drink before we get home?'

'Jed, I think I ought to practice a bit – I am not good enough – I have to please him.'

'I think you are perfect. Okay let's go then.'

She was not looking forward to going to the theatre that evening. When the time came to leave, her nervous mood returned. She hoped desperately that she would not encounter Greg after the performance. She realised how stupid she had been, she was embarrassed and ashamed that she had allowed herself to be so forthright. Greg caught her as she tried to slip unnoticed from the stage.

'Please Monsieur' she pleaded, shrinking away from him.

'Nicole, please listen.'

'I should not have been so silly. I am sorry Monsieur.' She attempted to leave but he held on to her.

'Come here Nicole.' He led her to a secluded spot amongst the props.

'If it makes you feel any better, you are on my mind every minute of the day. How could I fail to love such a sweet girl? I think I have been in love with you from the moment you walked across the stage.'

'Then why Monsieur.'

'Nicole my dearest. It cannot be. I am far too old.'

'Do not turn away from me Monsieur.'

'Oh my dear, do you really believe I wish to turn away?'

He took her face in his hands and kissed her lightly. 'You have no idea how much I have come to love you. How much I think about you, but as I keep trying to impress upon you, I am almost forty-four years old.'

'How can that matter Monsieur. I will never love anyone else.'

'How can you be so sure, you have your whole life before you.'

'I am sure Monsieur.'

'Oh Nicole, I wish I could make myself believe that.'

'It is the truth.' She leaned against him, 'Please believe me.'

He stayed silent for a while then turned her face towards his. 'Alright my love, we shall talk about it! Go now, dress quickly and I will take you to dinner.'

'No Monsieur, I cannot. I promised Jed I would be home this evening. He will be waiting for me.'

'Alright, tomorrow then. You have no rehearsal tomorrow and no performance. Perhaps we could spend the day together.'

'Jed was going to take me skating tomorrow, but perhaps he will not mind.'

'You see my love how busy you are, how much in demand you are.'

'I will tell him Monsieur.'

'No my dear. You enjoy your day. You have worked hard. If I collect you later, would that be acceptable to your young friend?'

'Oui Monsieur, it would be better.'

'Come here Nicole.' She went to him and he kissed her.

'I will take you home.'

Chapter 8

All that night Greg wrestled with his conscience, trying to reason with himself. There was no doubt that he loved her but was she just infatuated with him, her teacher. It had happened before, would it all end in disaster? If he went ahead as his heart dictated, would that be wrong? He would certainly be criticised. This did not bother him. From the age of 10, when the Hungarian uprising began, he had learned to survive, often amongst the rough 'justice of soldiers'. He'd had no time for loving then. No time for anything except striving to stay alive, and later he had only the time for work. He had been through much hardship and tragedy, but he had survived.

This feeling of love he had for Nicole was new. Should he not cherish it. It was a good feeling – a very good feeling.

He lay awake remembering the deprivations and terror he had suffered as a boy. Eventually falling into a troubled sleep.

He woke early the next morning and telephoned Amy's house and asked to speak to Nicole.

'Good morning Nicole' he said. 'I love you. I know that you have a date with Jed this morning, but do you think he could spare you for an hour – I will pick you up shortly and have you back home by 11. Would that be satisfactory?'

'Oui Monsieur.'

'You see my beloved, since I have settled my conscience, I do not wish to wait until this evening to feast my eyes upon you. I will see you in 15 minutes.'

'Oui Monsieur.'

Nicole's happiness was overflowing. At last he was saying he loved her.

She danced around the room for joy. Jed caught her as she danced past him.

'Hello Nicole, you are in a happy mood – shall we get ready to go to the rink?'

'Oh Jed,' she stopped skipping around. 'I am to go with monsieur Gregoire, but only for an hour. I will be back later.'

'What about skating, you promised.'

'I will be back Jed.'

'Does he want to rehearse you? You are supposed to be off today.'

'No, it's just for coffee. I'll be back before lunch.'

'It will be longer than an hour' Jed said.

He opened the door to Greg when he arrived to collect Nicole.

'Good morning Jed. I understand you are on holiday.'

'Just a few days.'

'Well, you must make good use of your leave time.'

'I'll try to,' Jed said cryptically. He hoped Greg would not monopolise Nicole,

'Oh Nicole, I see you are ready,' he said as she came running to meet him, much too eagerly as far as Jed was concerned.

Jed stood at the door watching as Greg helped Nicole into his shining black Mercedes, then he slammed the door. 'Why couldn't he leave her alone?'

They drove to the Kings Road, when after parking the car, they ordered coffee in the Old Copper Kettle on the main road.

'You look very beautiful my dear' Greg told her. 'I am still not sure if I am doing the right thing by you, but I have a good feeling that you and I, my beloved, will do very well together – I think perhaps that we shall be very happy.'

She looked at him, her eyes shining. 'I know it Monsieur,' she said. 'I will love you always, as I do now.'

He took her hand. 'The fact that you love me at all is a miracle, and listen my love, if at a later stage you might feel differently, I promise I will let you go, very reluctantly however. For if you should stop loving me I could not bear to witness your unhappiness.'

'I will never stop loving you Monsieur.'

'Oh Nicole, I do hope not.'

'I will never feel any differently Monsieur.'

'In that case, it will be a bonus for me. You are a sweet girl and I will do everything in my power to make you happy. Would you care for another cup of coffee?'

'Two cups are enough for me Monsieur and I have not the time.'

'What do you mean, why ever not?'

'Monsieur, you remember, I promised Jed. You said one hour, it is nearly two hours.'

He smiled, 'I do not think young Jed will suffer too much if you were to stay another few minutes.'

'He is on holiday Monsieur. I do not like to disappoint him. We are to go skating.'

'Well, well,' he joked. 'I am already having to compete with another admirer more than half my age.'

'Monsieur!!!'

'Come on Nicole. I need another coffee, would you prefer an ice cream instead – then I will take you home.' He looked at his watch. 'Well!!'

It was a command.

She nodded. 'Oui, another coffee.'

'Tell me Nicole,' he said. 'what do you two get up to when you are not required at the theatre?'

'Get up to?' she queried.

'I mean, how do you spend your time.'

'Oh, Jed writes songs and we sing and dance to them after he records them on the cassette. He is very clever Monsieur.'

'Of that I have not the slightest doubt,' he retorted.

'Sometimes we row on the lake or the river, sometimes we skate. Jed is teaching me how to skate properly.'

'Quite a programme. You must be careful when skating, you could break your ankle.'

'I will be careful.'

'You like to skate?'

'Oui, I love it.'

He lit another cigarette and gazed at her, a pang of guilt sweeping through him. She was a mere child, a very young eighteen year old. Naïve, innocent and trusting and there was something about her fée-like personality which endeared her to him. He loved her, wanted her, to protect, to hold her, keep her forever.

He sighed, paid the bill and helped her up from the table.

'Come my precious, your young friend will be getting anxious. It is getting late.' He stopped the car a few yards away from the house, leaned across and clasped her in his arms.

'You know that I adore you my beloved,' he whispered.

'I am so happy Monsieur. I thought perhaps, perhaps….'

'Perhaps what?'

'That you did not really mean it.'

He kissed her again, 'I mean it, you have captured my heart – you have cast your spell over me – I cannot escape, neither do I wish it – You will marry me my beloved, soon?'

'Oui, oui Monsieur I will.'

He removed his arms. 'we had better get along,' he said.

When he let her out of the car he took her chin in his hand, 'You are so very beautiful you know,' he said. 'Will you tell him?'

'Oui, I will tell him, we always share things. You do not mind.'

'Of course not, but I think that Jed loves you also. '

'He is a little boy.'

'Not so little my love.'

He took her once again in his arms. 'I love you Nicole, you have made me the happiest man alive. I will see you this evening; do not be late for the performance.'

She rushed in to find Jed playing his guitar as usual.

'Hey Nicki,' he looked at his watch. 'You have been over 2 hours.'

'I'm sorry Jed.'

'Never mind. Listen, tell me what you think of this new song.' He began to strum a very jazzy number.

'It's good Jed, have you recorded it?'

'Not yet, I was waiting for you.'

She pulled Jed's arm, unable to contain the excitement, 'I have something to tell you.' She sat down cross legged in front of him.

'What's up?' he asked.

'Jed, I am going to marry monsieur Gregoire. – Jed isn't it wonderful?'

Jed dropped his guitar and stared open mouthed at his friend.

'You can't. He is old.'

'I love him Jed. He loves me.'

'But Nicki you are only eighteen. He is so old.'

'I love him Jed,' she repeated, 'be happy for me, please.'

'I knew he loved you from the beginning the way he looks at you, even when he is angry,' he said bitterly.

'Jed,' Nicole clasped his hand, 'we can still be special friends can't we.'

'I don't know.'

'Please Jed. I will always love you. We are special you and I, but Gregoire, it is different, please understand.'

'But he is so old,' Jed said.

'He is not that old, he is only forty-three.'

'That's old.'

'You think I should not marry him.'

Jed ignored this, 'Are you going to leave here?'

'Of course not, where would I go.'

He looked at her. She was so young and innocent. Surely she must realise he would want her with him now.

'He will want you to go with him now.'

'Of course, when we are married, but until then I stay here if I may. Please Jed do not be unhappy. We can still have lots of fun.'

'I am sorry Nicki. Of course I want you to be happy. It was just such a shock. I am glad you are happy.'

'Do you really mean it?'

'Of course I do.'

'She threw her arms around him, kissed him recklessly. I love you Jed, we will always forever be special, won't we?'

'Yes Nicki, always.'

She jumped up from the floor, 'What about your song Jed?'

'Not now,' Jed did not feel like playing. 'We'll play it tomorrow. Let's go tell Gran your news.'

'Are you going to come to the theatre tonight?'

'No, I have too much homework. I'll see you later.'

'Well, I am to have dinner with monsieur.'

'Oh!'

'I will be here tomorrow, and I will not be late this evening. You will probably not be in your bed.'

'Maybe not. Have a nice time then.'

Chapter 9

Of course, it was not the same for Jed, even though she was still very loyal to him. She often insisted, especially if Jed was on holiday from school that she stayed home with him.

'Jed is home from school today Gregoire,' she told him, 'I think I shall stay.'

'Alright my love,' Greg indulged. 'When does he return?'

But he eventually became irritated. 'You know darling, I cannot allow you to accommodate that boy so much. I wish you to come with me tomorrow. You do wish to come with me surely?'

'Oui Monsieur of course,' and Nicole did not question or insist that she stayed home with Jed again.

'I will collect you at 10:30 tomorrow Nicole and we shall spend the day together – would you like that?'

'Oui, I would like that Monsieur,' she answered.

He took her first to meet Maddie, his housekeeper and friend. 'Maddie keeps everything running smoothly,' he told her. 'She has been with me right from the beginning isn't that so Maddie.'

'Indeed it is Gregoire. I am so pleased to meet you my dear.'

She disappeared to fetch some refreshment.

Greg took Nicole to explore the house.

'Do you like it Nicole.'

'It is beautiful, so grande.'

'Yes, it was very run down when I bought it, but with the help of Maddie, we have slowly improved things. However there is still much to be done and when we are married my love, you shall make your mark on it. I am sure you will be able to find things to enhance it further.'

He watched her walking around admiring ornaments and curios. She noticed there was but one photograph on the piano. She picked it up, studying it for a few seconds. There were no others, apart from portraits of famous artists.

He took the frame form her. 'It is a picture of my parents,' he told her.

'Your Maman is very beautiful. Do they live near?'

'They have been dead for several years now.' He glanced sideways.

'And here is Maddie,' he said guiding her to a chair by the fire. 'Sit down Nicole, when we have had coffee I intend to take you up into the country, you need a break, and although I have to be back at the theatre this evening you are free, you are not dancing this evening are you my love?'

'No Monsieur.' She touched his arm. 'I do love you so much Monsieur, my heart is full for you,' she declared.

He took her hand, 'Listen my love, I have so much to say to you, you know it has been very difficult for me to come to terms with my conscience; whether I have the right to ask you to marry me, whether your love for me was just an infatuation for me, your teacher.'

'But Monsieur...'

'Shush, it is done. I am sure it is right, that we are going to be very happy together.'

He smiled. 'What is it? Why are you looking so serious, cheer up now. Do you not want to go to the country with me Nicole?'

'Oui, I shall like to spend the day with you.'

'Good, come now, I really think we should partake of at least one or two of Maddie's excellent pastries or she will be most offended.'

'Oui Monsieur,' she said as she took one of the little cakes, but she did not smile.

He lifted her chin, 'What is it Nicole?'

'Nothing Monsieur, I am happy to spend the day with you.'

'But...'

She shook her head, 'There is nothing Monsieur.'

'Very well then, we had better get started. I want this to be a very special day Nicole.'

He pulled her up from the chair and kissed her, 'You know Nicole, I consider I am a very lucky man.'

'And happy Monsieur....You do love me.'

'Of course I love you. Have I not said it so many times?'
'And you really are happy?' she asked again.
'Yes, very happy Nicole.'
They drove to Westerham.

He smiled, 'I hope you are hungry, for this little Tavern serves an excellent breakfast.' He was fascinated and gratified as he watched her consume eggs, bacon, sausage, toast and coffee.

'Ah baum!' A frequent expression of hers. 'I am full.'

Relaxing after the meal Greg leaned back watching her. Listening to her chatter.

'Would you like anything else my beloved.'

She shook her head. 'I ate too much already,' she confessed.

'Come we shall visit Chartwell. I will show you the house where the great Winston Churchill came to escape his stressful duties in London during the war.'

They explored the beautiful grounds and the house. The studio where many of his paintings still hung on the wall. The chair in which he sat at the table to work – a glass and a box of cigars casually placed there.

'He had strength and vision,' Greg told Nicole, 'and an amazing aura. He was blessed with a gift which enabled him to talk, instil confidence of victory even when the odds were against him. He was a political giant. He raised the morale of the people and kept their spirits high, just by talking to them, when sometimes there seemed little hope. Yes, this nation has a great deal for which to thank Sir Winston Churchill.'

He turned to look at her, 'And let nobody convince you otherwise. He belongs with the greats of the world.'

'Could we see the upstairs of the house,' Nicole said.
'I am not sure, it is not always possible.'
They toured a few of the rooms above, but most were cordoned off.
'It is amazing,' Nicole was interested in some of the ornaments and of course the photograph of the family.
'It is so quiet.' she said.
'Yes, but I feel there is a happy atmosphere here.'

'They drove on further into the country, Greg pointing out different historical buildings and churches. They walked over the hills and she broke away from him to run through the tall grasses. He found a bench and sat waiting for her to return to him – when she did he caught her in his arms and kissed her.

'I have something for you my beloved.'

'What is it?' she said.

'Sit down here beside me.' She obeyed.

He reached in his pocket and drew forth a small parcel.

She took it. 'What is it?' she repeated.

She gasped, could not believe here eyes. The beautiful ring was set with diamonds and sapphires.

'Oh Monsieur, it is beautiful.'

He took the ring from her and slipped it on to her finger. 'As I thought, a little adjustment is needed. I will have it altered, perhaps we could go tomorrow?' He kissed her hand. 'You have such tiny hands beloved. Will you marry me soon Nicole.?'

'Oh yes, whenever you are ready Monsieur.'

'When I am ready! I am ready this very minute.'

She threw herself against him, then quickly pulled herself back, troubled.

'What now?'

'My parents Monsieur, they will not be pleased.'

'Then we shall wait until they arrive next month. Perhaps we can get married while they are here.'

They took tea at a small tea parlour, The Rose Garden, so named for the amazing collection of different species of roses growing around the building and in the garden. A single rose was placed in the centre of each of the twelve tables.

'Are you hungry Nicole, we seem to have missed lunch.'

Nicole's eyes were fixed on the selection of cream cakes.

'I would like one of these,' she said eyeing the little cakes with anticipation.

'Help yourself my love.'

The waitress poured tea from a rose painted teapot into dainty cups that matched.

Greg smiled indulgently at Nicole as she demolished a second chocolate cake.

'Be careful my love, or you will be getting fat.' But he could not envisage her anything but tiny.

She fell asleep on the way home and awoke with a start as soon as the engine stopped. Greg reached across to kiss her on the cheek.

He looked at his watch, 'Nicole, once again I am going to have to leave you. I am due at the theatre this evening. Come I will escort you to the door. Jed will be happy to have his companion back. I will see you tomorrow. Let me kiss you good night before anyone opens the door. Did you enjoy your day darling?'

'Oh yes, Monsieur, I did, thank you so much.'

The door opened and Jed appeared.

'Hi,' he said.

'Good evening Jed,' Greg smiled. 'I am afraid Nicole has not had dinner. Perhaps your Grandmother could find something for her.'

'Sure,' Jed said. 'Would you like to come in?'

'No, I think not. Thank you. I have to be at the theatre. Until tomorrow then Nicole.'

He rang her the next morning. 'Good morning Nicole. Are you well? I woke earlier and could think of nothing else but seeing you again this evening. And Nicole, after the show we shall dine out. Will that be satisfying for you?'

'Oui, thank you Monsieur.'

'And Nicole my love, I think perhaps you must try to get used to addressing me as Gregoire, instead of Monsieur.'

She giggled. 'Oui, Mons…Gregoire.'

'Until this evening then darling.'

Jed overheard her. 'What did he want?' he asked.

'Nothing, just to take me for dinner tonight.'

'Oh, will you have to go with him every evening now.'

'I don't think so. No, of course not.'

'Will you have to go with him on Sunday?'

'I don't know Jed.'

'I suppose we shall never go skating or rowing again will we?'

'Oh, Jed please don't be upset. I will come with you sometimes.'

'Sometimes!!'

'Well, I am sure monsieur will not always want to go out with me.'

'But if he does you will go!' Jed turned away form her. 'I'm sorry Nicki, but I really do miss you.'

'Look Jed, I will come with you on Sunday. I don't have to go with Gregoire.'

'He will want you to.'

'But I will come with you, I promise.'

'Will you really.'

'I promise, we can go to the river or to the skating rink, anything.'

'Great. Are you sure?'

'Yes I'm sure. I have to have fun with you sometimes. Perhaps we can listen to your tapes.'

'Nicki come and listen to the new one I wrote for you. It's fast and jazzy.'

'Let's eat first.'

* * *

'I wish we could borrow Greg's stage sometimes. This tape is really special. I think you'll love it. I tried to choreograph something for you – see what you think. He handed her his rough choreography – will you do it for me Nicole?'

'Okay, but let me work out the steps. Play the tape Jed.'

When they had perfected the tape to their satisfaction, Jed caught her arm, 'Go on Nicki, dance!'

It was fast, nothing like ballet – just the quick intricate movements Jed had mapped out for her.

She was perfect, fantastic. Jed was fascinated as she darted around. Her eyes shining, excited. She was exhilarated.

'Jed it is a wonderful dance,' she said, 'I loved it. You should do something with it. Try to get it published.'

'It's not that good except when you are dancing. Anyway it's for you.'

'I wish I could dance like this with Gregoire!'

'He'd hate it. But you can dance here for me Nicki – it belongs to you.'

She threw her arms around his neck, 'I will dance as often as I can Jed,' she kissed him several times. 'Shall I dance again?'

'No Nicki, it's quite strenuous. I think you should rest now.'

'I'm not tired and I loved doing it. 'Why don't you show it to Justin?' she said.

'I don't know – neither he nor Greg would like it. It's too jazzy. Ballet is what they do. I'd like to write shows one day. You could dance for me.'

'I don't think Gregoire would like that.'

'No he wouldn't – But you are fantastic Nicki.'

Chapter 10

Greg met Maddie in the hall when he reached home.

'Good evening Maddie,' he said

'Gregorie.' She waited until he had settled himself in his favourite chair then handed him a whiskey.

'Thank you my dear' he said. 'Sit down Maddie. I am sure you can spare me a few minutes.'

'Of course.'

'Pour yourself a drink Maddie.' He sat back, relaxing, took a cigarette and looked at her.

'Well now, what do you think of our future ballerina, is she not delightful?'

'Yes Gregoire, she is, quite delightful - as you say.'

'And what would you say if I told you that this old fool is in love with her and has asked her to be his wife?'

Maddie was quiet for a moment. 'Are you asking my opinion Gregoire?'

'I am not quite sure Maddie – I am not exactly sure, perhaps I am.'

'Has she accepted?'

'Oh yes, she has accepted me. She believes she is in love with me also.'

'But you are not sure of this.'

Greg sighed. 'Frankly Maddie, I am not sure at all. She is only just eighteen years of age, barely past childhood, in fact she still is very young. Many students think they are in love with their teacher.'

'Yes, and I suppose that could be possible.'

'And yet she seems genuine enough. She insists that she loves me. Do you think I should curb my feelings, Maddie?'

'Only you can answer that Gregoire, but don't you think that it is a bit late for that if you have already asked her?'

'Even so, do you think I am too old for such a young innocent?'

'If you are both genuinely in love and you understand, realise how young she is – I cannot see any problem regarding age.' She sipped the whiskey. 'There have been many such marriages over the centuries, which have survived as well as any other, perhaps more so.'

'Thank you, Maddie. She is perfect, in every way, she really is perfect.'

Maddie put her hand on Greg's arm. 'She is a young girl, Gregoire. You must remember that she will grow up.'

Greg seemed not hear. 'She is so beautiful, Maddie, exquisite and she dances like an angel.'

He poured himself another drink and topped up Maddie's glass. 'You must not expect too much of her my dear,' Maddie said.

'You and I, Maddie, have been friends for many years. I would be grateful to know I have your blessing.'

'Gregoire my dear, I am flattered that you think so highly of me – of course you have my blessing.'

'It will mean that we'll all be living in this house and because she is so young, she might lean on you a little, would you mind that Maddie?'

'You know I will do all I can to help her should she need me.'

'Thank you Maddie, you are a gem. I do not know what I would have done without you all these years.' He stood up, put his cheek against hers. 'I would never have survived.'

'Congratulations my dear,' Maddie said. 'I am sure you will be very happy. You deserve that.'

'And now I must go to the theatre. I have to relieve Justin; he is taking his wife out to dine. It is Cheryl's birthday. Goodnight my friend and thank you.'

Chapter 11

Jed watched as Nicole sorted through her meagre wardrobe.
'What is wrong with that dress, it's pretty,' he said
'It's old, it is not glamorous.'
'It is lovely and anyway, you are glamorous Nicky'
'Oh, Jed, you always such nice things but it is not an evening dress and Monsieur Gregoire is taking me out after the show tonight. He says it is special. Oh well, I suppose I will have to take it . There is not another – I will have to go shopping soon. I have hardly any clothes.'
'Could I come with you?'
'If you like, but it won't be very nice for you, you will get very bored.'
'No I won't, I'd like to come.'
'Alright – the next morning I have free.'
She wrapped the dress up with tights and other accessories, said goodbye to Jed and Amy and left for the theatre.
'You will look lovely Nicki. That colour suits you.'
'Thanks Jed. I still wish I had a better one.'
She did not see Greg before the performance. She was dancing tonight in a short sketch and would not be on the stage for long. He came to the dressing room for her at the end of the show.
'You look delightful, my love,' he told her, and she did.
She had swept her hair up into a ponytail, had persuaded one of the girls to put on her make-up and one of the other girls had draped her dress with a sheath of chiffon – had transformed it completely.
She opened her eyes wide at the splendour of the restaurant.
'You like it?' he asked

'It is magnifique.'

The manager greeted them at the desk. 'Good evening Dr. Fellini. I have reserved a special table for you and your guest. Please come this way.'

He smiled then poured two glasses of champagne from the ice bucket beside the table. 'I will send the waiter over directly.'

Greg raised his glass. 'To the most beautiful girl in the universe,' he said.

Nicole laughed and sipped the champagne.

'Now Nicole, tell me how you are enjoying rehearsing Coppelia'

'I like it Monsieur'

'Gregoire,' he corrected.

'And your papa has accepted my invitation – you will be superb darling. They will love you.'

He took her hands. They will be so proud of you.

'Oui Mon – Gregoire.'

'What is it Nicole?'

'Monsieur, please talk of you and me and not of the ballet.'

'I am sorry darling. Of course I should not be talking shop this evening. Well then my love, tell me something of yourself. I know you live in France on a farm, but that is really all.'

She told him a little more of her life on the farm, the wine having relaxed her. He watched her, could not take his eyes off her. She was so alive, her eyes wide with innocence and excitement. After a while she was silent, almost solemn.

'You tell me nothing of you Monsieur,' she said. 'Sometimes I think you look so sad.'

'But I'm not sad Nicole. This evening I am the happiest man alive.'

'What were you like when you were a little boy Monsieur?'

'Now that was a very long time ago,' he said.

'Were you happy Monsieur?'

'Nicole, my darling, I do not think that my life is the best subject for discussion this evening. Perhaps another time I will tell you a little.'

He passed the menu. 'What would you like Nicole?'

'Please order for me, as before.'

'Alright my love, are you sure you would not like to choose for yourself?' She shook her head.

Greg conferred with the waiter. He turned back to Nicole. 'I have ordered some caviar. Do you like caviar darling?'

'Oui, my papa always brought some at the weekend as a treat.' She looked around. 'This is a beautiful place Monsieur,' she said.

'Yes, it is. It has always been a favourite of mine. I hope it will become so for you my love!'

His eyes continued to watch her. She looked up, concerned. 'You do not like, Monsieur.'

He smiled. 'I like,' he replied. 'I like everything I see before me. Your beauty outshines everyone and everything here. I am happy that you have come into my life. You look absolutely gorgeous darling. That colour suits you. Are you enjoying your meal? Do you like what I have ordered for you?'

'It is very good Monsieur.'

Greg could not refrain from talking about the ballet. He was looking forward to launching his new protégée.

'There are only a few more weeks before your debut darling. How do you feel?'

'Nervous, of course. I hope I will not forget the steps.'

'Of course you will not forget. You are already proficient. Your parents will be proud of you, as I am my love.'

She smiled, causing his heart to race.

He laid his fork down, looked across at her, drinking in the beauty before him. He stood up.

'Nicole, my love, would you do me the honour. He extended his hand. She took it and followed him through to the circular dance floor.'

No word passed between them. There was no need for words as they danced, eyes locked together, oblivious to anyone around them, to the strains of the Invitation Waltz.

Towards the end of the dance, he stood still, his arms around her and brushed his lips across her forehead.

'I love you Nicole,' he whispered. 'I love you.'

He would have liked to take her home with him, to have her lying next to him, to make love to her, to wake up in the morning with her lying beside him. But he took her back to Amy's. Her innocence, her naivety and her complete trust of him was enough to curb his desires. She had been very sheltered. He did not want to frighten her. He could wait.

Chapter 12

Belle received her daughter's letter with a mixture of concern and anger.

'She is a child Pierre. She knows nothing of the world. This, this person is over forty years old – too old. What is she thinking of. I do not like it Pierre.'

'Now, Belle, let us not jump to conclusions.'

'Conclusions, what conclusions? The fact is, he is old enough to be her father. She must come home.'

'Shush now, Belle. She is in the ballet. We cannot deprive her of her great moment.'

'I insist she comes home. If she is so professional, she can dance here. It should not be difficult to join a French company.'

'We shall see, ma Cherie, we'll see.' Still, Belle wrote to Nicole demanding she return to France.

The next day, she informed all and sundry that her daughter would soon be returning and started to prepare her homecoming.

Chapter 13

'You look pale, my love. Are you feeling well?'

'I am fine, Gregoire.'

'Well, I will take you to Jenny this weekend.'

'Jenny?'

'Yes. she is an old friend of mine – she would like to meet you.'

'She danced for you?'

'No, my love, but she is a contemporary of mine. I met her whilst staying in Bournemouth. We became very good friends.'

'Did you love her?'

Greg laughed. 'I have only ever loved you my precious, but Jenny has always been a good friend to me. You will like her and I know she will adore you. We will drive down after the show on Saturday and you can rest all day Sunday. We shall drive back on Monday morning. The sea and Jenny's wonderful cooking will be good for you.'

They arrived just before midnight and Jenny had prepared a light supper.

'I am so pleased to meet you my dear.' Jenny clasped Nicole and kissed her.

'You both look exhausted and I am sure you are hungry. Come, eat and then you can relax.'

'Thank you, Jenny,' Greg greeted his friend. 'That would be ideal. Nicole can sleep and in the morning we can drive along the coast and have lunch in Boscombe.'

'As you wish, Gregoire, but I think perhaps that if you have promised this beautiful girl a rest, it would be better to stay here for lunch and then walk along the beach.'

'We'll see.' Greg replied.

Nicole was tired and excused herself after the supper. 'Would you mind if I went to bed,' she said.

'Of course not, pet,' Jenny said. 'I will show you your room.'

Nicole looked back at Greg.

'Alright my love. I will come and say goodnight.'

'It is a beautiful room, Madame,' Nicole said.

'I hope you will be comfortable darling.'

'Goodnight Gregoire,' Nicole reached up to kiss him. 'I am sorry I am so tired.'

'Sleep well, my love. I will see you in the morning.'

'She is a gem, Gregoire. Where on earth did you find her? Most delightful.'

'Yes, I know Jenny. I am so very lucky.'

He explained how he came to meet her. 'And now, Jenny, she is on her way to becoming a ballerina. She will make her debut in Coppelia next month. I fell in love with her the moment I saw her.'

'She is lovely.' Jenny said, then paused. 'Now, my dear, how are you. You work too hard. You must relax more.'

'I do relax more since Nicole and I became engaged.'

'You certainly look happy.'

'I am happy, Jenny.' He studied her, 'You have not mentioned the great difference in our ages.'

'If you love each other, what does age matter?'

'It shouldn't, I agree. But as you know I am almost middle-aged. She is barely eighteen years of age. I worry a little that she might get tired of an old man like me.'

'Nonsense, Gregoire. You are a very attractive, energetic man. I can see she worships you.' She handed him a brandy.

'And then, my dear, I think you should join her, get some rest. I will see you at breakfast.'

'Thank you, Jenny. You really do like her, do you not?'

'I do, Gregoire. Who could fail to like, even love, such a treasure.' She patted his arm. 'Take care of her. Look after her, my dear.'

'Jenny, it may or may not seem strange to you but Nicole and I, well, we – we have not shared a bedroom as yet.' He paused. 'I think I….'

Jenny put a hand on his shoulder. 'Of course my dear, I understand.'

'She is so young you see and I suppose I am a little old fashioned.

'I understand. Your old room is made up and ready for you. Goodnight my dear. Sleep well.'

Nicole woke early and was charmed with the room Jenny had given her.

'Did you sleep well, my dear?' Jenny asked.

'I slept perfectly, Madame,' Nicole said.

'Such a soft bed and such pretty colours.'

'Yes, it is a pretty room. You must make Gregoire bring you here often. He does not get away from the theatre often enough.'

'I will try.' Nicole could not imagine being able to make Gregoire do anything.

'It is so lovely here, and the sea is so near.'

'Yes, it is wonderful in the summer. You must try to come then.'

'I will try, Madame.'

'Please call me Jenny, darling.'

'Merci.'

They had a leisurely lunch and then Greg took Nicole for a walk along the coast road. The sun was shining although there was a nip in the air.

'I insist on taking you out for dinner, Jenny. Pity Sam is away.'

'I can cook you a meal here Gregoire.'

'No, I insist. The lunch was delicious. We will eat out.'

Nicole chatted through the meal, charming Jenny and Greg with her stories of the farm.

'Do you miss the farm dear?' Jenny asked.

'Sometimes, but I like being here, especially with Gregoire, and I love to dance.'

'Yes,' Greg said, 'she is a superb dancer, Jenny. Absolutely perfect.'

'It is really lovely, your house Madame Jenny. So pretty and grande.'

'Thank you, my dear. I hope you will both come again soon.'

'We will, Jenny, I promise.' Greg assured her.

They left early on Monday morning after farewells.

'We shall stop nearer to London, darling,' Greg said, 'and have a good lunch'.

'But I am so full.'

'Well, a light lunch, then. Whatever you wish, my love.'

'She is nice, your Jenny.'

'Yes, she is very kind. She helped me a lot when I was starting out. Introduced me to good dancers, and made herself useful in all sorts of ways. She even found the house I live in. Yes, Jenny is a good friend.'

They stopped at a small restaurant just before they reached London and although Nicole said she was full, she ate a good lunch.

'Did you enjoy your stay, my love?'

She nodded. 'I like the sea,' she said.

'When we get home, you will have time to relax before the performance and tomorrow you will rest again. There will be no show for you tomorrow evening. Natalie will stand in for you.'

'I am not tired, Gregoire.'

'Nevertheless, you may have all day and night free.'

'You look troubled., Nicole. What is it?'

'Nothing, Monsieur.'

He knew when she reverted back to calling him 'Monsieur', there was some problem.

'Nicole, you will be a superb Coppelia. You are not worried about that, are you?'

'It is my parents, Monsieur.'

'They will be so very proud of you, darling, as I am. You will marry me whilst they are here. I think they would like that. Have you heard from them?'

'Not yet.' She looked serious.

'What is it?' he said.

'I am so afraid the will not want me to get married. I think they want me to go back.'

'You mean they would like us to get married in France? That will be no problem. We could spare a few days away from the theatre as soon as Coppellia finishes.'

'No Monsieur, I mean they will not want me to get married at all.'

'We shall see, you must not worry so much about these things. I will talk to them when they get here. Would you like anything else?'

'No thank you.'

'Well, then, we will move into the lounge for coffee, it will be more comfortable.'

The waiter brought the coffee and they sat leisurely talking. He loved listening to her chatter. She always talked of the farm, of Pascal and the animals – and of Jed.

'He is so clever, Monsieur. He writes beautiful music and sometimes I dance to the tapes he has recorded.'

'I see. I dare say he misses you when you are with me.'

'But he does not mind, Gregoire. Still, I like to please him sometimes, he is my friend.'

'Which means,' Gregoire retorted, 'that I must not monopolise you too much.'

'Monsieur?'

'I am teasing, darling. I consider I am very lucky to be with you at all.' He lifted her hand to his lips.

On the way home she mentioned her parents again.

'They will not like it, Monsieur. I am a little worried.'

'Nicole, my love. Let us cross that bridge when we come to it. We can always set things right. Leave it all to me. I am sure your parents have only your happiness at heart. You enjoyed your break, darling?'

'Oh, yes Gregoire. Thank you so much. It was a wonderful weekend.'

'There will be many more my beloved,' he said.

After the novelty of escorting and nurturing her, Greg inevitably turned his thoughts to his work.

'You won't mind, my love' he apologised. 'I have been very lazy. I really must get down to some serious work.

This gave Nicole and Jed more time together and Jed was thrilled to have his friend with him again. However, if Greg decided he wanted to take her out to dinner or away at the weekend, he expected her to accept his invitations without question. He became demanding if she intimated that she had promised Jed.

'For goodness sake, darling,' he said. 'The boy is with you all the time. Surely you do not wish to spend your time with a schoolboy, rather than accompanying me in a more sophisticated activity. Is he becoming a nuisance to you?'

'Of course not. It is just that I had already promised to go with Jed.'

'Well, I insist you come with me this evening. You may do whatever you like Sunday. I have an appointment most of the day.'

She never argued with him, and she always did what he wanted but often felt sorry for Jed. Greg sensed her feelings.

'Listen, darling. Jed is a schoolboy. He will get over his disappointment. In any case, I think he relies on you far too much. It is not good for him. Has he no friends of his own age?'

'Yes of course he has but they are not interested in show business. We talk a lot about that and dancing.'

'Oh well, as long as you are happy. Perhaps if you would like, we could take him with us sometimes.'

She jumped at the suggestion. 'That would be wonderful Gregoire.'

Greg noticed how she brightened up at the suggestion and he was sorry he had been so rash. However, he found that Jed was good company and popular with his guests. But he never accompanied them in the evenings.

'I prefer to be alone with my beautiful fiancée.' he told her. He also became protective towards her, decided he did not want her skating.

'You might injure yourself Nicole. Think of your dancing.'

If he discovered she had defied him, he showed his anger and forbade her to go again. They ignored him and made sure he did not find out.

One of the instructors noticed Jed, approached him during one of the dance intervals.

'You're good,' he told him. 'I'd like to train you up for competitions and then for the championships.'

Jed laughed. 'Couldn't afford it,' he said.

'I'll train you for free,' the instructor offered. 'You are a natural. You have a good style.'

'I taught myself to skate. It is not possible I'm that good. I am just an amateur who enjoys skating. Thanks all the same but I am not that good.'

'Oh, but you are, kid. I know talent when I see it. Think it over. I'd love to train you.'

Jed shrugged. 'Okay, I'll think about it.'

'Gosh,' Nicole was impressed. 'Why don't you, Jed?'

'Costs a lot of money and although he says he wouldn't charge, as soon as I get half way through, he'd want his pound of flesh.'

'He sounded as though he meant it,' she said.

'Costs a fortune, unless you are good enough and lucky enough to find a sponsor. Even then, my granddad has not got that sort of money. Anyway, I want to dance. I have an excellent teacher. The best. I hope Dr. Fellini will take me into his company when I leave school. He half promised me something in the Christmas show. I hope he remembers.'

'I'll remind him,' Nicole promised.

'No, I'd rather you didn't thanks.'

'Well, if he promised, he will – he is very honourable.'

Jed grinned. 'You think he is a god, don't you.'

'I love him, Jed, but I love you too. You do not understand, I think?'

'No of course I don't. I'm just a kid, aren't I?'

'Please, Jed. Don't be cross.'

'Sorry, it's just that I miss you when you aren't here and I wish I was older!'

'I like you as you are, Jed. You are my dear good friend.'

'Yeah!'

'Anyway, I'll be here all day Sunday. Gregoire is going out all day.'

'Good. Perhaps we could go somewhere different. There is a funfair in Clapham.'

'That would be fun. We'll go there!' She looked at her watch. I'd better get ready now, though.'

'I'll walk to the theatre with you.'

Nicole received an answer from France the following week and although she had expected opposition, she was shocked and upset at her mother's vitriolic words. Jed found her sitting on the window seat in the dining room.

'What's up Nicole?'

'They want me to go home. I do not think I can fight them Jed. They do not wish me to marry Gregoire.'

'You do not have to go. I told you before, you don't have to. You are eighteen; they can't make you go.'

'I know all that but they are my parents and I am not a fighter like you.'

'Tell Dr. Fellini. He will know what to do. Take the letter to him, Nicole, when you go to the theatre later. Tell him. Promise me you will tell him.'

'Yes, I think that will be best, but they will come and fetch me. They will insist I go back. I will have to obey. It is my duty.'

'That's rubbish, Nicole. Nobody thinks like that these days. Tell Dr. Fellini. He'll know what to do.'

She went early to the theatre and found Greg in his office.

'What can I do for you, my angel?' he said. He turned and caught her in his arms, kissed her and smiled. She handed him the letter. He looked at her after reading it.

'Come here, darling.' He drew her close.

'Nicole, my love. They do have a point. You are very young.'

'You do not wish to marry me?'

'Of course I do, darling. Of course I do.'

She began to weep. 'They will come for me. They will insist I go back with them.'

'No, Nicole. I will write to them, explaining how much we are in love. Why did you not wait for me to do that, sweetheart?'

She shook her head resignedly. 'Monsieur, it would have made no difference. They will make me go.'

'No! They will not,' he said vehemently. 'You do not wish to go, do you Nicole?'

'Oh, no Monsieur. It will not be the same in France. I do not wish to leave the ballet here.'

'And me, Nicole. What about me?'

She threw her arms around him. 'I never wish to leave you, Monsieur.'

'Well then, you will stay here with me.'

'But they said they would come soon. I don't know what to do.'

'I do,' he said. 'Are you absolutely sure you wish to marry me, to make your home here?'

'I am sure, Monsieur. I love you. I want to marry you. I don't want to go back to France.'

'Alright.' he took her shoulders and bent to kiss her. 'Would you be prepared to marry me in the next few days?'

'Yes. Oh yes, I would. And then I would not have to go back.'

'Yes, you wouldn't feel obliged to leave me.'

He procured a confidential licence, the details of which could not be disclosed to anyone. They married quietly the following week, just with closest friends. Jed, Justin, their families and Maddie. It was a warm sunny day in July. There was a performance that night and Nicole had never looked more radiant. At the end of the show, he took her for dinner at the Caprice and afterwards to his house.

'Sit down, Nicole,' he said. 'Maddie has left some champagne.' He produced glasses and handed her one.

'Are you happy, my beloved? You have no regrets? You did not mind being married in such haste? I will make it up to you, darling. I will take you to some beautiful spot for our honeymoon as soon as the show is at an end.

'There is no need, Monsieur. I do not need such things.'

'But you deserve them, darling.'

He took the empty glass from her hand and kissed her. 'You have had a very long day, beloved. You must be tired. Come, my precious.'

He led her towards the stairs and to the room which Maddie had prepared for them. There was a small fire burning in the grate and a huge bouquet of flowers on the table. He left her, went downstairs for the champagne. Suddenly, he felt guilty. He had deliberately taken her from her family because in his heart he was afraid of losing her. Afraid they would have persuaded her, bullied her to go back with them. She would have obeyed out of a mixture of love and duty. Perhaps he was wrong. He should have trusted her feelings for him and yet he had been afraid. He could not bear the thought of her leaving. He hoped she would not regret the haste. He went slowly back up the stairs with the champagne. He pushed open the door. She was waiting. Refreshingly uninhibited, she stood before him unsmiling, pure and innocent, her great eyes staring up at him. He felt incredibly humble, as though he was standing before a goddess. He could not move.

Sensing his reluctance to take her, she proffered her hand.

'Monsieur,' she whispered.

He slipped the soft white gown from her shoulders, letting it fall to the floor and gazed reverently at her beautiful unblemished body, his for the taking. He began stroking her tenderly, felt her tremble to his touch. Gathering her close, he picked her up and laid her gently on the bed. He stood gazing down at her.

He threw off his clothes carelessly. She watched his every move as he climbed up beside her, a mixture of fear and love in her beautiful eyes. He smiled down at her reassuringly. After caressing her, whispering his love for her. He moved across her, sat astride her, lowering his head, enabling him to kiss her, at first softly, gently – his lips searing across her face, neck, arms. Her wide eyes were still fixed on his. He could see she was suddenly afraid. He put his hand up to stroke her hair, whispering words of encouragement and love, kissing her again. He began to caress her gently, his hands travelling her body, her nipples hardened before he even touched them. Then he brought his mouth down on hers, his tongue swirling inside sensuously, tasting the sweetness of her. She moaned, kissing him back, her arms clinging to him. He stopped kissing her, raised himself above her, gazing down at her beauty.

'You are so lovely, Nicole,' he whispered, 'So perfect.'

Once again his mouth crashed down on hers, fiercely this time, his kisses sweeping across her face, his hands probing every inch of her and as he cupped her breast, flicking the nipple with his fingers, she was unable to stifle a little cry. As he continued kissing her, she whimpered, not understanding the strange sensations he caused her. Over and over he kissed and caressed her, murmuring words of love into her ear, trying to reassure her. She responded passionately at first to his love making, then as his knees began to prise her thighs apart she trembled with fear and desire.

Greg sensed her fear. 'Don't be afraid, my beloved. Trust me.'

He gently eased himself inside her and as he penetrated further, she cried out. She opened her eyes, looked at him questioningly, accusingly, trying to push him away from her. He held her still.

'It is alright, darling,' he soothed her. 'It will be alright'. And when she cried out again, he pressed his lips against hers, kissing her gently, quietening her. He lay still with her for a moment, so that she would get used to the feel of him inside her. Then knowing the discomfort he was about to cause her, he pushed purposefully, plunging deeper into her. She gasped, letting out a squeal of pain as he continued relentlessly. Kissing her, loving her, all the time allaying her fear of him. Then, as the pain ceased, she relaxed, clasped him to her, pulling him closer, sighing with pleasure as she felt his body warm against her own. Trembling with a passion so great, it sent Greg's head spinning, she dug her fingers into his flesh, abandoning herself to his lovemaking, her whole being awakened with a blinding ecstasy. She lay exhausted beneath him, a feeling of contentment and love enveloping her. Greg pushed the damp hair from her eyes and brushed his lips across her forehead.

'You are my own sweet love,' he said. 'I am sorry I hurt you, it will be easier next time, I promise you.'

'You are pleased with me, Gregoire?' she said, anxious for his approval.

'Oh, Nicole. I am the luckiest man alive.'

He caught her in his arms, cuddling and kissing her until in a little while they were loving again. This time Nicole felt nothing but pleasure. Afterwards he held her against him, his arms encircling her tiny body, her head resting against his shoulder.

'Are you happy, my love?'

'I am happy Monsieur. I love you very much.'

When she awoke the next morning the sun shone through the window, a shaft of gold streaked across the bed. She turned and gazed at her love. As she moved her arm to touch him, he awoke, smiled and drew her close to him. She bent to kiss him.

'Did you ever see a more beautiful day?' she exclaimed.

He looked lovingly at her. 'I never saw a more beautiful girl,' he replied.

'I am so happy,' she cried. 'I love you so much. I will love you all of my life. The world is a heavenly place.'

'Wherever you are, my precious, that is where heaven will always be.'

And it was so for Greg. Every moment he spent with her was pure unadulterated heaven. He was a very happy man. For the first time in years the haunted look disappeared from his eyes. He worshipped her. He loved the way she always skipped instead of walking. The way she sat cross legged in front of him. The way she laughed, or pouted when she was angry. The way she called him Monsieur sometimes. The way she pronounced his name. He loved her naivety and innocence, her gentleness and loyalty. She was young, he gave her space, never restricted her. She was free as a bird and he knew she would never betray him.

She was loved by everyone, men and women alike, for she had no meanness about her.

Greg asked Justin to run the company for a few days so that he could stay at home with Nicole. He was aware that moving away from Amy and Jed would be a little traumatic for her at first. He wanted her to like being in his house; also he knew she would miss Jed's company. They had always been inseparable and this fact made him slightly envious of their close relationship. When he returned to work, she did feel at a loose end in this large house. But she had some of Jed's tapes and spent much of her time listening and dancing to music. She wandered about, looking at the many books in the library, walking around the garden or knocking on Maddie's door asking her if she could help her, waiting until Jed called her after school, when they went for a walk.

Greg continued to groom her for Coppelia. She was virtually ready to perform. He could almost present her next week, but he must wait until her parents arrived. He had promised them seats for her debut. After all they would be arriving in a couple of weeks.

Chapter 14

Pierre and Belle arrived the day before the opening of Coppelia. Greg met them at the airport and settled them in the Savoy Hotel where he had booked them in as guests. Although Belle was distant, she made a great fuss of her daughter and was polite to Greg and they were left to settle in until the next day. Nicole's conscience had bothered her since her marriage. She felt she had betrayed them and although Greg had implored her to keep silent until the first night, she could not do it. She felt it would cause too much hurt, to them if she delayed telling them that she had married without their knowledge, but she did not expect the tirade that followed.

Belle could not believe her daughter's deceit.

'This is too much!' she cried. 'First you lie about leaving Madame Trudi and now this.' She started to weep.

'Please Maman don't cry, I am so sorry I did not tell you before.'

'Why? Why have you deceived us Nicole?'

'I don't know Maman. I was afraid you would not allow it. I was afraid you would take me home.'

'That is for sure, I do not approve of this, this Dr. Fellini. He is far too old. He has poisoned you against us. You are a child, he has taken advantage of you. You should have returned home after you left Madame Trudi.'

''I love Gregoire, Maman. Please understand.'

Belle ignored her tears. She put her arms around her daughter. 'Oh my poor baby, you must return ma petite cochon. You are too young to be alone.'

'I am not alone Maman, I have Gregoire, and Jed and Jed's grandparents. They love me.'

'We can get the marriage annulled,' Belle continued, 'your Papa will arrange it.'

'No Maman, Gregoire is my husband. I love him.'

Pierre tried to intervene, but Belle was always the forceful one and she was genuinely upset. She truly believed her innocent child had been coerced into marriage by this reprobate. She glared at Greg.

'How dare you Monsieur take advantage of a girl as young as Nicole. She is an innocent child. How dare you.'

Greg drew Nicole away. He kissed her tenderly. 'Nicole, my love, they are absolutely right. I did persuade you, didn't I darling?'

'No Gregoire, you did not.'

'You see, I was so afraid of losing you, that they would persuade you to go away with them. It was wrong of me – I know how much you love your parents. Listen darling, would you like to go back for a while? I can arrange that in a month or two. I will wait for you to come back. You would come back to me, wouldn't you darling?'

She was crying, he clasped her close to him. 'You are torn between us, aren't you?'

'No Monsieur, I want to stay here with you. I love you. I do not want to go back to France, but I wish they would not be so angry and upset.'

They returned to the others. Belle had become quieter, but she did not look or speak to Greg or her daughter, and during the next few days she made her contempt for Greg very plain.

The first night of the ballet, Pierre came to Nicole's dressing room, kissed her and wished her good luck.

'I am sorry, cherie, your Maman is still upset. Perhaps in time, when she sees how happy you are, she will forgive. You are happy, ma petite cochon?'

'Oh Papa, I am, I love Greg.'

'Good, but Nicole, to marry without telling us was not an honourable thing to do.'

'I am sorry Papa.'

Pierre patted his daughter on the head. 'Alright, ma cherie. We shall always love you, remember that. I am looking forward to seeing you dance.'

The ballet was a great success. When Nicole retreated to her dressing room, she was hoping that her mother would be there, but neither of them came and she burst into tears.

'Don't my love, don't do this.' Greg held her tightly. 'We shall see them later. The audience adored you, beloved, as I do. Get changed, we will join them for supper at the hotel. Everything is laid on. I am looking forward to showing you off. They will all be there.'

Her eyes lit up. 'My parents will be there?'

'Yes, they will all be there to toast your success. Dry your eyes. I will come back for you in a few minutes. I must see the other artists.'

'Gregoire,' she called, 'you were pleased with me, yes?'

'You were superb, darling.' He kissed her. 'I will see you directly.'

He turned to her dresser. 'Look after her Sophia,' he said. 'I will send Jed to you my love. There are a lot of people wanting to congratulate you. Smile for me now.'

Greg had suggested they celebrated as usual at the Arts Club, but Belle refused to leave the hotel, so attempting to please her, he arranged a dinner party at the Savoy with Jed, his grandparents, Justin, Yanni and their families.

At first, Belle refused even to attend this gathering, but Pierre persuaded her. Perhaps he sensed that it would be a long time before they saw their daughter again. Even so, Belle was still extremely upset, still angling to take Nicole back to France, and although Nicole looked happy and excited, she could not help feeling unsettled because of Belle's attitude. Greg sensed her anguish and was livid with Belle.

When they left to go back to France, Belle unbent enough to embrace her daughter, to kiss her and to warn her of the danger she would certainly encounter – especially with a man 'old enough to be your grand-père' she said.

'Maman, Gregoire is not old.'

'Too old for you Nicole. Please ma cherie, would you come back with us?'

'We will come and see you when the show has finished its run, Maman. Please forgive me, I did not mean to hurt you.'

Belle ignored Greg's outstretched hand, she never wished to see nor hear from this man again, she told Pierre.

'She will get over it, ma cherie,' Pierre told his daughter, trying to comfort her, 'I will talk to her.'

He kissed her goodbye and looked harshly at Greg. 'You should never have done this, Monsieur, and now I must ask you to please take care of our daughter. She is very precious to us.'

They shook hands and Pierre hurried to catch up with his wife. Nicole cried all the way home from the airport.

'I am sorry my love,' Greg said 'I suppose we should have told them earlier.'

'They would not have come to England Monsieur. They would just have tried to make me go back. I have hurt them very badly; they did not even tell me that they had enjoyed the ballet.'

'I'm sure they did darling – come, as your father said, she will get over the shock. I love you. Try not to be too disappointed. There will be other times.'

'I will be alright tomorrow.' she said.

Chapter 15

During the month that followed, Greg took her to special places after the show. She always looked exquisite, he was pleased to have her beside him. He never tired of looking at her. She in turn worshipped him – it was a perfect love match.

Wherever they went men and women turned to look at them, she was so astonishingly beautiful, but she had eyes only for Greg. Jed missed his friend, especially during the holidays, but she spent time with him sometimes when Greg was busy.

'I do miss you, Nicki,' he said.

'Never mind we can go on the river on Sunday. Gregoire has to go out and today we are free to go anywhere you like.'

He sat rubbing his finger along the edge of the table.

'Cheer up Jed' she pleaded.

'Shall we go to the rink then, we could stay all day.'

'Yes, I'd like that. We haven't been for a while have we?'

So they went skating in the morning but decided to work together on Jed's music after lunch.

He had written a number of songs; some good, others not worth keeping. When Greg learned that Nicki had been skating he reprimanded her and ranted at Jed for taking risks with her.

When they were in bed Nicole kissed him, folding her arms around him.

'I love to skate, Gregoire, do not be angry with Jed. I am always very careful.'

'You are a dancer, Nicole – if you break any of your limbs it would ruin your chances.'

'I will be extra careful, Gregoire. Please say I can go.'

He took her face in his hands. 'Well I suppose if you love it so much, but please my love be very careful. Do not get silly with Jed's stunts.'

'I won't. And thank you Gregoire, I love you'

The Christmas season was always a busy time for Gregoire and Justin. They decided to stage the Nutcracker.

'You promised Jed something in the Christmas show, Greg. He has worked bloody hard and is raring to go.' Justin said

'I'll think about it' Greg replied, 'he'd have to get clearance from his school for rehearsals etc.'

'That shouldn't be a problem, should it? We have had youngsters before.'

'Depends on the school. As I said, I'll think about it.'

'He's good Greg. Time he had some sort of recognition.'

Greg was still a very formidable character but had mellowed a little since his marriage. Nicole still wrote regularly to France. Only her father answered her letters. He never mentioned Greg. 'Your Maman is still very upset, Nicole,' he wrote, 'it was not a good thing to do, ma cherie.'

Every time she received a letter it infuriated Greg, because it was the only thing that made her miserable. At these times, he would take her in his arms, trying to comfort her, often carrying her to the bedroom to make love to her when she would forget her misery.

Greg became so frustrated with the hurt they caused her that he wrote humbling himself, apologising, asking for a truce. 'I will bring Nicole to see you very soon, and we shall talk Madame, or perhaps you will visit us.'

He sent pictures of her, telling them how well she was and how happy they both were. They never answered his letters. Nicole started to write less frequently but she never gave up hope of receiving forgiveness from her mother.

'I am so sorry my love, I cannot bear to see you upset, however it is me with whom they are angry…'

'I do not mind – you are all I ever want. I do not feel so sad any more Gregoire, I have you. It does not matter what they think' she smiled at him, 'truly it does not.'

'Good, you know how much I love you, don't you.'

'Yes, I know and I love you too.'

'Well now, here is something which might please you beloved. Justin has suggested we should use Jed in the Christmas production. Do you think he will be pleased?'

'Oh Gregoire, I know he will and I am so happy for him. He is really good, isn't he Gregoire?'

'Yes, he is, I admit, he has worked hard.'

'May I tell him?'

'I suppose so. You are very fond of Jed aren't you?'

'Yes, I love Jed, he is such a nice boy, so exciting, you know. I told you he writes songs.'

'I must hear them sometime' Greg said. 'How is your skating, I presume you still skate?'

'I love skating. I can do a lot of things now. I have learned to do a salco – Jed has taught me so many things.'

'You must be very careful Nicole. I hope Jed is not reckless.'

'I am very careful Gregoire, but Jed says I learn to do things very quickly. He is teaching me to dance.'

'It is good job I am not jealous,' Greg said.

'But Jed is young boy, and there is no one else I love like you, only you'

He kissed her. 'I hope you will always enjoy life the way you do now my love. I want you always to be happy and of course you may tell Jed he is included in the show.'

'May I tell him now?'

'Of course.' He smiled as she threw her arms around him.

'Jed will be so thrilled,' she cried 'Do you mind if I go now?'

'So anxious to get away from me.'

'Oh no, Gregoire,' she was full of remorse.

'I am teasing darling. Off you go. Don't be too long.'

He watched her skipping off excitedly. God how he loved her. Before she reached the door, she turned, rushed back and throwing her arms around him she kissed him.

'I do love you Gregoire. I will be back soon' then she rushed off again.

Greg telephoned Justin to tell him he was in agreement to include Jed in the Nutcracker.

'Nicole is with him now imparting the news to him. I'll leave it up to you to cast him.'

'Right, I think you have made a good decision.'

'Your decision, Justin' Greg corrected.

'Well, whatever'

'Just remember it will be his first real part.'

'He is more than up to it, Greg.'

'Better start casting – you will not need me for a few days – get it all sorted and I will see you next week.'

'Of course, Nicole will be dancing Clara, I presume.'

'Of course, she will be with you on Monday as well as Jed. I have an appointment and will not be back until Thursday next. I'll try to look in on Thursday or Friday.'

'What do you want me to do with Jed?'

'I'll leave it to you. Try him out. Maybe he'll have to have time off. How old is he now?'

'Fourteen, I think. He is tall, looks older and as you know, dances almost professionally.'

'Well, you'd better get Amy to sort out the school. I don't want any sort of aggro, Justin. If they won't cooperate, find someone else.'

'Greg, do you want to direct Nicole?'

'Why? Justin, I am leaving everything to you. Nicole will give you no trouble.'

'I wasn't suggesting she would.'

'Alright Justin, I'll see you later today to discuss the production.'

Later Greg and Justin met to discuss some minor details. At five thirty Nicole appeared, bubbling with excitement.

'Jed is so thrilled, he could not believe it.' She flung her arms around Greg.

'Well, it is Justin he has to thank,' Greg told her 'It was he who suggested we include him. I hope he appreciates it and will work hard.'

'He will. He is so grateful. Thank you Justin.'

When Justin finally left, Greg drew Nicole onto his knee. 'Listen darling, I have to go away for a few days and you must report to Justin on Monday for casting. I will be back on Thursday. Maddie will look after you. You will be alright. I shall miss you, my love.'

'Greg, if you are not here, I would like to stay with Jed's grand-mère. Is that alright?'

'But this is your home now, darling.'

'I know and I love it here, but I will be lonely. Just this once, please Gregoire? You would not mind, would you?'

'Alright, I will tell Maddie and I will drop you off at Jed's tomorrow morning. It will be early because I have to be on the train at eight.'

He touched her chin. 'You will have the whole four days with him. You must be careful when skating or if you go on the river.'

'I will. When will you come back?'
'On Thursday, after lunch I think. Will you be back here for me?'
'Of course I will.' She smiled and snuggled onto his shoulder.
'Shall we go to bed then' he said, 'it's getting late.'
'I love you Gregoire, I love you so much.'
'And I love you my love. Come closer, let me feel you close to me. You are the most wonderful girl.'
'And I make you happy?'
'Yes you make me happy, very happy Nicole.'

They lay for a long time, talking and kissing and eventually making love, after which he held her tenderly in his arms until she slept. When he left her at Jed's in the morning, he said 'Take care of her Jed, I rely on you to be sensible.'

'I'll look after her, sir' Jed answered him.

It never occurred to Greg how strange it was that he should be asking Jed to take care of his wife who was four years older than the boy.

He watched the two of them run to the back of the house and thought 'My god, she is just a child, unspoiled, innocent and yet she was eighteen years old. He hoped she would not change too quickly, hoped she would not become wise to the world too soon.

Chapter 16

Jed was thrilled to have his friend with him for three whole days. In the afternoon, they spent time on the river. It was a bright, sunny day, a little cold, but pleasant. He took his guitar. They moored a little way up stream, when they sat on a grassy bank, enjoying the river scene while he strummed his guitar.

'You should ask someone to publish some of these songs, Jed. They are very good. Try to get them published.'

'Nobody would be interested. I don't think they are that good anyway.'

'I'm sure you are wrong.'

'They are just simple songs, Nicki. It's wonderful sitting here, isn't it? I wish Greg would go away more often.'

'I don't want him to go away, Jed.'

'I know. I'm sorry.'

They stayed singing and talking for about half an hour when it became cold, and they decided to return home. Jed put his arm around her to warm her. He squeezed her.

'Oh Nicki, I am so glad to have you back, even for so short a while. I really miss you not being at home with us.'

She smiled, 'We have to see Justin, tomorrow. You'll have to miss school.'

'I know old Simmonds wasn't too impressed but thank goodness he agreed to let me off in the end.'

'We must not be late,' she said.

'We won't be late.'

It had started to rain when they finally reached home and Amy reprimanded Jed. 'What on earth possessed you to go on the river in this sort of weather?'

'It's only just started to rain Gran and the river was fantastic,' he said convincingly, then added 'We're going out now to get a hamburger for dinner.'

'Oh no you're not – I have a perfectly good meal prepared here. Dr. Fellini will expect Nicole to have a decent meal.'

'Oh alright Gran, but afterwards we are going to the cinema. That's okay, isn't it?'

'I suppose so.'

Greg telephoned Nicole later that night. 'I miss you already, my love' he said. 'Are you enjoying yourself?'

She told him what they had been doing and that they were going to a fun fair the next day.

'Don't forget you have to be with Justin at ten in the morning.'

'I know, Gregoire, we will be going in the evening. I am not dancing tomorrow.'

Justin cast Jed in the role of Fritz. 'Are you familiar with the Nutcracker, Jed?'

'Yes, I've seen it several times.'

'Then you know more or less what is expected of you?'

Nicole was, of course, cast as Clara with Matthew, one of the senior male dancers, as her partner. The Monday morning rehearsal ran as smoothly as any rehearsal could.

'Dr. Fellini wants some sort of rough sketch when he gets back on Thursday, so tomorrow we will start rehearsing in earnest. However, we'll finish now for today. Be here sharp at 10 tomorrow,' said Justin, before adding 'Jed, I'd like a word with you before you go.'

'I'll wait outside for you Jed,' Nicole said.

'Now then Jed, we are going to try to rehearse you as much as possible in the morning so that you can attend school in the afternoon.'

'But I thought you wanted us all day.'

'Not you. I want you to attend school as much as possible.'

'They wouldn't mind you know. Gran has already squared it with Mr Simmonds. I was there,' Jed answered, 'He said as often as possible.'

'Exactly.'

'I don't have to go Justin.'

'Jed, either you turn up for school or I don't give you the part. You are still only fourteen years old, even though you look older and think you can do whatever you like. You are lucky the school agreed to let you do this. So we'll play it our way. Now can I trust you to get back to school?'

'Yes, okay.'

'Right – your time will come, don't fret.'

'Could I stay sometimes in the afternoon?'

'I don't know. You might have to.'

Justin rehearsed most of the cast in the morning and some later, so that Jed did not see Nicole much during the day.

'At least we have the evenings sometimes, Nicki.'

'Do you like rehearsing, Jed?'

'Yes but I wish I could rehearse with you and the rest of them. Justin has given me another part. I am to be on one of the mice as well as Fritz.'

'Oh, good.'

Chapter 17

Greg did not get back until late afternoon on Thursday, and Nicole was sitting by the window reading. She ran to him as soon as he appeared.

'Hello beloved,' he said gathering her into his arms. 'I didn't realise how much I would miss you. I thought of you every second. I could not get back here fast enough. I daresay you have been very busy with Jed. Come here, I am so glad to be back. Did you enjoy being with Jed, my love?'

'Yes, but I'm so pleased you are here with me Gregoire.'

'How did the rehearsal go?' he asked 'How did Jed get on? Did Justin try him out with Fritz? That is quite a straight forward part.'

'Yes and he is one of the mice as well.'

'Well, well. Tell me all about it.'

'He was good Gregoire, but I don't want to talk about the ballet. I want to talk about you and me. I have been thinking about you.'

'I am gratified to hear that, my love, but I am sure Jed kept you amused.'

'You are not going away again, are you Gregoire?'

'Not for a while- now tell me everything.'

'I love you Gregoire. Stay home with me today.'

'Of course darling,' but Greg wanted to know more about the ballet and after a suitable time he once again brought the conversation round to Justin and the rest of the cast.

'How did you get along with Justin on Monday?'

'Okay. I like Clara.'

'You will be superb, my love.'

'Jed wanted the Nutcracker.'

'Did he indeed. He will have to gain a great deal more experience to partner you my precious one. Tell me how did he cope with Fritz? Was Justin pleased with him?'

'Yes, he knows he is lucky just to have a part. He was joking about the Nutcracker. But even so I bet he could do it. He is very good.'

'I know that. But he has to learn to walk before he runs. He will get there in the end I am sure. I will keep an eye on him.'

'He wants you to take him into the company.'

Greg smiled at her. 'He would do well to employ you as his agent – as far as you are concerned, he can do no wrong, can he?'

Nicole lowered her head and her eyes clouded. Immediately, Greg lifted her chin so that she was looking at him. 'What is it, Nicole darling?'

'It's just that I have no one. I never hear from my home, and Jed is like my own brother. He makes it better for me.'

He gathered her to him. 'Oh Nicole, I know you are often still sad and I'm sorry my love, I was not criticising you. I know how you feel.'

He kissed her. 'He loves you, you know and who can blame him for that?'

'Do not think I have any regrets, Gregoire. I would rather be here with you than any where else in the world. I would die without you and sometimes I think I am too happy, I get afraid. I love you so much.' She clung to him, kissing him passionately. 'I would die for you Monsieur.'

'Here now, I don't think there will be any need for you to do that my beloved. Come now, give me one of your captivating smiles. That's better, you know something? Jed is a very lucky young man, maybe I should feel a little jealous.'

'Oh no Gregoire. No.'

'I'm just kidding, darling. I'm happy you have him as your friend. I will make sure he is alright. Don't you worry.'

As long as the rehearsals for the Nutcracker were taking place, Jed was in his element. He was able to have lunch with Nicole and the stars. But he missed Nicole in the evenings now that she was married to Greg. Even during lunch break she often now went off with Yanni or Matthew. Jed felt left out. He moped and hurt.

'What is the matter with you, Jed?' Amy enquired of him. 'You have been like a bear with a sore head lately. Are you not well? What is it? Dr. Fellini has included you in the ballet, you are even getting paid. I thought you would be on top of the world.'

'I'm sorry, I miss Nicki.'

'Jed, she is married to Gregoire. She is a star; sometimes she is busy with her dancing and other things. She can't always be with you son. She has her own life and other things to do now.'

'She used to be pleased to be with me.'

'Jed, you have to understand. You must let her have time to herself. If you crowd her, she will stop coming here altogether.'

'I suppose she considers herself special now. She can't be bothered with a kid like me,' Jed pouted.

'I am surprised at you Jed. You know Nicole would never think that way. She is not that kind of person and she is extremely fond of you. You know that.'

'Yes, I know. I didn't really mean that, but I wish it could be like it was Gran.'

Amy put her arm around her grandson. 'You'll find your feet son; just give it a little time. Be there when she needs you. Cheer up now. I am looking forward to seeing you in the ballet next month.'

'It is not a very big part,' Jed said.

'Big enough son, and it is a start. You know Grandad and I will be very proud of you.'

Jed allowed himself a smile. 'One day' he said, 'I mean to get my own company and write my own musicals.'

'That's the ticket. Come now, help me get this dinner on the table.'

Amy felt for her grandson. He was fourteen years old and he was in love with Nicole, and who wouldn't be? Everyone was in love with her. She was different, saintly as well as fun-loving. A lovely girl in every way – she was his first love.

She sighed, 'Poor Jed', but he was a sensible lad. Things would work out for him, hopefully soon.

A few days after the Nutcracker had commenced, Jed had the chance of a lifetime. Yanni playing the lead contracted pneumonia. Having tried the understudy, Justin decided to call Greg.

'This guy is not right, Greg. He has no spark, no imagination. Not a patch on Yanni.'

'Well, get someone else. You must have someone.'

'It's difficult at such short notice.'

'Well, what the hell is this person doing if he is not up to standard?'

'There is Jed.'

'Don't be ridiculous – he has only just started.'

'I reckon he could do it.' Justin said. Greg shook his head.

'We need someone right now and he takes direction well, he learns quickly and he has what it takes.'

'He is only fourteen years old, Justin.'

'Who's to know that? He's so tall, looks the part.'

'He's good. Will you at least agree to try him?'

'Very well, I suppose we have little choice.'

Justin summoned Jed. 'You know about Yanni,' he said.

Jed nodded. 'How is he? Is he very ill?'

'He'll be okay with the antibiotics, but it leaves us in a difficult situation.'

He studied Jed. The tall lanky schoolboy was agile and keen, but he was not absolutely certain. Was he being fair to him, with hardly any experience - however what choice had they? It was an energetic part.

'Jed,' he said, 'I have suggested to Dr. Fellini that you step in to play Yanni's part. It will probably mean for the rest of the show. Yanni won't be fit enough to come back for at least a month. Do you think you can do it?'

'I don't want to sound big-headed' Jed replied, 'but I believe I could Justin.' He was excited, could not believe his luck.

'You will have to rehearse this afternoon after school. How soon can you get back here?'

'I'll ride my bike and then I could be back here within fifteen minutes.

'Right. If Dr. Fellini thinks you are okay, we shall have to try and persuade your headmaster to let you have more time off for a while.'

'He won't stand in the way, I know he won't.'

'Hmmm'

'Justin…'

'What?'

'Do you think it would be possible for you to rehearse me before Dr. Fellini sees me?'

'Oh for god's sake Jed. I really don't know. Surely you are man enough to cope with his criticism?'

'He makes me nervous. I feel like a small boy, a child.'

'You are a child, Jed. However, I'll try but I can't promise. And you will have to suffer him eventually.'

'I know, it's just for the first rehearsal.'

'Be here as soon as possible later this afternoon. Better get off to school now.'

As Jed was walking out of the dressing room he bumped into Greg.
'Ah boy, where are you off to?'
'School, sir.'
'Ah, have you spoken to Justin?'
'Yes sir'
'What do you think?'
'About taking over Yanni's Mouse King?'
'Of course that is what I mean.'
'I'm sure I can do it sir. Just give me the chance. I won't let you down.'

'If I agree to Justin's recommendations you had better not, you are going to have to convince me, you know. Rehearsals start with Justin after school this evening. Let your grandmother know you will be very late home.'

'Yes sir'

Jed put his heart and soul into the rehearsal. Between the two of them, Jed managed to convince Greg that he was up to the part. He was terrified and exhausted by the end of the afternoon. Greg had yelled hard at him, but was not too vitriolic – and he was sweating all the way through.

'Not bad,' Greg said. 'You rehearse for the rest of the week. Then you will take over from the understudy. I agree with you Justin, that one is useless. Why is he here?'

'He is okay with the chorus scene. There is no reason to throw him out. It would devastate him.'

Greg looked at Justin 'I'll leave it up to you then, but remember Justin, we are not a philanthropic society.'

'He's useful Greg.'

'Alright, if you say so.'

Chapter 18

Every evening Justin worked with Jed. There was no time to moon over Nicole. Justin worked him hard and he was tired when he came home. After his meal, he more or less tumbled into his bed. Greg watched his progress, but did not interfere. Justin was right. The boy was dynamic. He learned quickly.

'He is a genius, Greg. We are lucky to have him.'

'You are right' Greg agreed 'But he is still at school.'

'That's true.'

'So, if he is to carry on, he will need a lot of time off.'

'What on earth for?'

'Greg, his grandparents would at least like him to finish his O's and possibly his 'A' levels. He will be rehearsing straight after school, then preparing for the evening show at least for a few weeks. On top of that he has his homework. If we had a tutor on tap, it would make it less exhausting for him.'

'Yes, maybe you have a point, but we are coming up to the Christmas holidays, he will not be at school then, by the end of which we will probably be closing the Nutcracker and Yanni will be fit then.'

'We can't just leave Jed with nothing after this.'

'Why not? He has plenty of time, let us leave it as it is now.'

'Greg, he is a very attractive boy, has talent and loads of charm. For a youngster he has a presence. We could include him in future productions. He has stamina and I am sure he would cope anyway, but we could make it easier for him. From now on, he will be working flat out at school.'

'I'm still not entirely convinced he should be taking over from Yanni.

'He is too young,' Greg sighed. 'Alright Justin, as I said I will think about it.'

'You do agree don't you?' Justin persisted 'He is unique'

'Oh yes, he is unique, but I'm not sure. I'm still far from comfortable with this arrangement.'

'I don't understand.'

'It's just a feeling. Who ever heard of a boy of fourteen playing the lead with no experience? I am a little more cautious than you, Justin.'

'I have a great deal of faith in him' Justin said.

Things came to a head when Greg joined Jed bent over the makeup bench with books, a sandwich and a flask of coffee beside him.

'What the hell are you doing boy?' he yelled.

Jed jumped. 'I didn't think anyone would mind if I did some homework in here.'

'When did you last eat a decent meal?'

Greg pointed to the sandwich. 'What the hell is that you're eating?'

'I'm sorry, sir, I thought I could save some time if I brought some food here, instead of going all the way home.'

Greg lowered himself into the chair beside Jed and stared, 'And what about the occupants of the dressing room?'

'I always finish eating before they arrive,' Jed answered.

'Indeed – I understand from Justin you are studying for you exams.'

'Yes sir, but I can manage to do the show as well.'

Greg rose from the chair. 'Come to the office when you have finished eating, we cannot have this,' he said and left the room.

He telephoned Justin to meet him.

'Alright Justin' he agreed 'I'll take a chance on Jed. Get him a tutor. I have just caught him in the dressing room. He was so engrossed in his books, he did not even hear me knock. He was eating some sort of rubbish at the same time. Instead of going home for a decent meal. Get him a tutor. Does he think he is some sort of superhero? He looks exhausted. I agree we need to help him. I'll talk to him and perhaps you will talk to his grandparents. See how the land lies. It would be a pity to lose him.'

'Greg, I think it would be better for you to talk to the grandparents.'

Greg looked aghast. 'Good god man, surely I can leave this sort of thing to you. I have other things on my mind.'

'I think you should talk to them Greg. They hardly know me. Nicole is practically one of the family and you are her husband. It would be better for you to approach them.'

'You think there will be a problem?'

'I don't know, probably not, they raised no objection to him being off school. But I know they are keen for him to finish his education.'

'Oh alright, I'll see to it if I must. Get Trudi to arrange a meeting with them next week. By the way, what are you doing about the part of the Uncle. Who is playing at the moment?'

'That's all settled, we have Dexter. He is older than Yanni, but he seems to be carrying it off okay.'

'Why didn't he take over the King?'

'I just thought Jed would be more dynamic. Dexter was not right.'

'I see, well let's get everything tidied up Justin. Do you know of a tutor?'

'Yes, he is a friend of mine, Ben Daniels, he is dedicated and will keep Jed working. I'll contact him.'

With Nicole and Matthew as principals and Jed nervously making his debut in his first important part, Greg's production of the Nutcracker soon got underway and by the Christmas period Jed grew into the part and eventually inspired the audience. Being lithe and good-looking, after a few performances he claimed almost as much admiration as the principals, but he continued to moon about Nicole. They spent little time together off-stage. Justin had arranged for Jed's tutor to be based in the theatre. Jed left school and studied each morning. If there was a rehearsal, he studied during the afternoon.

Greg insisted he ate a nourishing meal each day. It seemed to work with improvisations and after the first week he found he had more leisure time. Most of his afternoons were now free apart from the small amount of homework Ben set for him so that he could either relax or study at home.

When the Nutcracker came to an end, he was already an established member of Greg's company, often included in the productions which followed.

Now he was able to spend more time with Nicole including sometimes on a Sunday when they either rowed on the lake or visited the ice rink. Greg seemed not to mind as long as she was back in time for dinner with him. In any case, he was always busy with some project and he was not one to sit down for long so that if Jed could keep his young wife amused for a while, he did not complain. Nicole still wrote to her parents but not so regularly. She had come to terms with their disapproval of Greg. Although she confided in Jed regarding her great disappointment, she tried not to involve Greg.

'It does make him so angry' she said 'I know it is because he does not like me to be upset, but I do not like to see him when he is angry. Jed, it frightens me.' Jed knew what she meant. Greg's angry moods were to be avoided as far as possible.

Jed worked solidly each morning with his tutor and by the time he was fifteen, he had obtained five 'O' levels.

'Do you want to go on to take some 'A's?' Ben asked him.

'What do you think' Jed replied 'My future lies in the theatre. I'm not sure if this would be of any use to me.'

Ben studied Jed. 'If you can stand the pace, I would suggest you have a go. It would be worth it. It is always *worth* gaining extra knowledge, still it is up to you. What about your grandparents? Education is never a waste of time, Jed.'

'It means at least another year and more. I'll think about it' Jed mused.

His grandparents made the decision for him.

'Listen son,' his grandparents said 'You are fifteen, you have your whole life before you. One or two more years of study with Mr. Daniels will not go amiss as long as Dr. Fellini is willing to help. I honestly think you should give it a go. You may wish to do other work entirely different when you are older.'

'No, I won't.' Jed said.

'Well, why don't you try it? If you find it is more than you can manage, there would be no harm in having attempted something would there.

Jed found the work hard going, a lot of time taken up with reading and absorbing the classics. He begrudged the lost hours with Nicole and began to regret the decision he had made.

'You are doing well, Jed.' Ben encouraged.

'Don't slack now, you will be glad you decided to carry on. In a few months time you can take English and you'll pass for sure.'

'Could I take maths at the same time?'

'Good god, no. I don't think so.'

'Why not? I'm doing okay, aren't I?'

'Well yes, but with all the commitments you have it would be pushing it, unless you want to work all hours god sends. I suggest you wait.'

'I'll work,' Jed said.

'Jed, no one is forcing you to do this. It's not some sort of punishment and its not a matter of life or death. Give yourself breathing space.'

'It is to my grandparents. They have been fantastic coping with everything. I don't want to disappoint them.'

'Your grandparents would not want you to drive yourself into the ground Jed. Why don't you talk to them?'

'I don't need to. I know how they feel. I'll do it.'

Within a few months, Jed braced himself to sit for his English exams. Ben approached him. 'Give yourself a few more months before you take your Maths, Jed.'

'Do you think I'll pass English?'

'I'm certain of it. Your knowledge of the classics is excellent.'

'I'd like to take Maths as soon as possible. Ben I want to get shot of them.'

'I advise you to wait – at least for another few months.'

'Okay, I suppose three to four months is not a lifetime.'

'Exactly.'

Greg continued to include Jed in most of his productions. Both he and Justin watched with interest. He was dynamite. The audience loved him. He had matured of late, grown taller. It was difficult to remember that he was barely fifteen years old.

There had been many requests for Greg and Justin to stage another production of La fille mal gardée. It was over a year since the last production. Justin gave Jed the part of Colas and Matthew was to be Alain. Nicole would be superb as Lisa, beautiful and graceful and Matthew had been a favourite with the audiences for years.

They recognised Jed from the Nutcracker and showed their appreciation as soon as he appeared on stage. The show ran well through Christmas and well after the Christmas holidays, enabling Jed and Nicole time to get together during most days. However, in the evening after the show, Nicole would rush eagerly to Greg, her arms encircling him. Both were ecstatically happy.

When the holidays were done and Jed started studying, Nicole did not see quite as much of Jed, but he made sure he was available most Sunday afternoons unless Greg had something planned. Often though, he was preoccupied in his study, and when she asked if he minded her joining Jed, he said, 'Of course not, my beloved. Enjoy yourself. I have things to do.'

'I will be back soon.' She always assured him, throwing her arms around him and kissing him several times before rushing out to join her friend.

'When will you finish studying?' she asked Jed.

'I'm waiting for the results of my English, if I pass, it will be another two months before I take Maths.'

'You are a clever boy, Jed' she said.

'I don't know about that. It's been a hard slog. Ben has worked hard to get me up to standard, I found Maths much more difficult.'

'You will pass both Jed.'

'I bloody well hope so. I'd hate to have to take them again.'

'What about your music?'

'Haven't had a lot of time for that lately.'

'But you still want to write songs?'

'Can't wait to get back to it. We have some free time this afternoon.'

'Why don't we listen to the tapes. I love the music you write, Jed.'

'Alright, will you dance for me?'

She nodded, she loved the jazzy numbers he had composed for her. He watched her, she was like a wood nymph obsessed with the sexy movements. She danced expertly, carrying out the energetic choreography Jed had devised. Suddenly, she stopped.

'Dance with me, Jed,' she called.

He glided towards her, held her, twirling around, complimenting her movements exquisitely until the tape finished, then she threw her arms around him, kissing him impulsively.

'You are so talented.'

He looked down at her. She was so innocent, so beautiful, graceful. She had no idea what she did to him. She released him just as impulsively as she had embraced him, then ran to change the tape, returning to him ready to dance again, and he could not resist her. He knew that Greg was her world, but to hold her was sheer heaven. In one hour she would be back with Greg. She worshipped Greg. They were both obsessed with each other. He wished he was older but he knew there would never have been anyone other than Greg for Nicole. He would have had no chance.

'But I will always love you Nicole' he murmured to himself, 'always, forever.'

La fille mal garde proved so popular that Greg was reluctant to change it, and he let it run for another two months. In the meantime, he and Justin discussed the next production. They both noticed that Jed looked pale and gaunt. Greg took him aside.

'Are you alright boy?'
'I'm fine,' Jed replied.
'You don't look it, are you eating properly?'
'I'm okay Greg, it's probably the fact that I'm just about to take the maths exams. It's a bit nerve racking.
'Do you want some time off from the ballet?'
'No!' Jed was emphatic. 'I'm okay'.
It was the one thing Jed did not want. He could fantasise on stage. He could play it out and he got to dance with Nicole each performance.
'Are you sure?'
'I am sure sir. I don't want time off.'
'You are too thin.'
'Don't worry about me Greg.'
'Come for a meal with Nicole and me this evening after the show.'
'Thank you, I'd like to.'
'I'll pick you up here.'
'Thanks.'
Greg had booked at Overton's in Victoria.
'My god you certainly need feeding up boy. You are as thin as a garden rake. I don't want you to land up with a nervous breakdown or worse.'
'Greg there is nothing wrong with me, honestly. I guess I am just sick of the exams.'
It was true, he desperately wanted to be rid of them. English was no problem but he did not feel at all confident with maths.
'When are you sitting them?'
'Next Thursday and Friday.'
'Oh well, let us try to forget them for now,' Greg said. 'Just eat my boy.'
Half way through the meal, Greg put his knife and fork down.
'I want to talk to you Jed. I guess this is as good a time as any. It might cheer you up. I'd like to put you under contract when you are a little older.'
Jed dropped his fork making a clatter on the plate.
'A contract Jed. Close your mouth boy. A contract with a salary.'
'What?'
'Yes, I think you deserve recognition. You have done well under difficult circumstances.'
'But..'
'But what?'

'Nothing sir, I am just surprised, thrilled but surprised.'

'You should not be, Jed. In a year or two, or perhaps sooner, you will surpass even the best of them. You are popular with the audiences and an asset to the company. What do you say, Jed?'

'I, I don't know what to say. I'm just thrilled that you think I am worth it.'

'You deserve it my boy. Just get these stupid exams over, put a bit of flesh on and get that starved look off your face. I will make you a star in no time at all.'

Nicole was beaming. I knew you would make it Jed, you dance so beautifully and you look so handsome. It's wonderful, isn't it? I'm so fond of you.'

Jed looked over at her, his look full of love for her. He smiled slowly.

'I suppose it's a bit better than hiding behind scenery sir, so that I could escape without you seeing me.'

'What you don't know is that I invariably did see you. Now, I have only mentioned this to give you a little encouragement. Now then, let us celebrate our good fortune, yours and mine, Jed, and we must also remember that it was Justin who just insisted we use you in the first production. It is Justin you should be thanking. From now on though, you will skip rehearsals until your exams are over. You need to relax a little.'

'That isn't necessary sir, I can handle it.'

'No Jed, you cannot. Ben tells me you start the exams next week.'

'I have maths at the end of next week. I said I can handle it.'

'And I say you cannot and you will take a break as soon as this production is over.'

'But I...'

'Remember what I said. You obey me at all times regarding your work in the theatre!'

'But...'

'Don't argue with me Jed. If you persist I will replace you tomorrow.'

Jed clamped his lips together in anger, but resisted further comment. Greg looked at him.

'You will thank me in the end, boy' he said.

For the next week Jed worked relentlessly day and well into the night. He began to wish he had not agreed to do these 'A' levels. He would never need them, so why was he driving himself? He missed the hype of the stage and worse he missed Nicole.'

In three days, he was sitting for the English exam and he had got to the stage where he could not care less if he passed or not. The next day he did not turn up at the theatre for his lesson. Ben waited and after half-an-hour telephoned Jed's house. Amy answered.

'I'm sorry he is not here' she said ' I thought he was at the theatre with you.'

Ben waited for another half an hour, then left after informing Greg that Jed had not shown up.

'Do you think there is any need for concern Justin?'

'No, I don't think so. He is almost sixteen, I'm sure he is okay. He is fairly level headed. Well if he doesn't show up tomorrow, we had better do something. I'll telephone Amy this evening, no point in worrying her unnecessarily.'

Chapter 19

Jed had worked solidly and had fallen asleep at his desk at about five am. He woke at seven fifteen, closed his books, made himself a coffee then called to his grandmother.

'I'm going now Gran.'

'Aren't you a little early, son?'

'Yes, but I'm not going straight to the theatre. I'll see you this evening.'

'What about lunch?'

'I'm seeing someone for lunch, Gran.'

'Oh, alright.'

He walked around the square until he saw Greg leave the house, then ran up the steps and knocked at the door.

Maddie answered. 'Oh hello Jed. Dr. Fellini has just left.'

'I know, is Nicole in?'

'Yes, she does not have a rehearsal today. Come in, I shall call her.'

'Hello, Jed,' Nicole came running down the stairs. 'Are you okay?'

'No, I'm not.'

'What is the matter.'

'Oh, nothing really, I suppose I just wanted to see you, talk a bit. How are you?'

'I'm okay. I thought you were at the theatre with Ben.'

'I am sick of studying and Dr. Fellini has stopped me rehearsing. He has even said I have to take a break when the show finishes. I hope he doesn't really mean that. I was promised to dance in the next production. It's bad enough missing rehearsals. It's the only thing that keeps me going after slogging all morning.'

'Never mind, your exams finish soon don't they?'

'Yes, thank god. I wish I'd never started them. I'm certainly not taking them again if I fail.'

'You won't fail Jed.'

'I might – listen Nicole I've brought a couple of tapes. If Dr. Fellini is not coming back for a while, could we play them somewhere? Would you dance for me?'

She took him into the lounge and he sat watching her. She was wonderful. He started to relax and after a while he was laughing and chatting with her until Jed remembered about Ben.

'Oh god,' he said 'I'm meant to telephone him. He will be furious.'

'Ring him now.'

'He will have gone.'

'Well, you can ring him at home.'

'I guess I should – He is going to be angry with me.'

He dialled the number. 'It's Jed, Ben. Look, I'm terribly sorry, I meant to have phoned you before but…'

'Before you go on Jed, don't lie to me. I know you are not at home with some obscure malady. I telephoned them earlier.'

'I wasn't going to lie.'

'Where are you?'

Jed hesitated.

'Where are you?' Ben repeated.

'I'm with Nicole.'

'I see, well I daresay Dr. Fellini will appreciate that,' Ben said sarcastically.

'Ben, I'm sorry.'

'Be at the theatre at nine thirty tomorrow.'

'Ben!!'

'I'll see you tomorrow.' and Ben put the phone down.

'What did he say?' Nicole asked.

'He's angry but I did mean to phone. It was worth it just to see you. Shall we go out first? I'm a bit hungry.'

'Yes, I'll tell Maddie. Shall we go for a hamburger?'

'Sure that will be good, just like old times. Where is Dr. Fellini by the way, he's not coming for lunch, is he?'

'No, he has an appointment for lunch.'

They went to the park and Nicole talked about her parents. 'They are still angry with me. My Maman never writes. It's as though she does not love me.'

'I'm sure she does Nicki.'

'Maybe. Gregoire gets so angry because he knows it makes me upset.'

'I'm sure they will come to terms with everything soon Nicki. Don't be sad.'

'It doesn't matter so much as it did. I have got used to it now.'

'Do you think we have time to hire a boat.'

'Better not – I told Maddie I wouldn't be too long after lunch.'

She turned to see Jed smiling.

'Why are you smiling like that?'

'Do you have to tell Maddie every time you go out?'

'Gregoire might phone. He likes to know where I am.'

'So you never get any privacy?'

'Of course I do. Don't be mean Jed. I don't mind telling Maddie.'

'Sorry I'm just joking. Come on, let's get some lunch.'

They arrived back at about four thirty.

'Come into the kitchen, we can make some tea,' she said.

Jed brought the tape with him and Nicole inserted it into the cassette.

'I really love this tape, Jed,' she said.

'It's yours. I told you. I made it for you.'

She started to dance in the large kitchen and Jed eventually joined her complementing her with his lithe movements. It was thus that Greg came upon them. His astonishment turned to anger.

'Turn that thing off.' he said 'What the hell do think you are doing here? Do you know what inconvenience you caused to Ben. Where have you been all day? Not here I hope.'

'I'm sorry, sir.'

'You mean you have been here. My God I would have thought after the discussion I had with you at dinner the other evening, you would have been a little more responsible. I ought to dismiss you this minute, get out of here. Go home. I'll deal with you tomorrow.'

Jed fled from the kitchen and out through the front door. He was nervous now. Dr. Fellini might sack him from the company. He sat on the coping outside, tears gathering behind his lids. He would have to face him this evening. Greg turned to Nicole.

'I'm sorry Monsieur,' she began.

'My name is Gregoire for god's sake – remember Nicole.'

She bit her lip. 'Please don't be angry.'

'Angry, what the hell do you expect me to be? Did he tell you he was supposed to be studying? He did not even have the decency to telephone Ben. We did not know where he was. I did not expect him to be here.'

'He did phone.'

'Did he now? Not for one hour at least though. We had no idea where he had disappeared off to.'

'He didn't mean to be…'

'To be what? You know Nicole, you should have sent him packing. He had no right to be here in the morning.'

She was near to tears as Greg's anger persisted.

He relented 'Come here my love, I'm sorry. It was not your fault. I am not angry with you. I am sorry my beloved. I should not have yelled at you. But Jed, he has to be taught a lesson.'

'Gregoire, don't be too hard on him, he is only a boy. He is only fifteen.'

'Nearly sixteen. However I suppose we should not judge him too harshly. As you say, he is young.'

'He doesn't want to stop rehearsals and he is very upset that you are making him miss out on the next production.'

'Is he now? Well he will do as I say and he should not be worrying you with such things.'

'You won't dismiss him Gregoire, will you?'

'I'll think about it.'

She put her hand on his arm. 'Please Gregoire. He was just tired of working all the time.'

'Oh dear! He is such a lucky boy that he has you pleading for him. Alright maybe I'll just frighten him a little.'

'Thank you. I love you Gregoire.'

'Hmmm, that is what we call cupboard love, my beloved. Come along, cheer up, your young friend is safe, at least this time.'

Jed was not to forget the next morning when he gingerly walked into the theatre, where Ben was sitting on the corner of the table waiting. He looked up as he approached.

'Ben,' Jed faltered, 'I'm sorry I didn't phone earlier yesterday.'

Ben did not reply.

'I mean,' Jed continued, 'I didn't intend to skip the class at first.'

Ben lowered himself from the table.

'Jed' he said 'I am waiting for an explanation. I assume you do have one.'

'I'm sorry, things just got on top of me. I wasn't thinking straight.'

'Straight enough to take yourself uninvited to Dr. Fellini's house, to see his wife.'

Jed closed his eyes, 'I needed to talk to someone.'

'By someone you mean Nicole.'

'Yes, I suppose so.'

'You know, of all places you should not have been there, don't you.'

'I didn't mean any harm.'

I don't think Dr. Fellini was too pleased at finding you there, when you should have been working here.'

'Did he say anything to you?'

'If he did, I would not be telling you. However he wants to see you, after I have finished with you.'

'Is he going to throw me out?'

'You will have to ask him that. I am only concerned with you missing your lesson with me. You seem only concerned with the theatre and Nicole. Perhaps you do not need me. You could possibly work on your own now. It's just revision after all.'

'No, I couldn't, I do need you Ben. Please don't give me that sort of punishment, it isn't fair. I've never done it before.'

'No, well maybe you're right. You know Jed, if you needed a bit of time off, you only had to ask.'

'I know, I told you I didn't mean to skip the class. It was on the spur of the moment.'

'You are doing well and if you want any more time off, that's no problem.'

'I'm alright, and I'm sorry.'

'We are more concerned for you. You have been given a lot Jed. I hope you appreciate that.'

'Of course I do. It won't happen again. I promise.'

'Good. Better go and see Dr. Fellini. I'll wait here.'

'Suppose I don't go. He may have forgotten.'

'That could be extremely unwise and I can't believe you would even think of such a thing.'

'Wish me luck then.'

He went slowly through to Greg's office, beyond the pass door, knocked and was immediately called in.

After finishing the page on which he was working, Greg sat back contemplating Jed.

'You asked to see me sir.'

'I don't know if you mean to be as impertinent as you sound boy.'

'I am really sorry sir.'

'And I am waiting for an explanation regarding what you were doing at my house yesterday, when you should have been studying with Ben.'

'I...I don't know what made me go there sir.'

'Then I suggest you think about it.'

'I needed a break'

'Really! I understand from Nicole that you do not need any kind of break. In fact she gave me to understand that you were quite definite about that.'

'I don't know what to say sir.'

'Don't you now, well let me tell you that yesterday I would have had no compunction in suspending you. However, thanks to Justin's great faith in you and Nicole who begged me to go easy on you, I have decided to let you carry on. But remember in future that you are not free to go wandering anywhere you choose during your study time. Also, my house is not a refuge for slacking.'

'I wasn't slacking sir'

'Don't interrupt me. You are in deep trouble boy'

'I'm sorry sir, I was just spaced out'

'For god's sake boy, speak English! 'Spaced out' – what is that supposed to mean?'

'I meant I was going a bit crazy with the exams. It was getting me down, I needed to talk to someone.'

'What about Ben, or Justin, or even me? You could have approached any of us. Instead you decide to bother my wife with your troubles, and I will not have that, do you understand? Now get out of here.'

'I'm sorry sir'

'Go!'

'I didn't think that he would mind if I went to Nicole,' Jed said to Ben, 'He's never minded before.'

'I don't suppose he would have minded in normal circumstances, but you should have asked me for a bit of time off. Jed, you do realise we were worried. We had no idea where you were. Not even your grandmother knew. Nobody thought of ringing Nicole at nine in the morning. By the time you telephoned, Greg was in a state – of course I didn't tell him where you were. He was steamed up enough that you had skipped class without permission. Greg is old fashioned, he would consider your behaviour the height of bad manners. Anyway, there is not much left of this morning.' Ben said.

He noticed how distressed Jed was. 'It's not worth getting the books out. We'll visit some art galleries. I'm sure it will all blow over in a couple of days.'

Jed did not see Nicole except in passing and sometimes at rehearsals. He did not dare approach Greg's house. He was tired and miserable.

'Would you like a few hours off Jed?' Ben asked .

'No! It's okay I will have finished on Friday, won't I?'

'You look tired.' Ben closed his books. 'Let's finish in the morning. I'll buy you some coffee and you can talk, relax, whatever.'

Ben came back with the coffee and some buns. 'Now then, what's troubling you apart from the exams?'

Jed shrugged 'Everything has changed since I have started these exams.'

'How do you mean?'

'I don't know. It's different, not so friendly anymore.'

'You are imagining things. You are just strung up.'

'No! I feel different, older, I don't think life is fun anymore. It isn't other people, it's me, the way I feel. Also, Dr. Fellini treats me like a stranger now and I never see Nicole anymore.'

'Dr. Fellini treats everyone the same way and you stepped out of line. You have been with us for three years, you should know him by now. And Jed, Nicole is his wife, you can't always be gadding about with her, the way you used to. You must have other friends, from school for instance?'

'They are not interested in theatre or dancing. I don't' feel comfortable with them anymore.'

'That's a pity, but you are just growing up Jed. Sometimes a painful experience, but the feeling will pass, believe me.'

'I hope so. Anyway I should be thankful to you and Dr. Fellini. I would be slogging at school but for you.'

'Perhaps you would have been better off, more contented that way.'

'Oh god, no I wouldn't. I certainly wouldn't be dancing professionally and that is very important to me. I don't think I have wasted my time. I feel I'm pretty good generally'

'I agree you are Jed, but don't let it go to your head.'

'You don't think I would do that do you Ben?'

'Maybe not.'

'Trouble is I have annoyed Dr. Fellini. He probably won't let me dance now. He has never mentioned casting for the new production.'

'He will'

'Maybe he won't. He was really mad at me.'

'He doesn't bare grudges. I'll have a word with him, tell him you are ready for work, I'm sure he will have you slaving away pretty soon. And he was absolutely right to make you take a break. You needed rest.'

'Not from the ballet.'

'Yes from the ballet. Come on, get your things together, we'll finish looking around here then we'll get some lunch. After that I suggest you go to the cinema or the rink. Relax, enjoy yourself for a few hours. You need to take a few days off before Greg gets his clutches into you. You know what a slave-driver he can be, I'm sure he'll have you working before long, then you'll wish you were back with me slogging away for you exams.'

Jed grinned. 'I really enjoyed studying with you Ben. You're a great teacher but I'm glad it's all over. But I couldn't have done it without you. Thanks'

Ben was right; Greg called Jed into his office the week after the exams were over.

'Come in boy, don't hover there. How are you feeling now?'

'I'm okay, sir'

'You don't look it, you pushed yourself too hard. You should have allowed yourself more time and I should have let you off the evening performances.'

'I've finished now, sir'

'So Ben informs me.'

'My maths was last Friday. I'm waiting for the results now.'

'Well, I was thinking of casting you in the next production. Rehearsals will start next week. Do you think you are up to it?'

'More than up to it sir. I've missed rehearsals.'

'Alright, it will probably do you good. The part is not too strenuous, fairly small this time, but a good part Jed. Are you sure you feel ready?'

'I am ready sir.'

'Good'

'Dr. Fellini?' Jed hesitated

'Well?'

'Would you mind if I called in on Nicole this afternoon?'

'Of course not. She has missed you. Off you go. She'll be glad to see you.'

'Thank you sir.'

Because of the exams and the brush with Greg previously, he had not attempted to go to the house and over the last weeks he had hardly seen her, so that when he rushed in, she was delighted and thrilled to see him.

'I asked Dr. Fellini if I could come, it's okay,' Jed said. 'He has given me something in the next production. Are you dancing in it Nicole? I hope so.'

'Yes. We start rehearsals on Monday. It's a new one Gregoire and Justin wrote between them. It's called Punch Lines. They have choreographed different sketches based on the magazine. I think the idea came from Justin. It's quite new.'

'Greg said he wasn't sure about it.'

'That's because it's different.'

'You mean it's not all ballet?'

'I'm not sure, but I know there will be several different sketches.'

'Sounds exciting.'

'I know, I don't think Gregoire is totally comfortable with it but Justin is thrilled and excited about it.'

'Are you dancing this evening Nicole?'

'Yes, are you?'

'No, Dr. Fellini won't let me. Where shall we go? It's too late to go skating. Let's go to the park. We can talk.'

'Okay, but I mustn't be out too long. I need to rest a bit before this evening. I promised Gregoire.'

'How long?'

'An hour. Look we can stay here today. I have some things to do. You can help me.'

'Alright.'

The fact was that although Nicole was pleased to see Jed, she was also growing up and was getting used to being married to Greg. Quite often she would meet him for lunch, after which she was content to go home, gather her own things around her as one does when one settles down, and Nicole loved being married to Greg. Still there were times when she wanted childish amusement - to skate with Jed or to row on the lake and of late they had taken to visiting a pop concert if she was not working herself. Jed was always ready to amuse her. They were young and resorted at times to ridiculous activities. He was very handsome, taller than she. They looked good together.

He was sixteen years old when the results of his 'A' levels came through. He had passed with flying colours. He had been on edge since his last exam. Suddenly he flung himself on the bed, his relief so great that tears flowed down his cheeks. He rushed to the bathroom, calmed himself, he flung his arms in the air, and let out a whoop of joy. The next moment, with a huge grin, Amy was clasped in his arms – swung around.

'Look!' he cried. 'It's all done, finished, I've passed the exam. I've passed. I don't have to study anymore. I'm free, I can do what I want when I want. It's wonderful Gran. Wonderful.'

'Come, tell your Grandad. We are all so proud of you son. I know you did it all for us. You are a good boy, Jed.'

He telephoned Nicole, and Greg told her to ask him to have dinner with them.

'I can't Nicki. I promised to go out with my grandparents, but I'll see you tomorrow.'

Chapter 20

Punch Lines was not the success Justin hoped for at first, but after two months people started to patronise the show and eventually it was considered one of the best and most sophisticated in the West End. Funny, different, witty.

But in the next few months it was noticeable how much Jed had matured in contrast to Nicole, who had grown more slowly under Greg's protective care of her. He nurtured and sheltered her, so her life was almost an extension of life with her parents in France. She wanted for nothing and he usually indulged her in anything she desired. She and Jed had ceased racing around the park although they still attended the skating rink and on fine Sundays if she was available they sometimes rowed on the lake. More often than not though they spent much of their spare time listening and dancing to their tapes, Nicole enjoyed the fast jazzy numbers. She found them exciting, exhilarating a relaxation from the strict discipline of the ballet. Jed watched her avidly, with adoration

'You look so good Nicki.' he said. 'Those dances really suit you.'

He was right, she positively glowed, her eyes shone, her body movements were provocative, almost intimate as she became totally engrossed in the dance. When the music ended, she ran to him, flung her arms impulsively around him

'Jed,' she cried, 'I really love dancing like this, you are such a clever boy.'

He lifted his eyes, savouring the closeness of her beautiful slim body against his, although he was perfectly aware that the gesture meant nothing to her. It was just exuberance on her part. She released him as suddenly as she had embraced him, Jed smiled

'If you danced like that in the show, you'd have everyone climbing on to the stage, you really are terrific Nicole.'

He caught her hand as the music began.

'You know something, this production of Punch Lines would benefit from a bit of Jazz in some of the sketches, with you dancing about so dynamically – it would be wonderful don't you think if he would include some jazzy numbers. But Dr.Fellini would not like that - it would not fit in.'

'I don't know, Gregoire is a genius – it is a wonder he doesn't think of it.'

'I'm sure Justin would do it.'

'I do not think it is wise even to say it Jed.'

'No! I guess not. He would blow up. But you are like dynamite. The audience would go crazy. They would love it.'

'I dance only for Gregoire,' she said unsmiling, not liking any sort of criticism of Greg.

'But you do like it don't you, and you dance here for me,' he said.

'It's just for fun – I love the ballet'

'Pity. You look so good – like a water nymph, a firefly, a jumping jack.' He looked at her – touched her face, 'you really love him don't you.'

'Yes I love him. He is my life Jed.'

'And he wouldn't really like you doing this sort of dance.'

'I do not think that he would mind - he never minds what I do – you must not think he dominates me Jed. He doesn't – it is just that I like to please him.'

'It's alright Nicki – I wasn't criticising.'

'Weren't you?'

'No! Honestly, of course not'

'Gregoire is very fond of you Jed.'

'Yeah. I know.'

It had been arranged that Jed and his family would join Greg, Ben, Justin for a celebration dinner on the Sunday following Jed's exam results.

Greg had reserved a large table at the 'Arts Theatre Club'.

'Well my boy, I daresay you are relieved to have finished studying. Ben tells me you were one of his most rewarding pupils.'

He also congratulated Amy and William, Jed's grandparents

'He is unique' he told them 'to have gained his O Levels and two A's before reaching the age of seventeen is something to be proud of. He also has exceptional talent as a performer – he will go far believe me.'

It was a pleasant evening – Greg always enjoyed a celebration, especially when it was organised and financed by himself. He was at his most amiable and charming, the complete opposite from the strict sharp tongued character he showed to his dancers.

Jed had never seen him like that before and was completely stunned by his wit and charm. His strong handsome features transformed and from the stern alter ego he assumed when teaching, and he understood why they all worshipped him and why he felt privileged to have been allowed to join his classes.

On his birthday a couple of days later, Greg called him into the office.

'Sit down Jed' he said 'well now you have been with us now for 3 years or more. How do you feel about the Company?'

'The Company, it's great sir, everyone knows that'

'Do you enjoy the ballet?'

'Yes sir I do.'

'You are sure'

'Yes, I'm sure'

Greg studied him 'Nicole has been singing your praises, I understand you have many talents, amongst which you are a budding choreographer and song writer. Also your prowess at the skating rink is exceptional.

'It's just a hobby sir'

'What is, the music or the skating'

'Both sir.'

'You were approached I understand by one of the instructors. Would you like to be a professional skater?'

'That would be impossible and very expensive'

'And that is not what I asked.'

'No sir, I just enjoy it. Anyway I'm not that good – it's just that I have a certain style.'

'I see, but you must never underestimate yourself Jed. I am quite convinced that you would be excellent even excel at anything you put your mind to.'

'I don't know about that sir.'

'I do, that is why I wish to talk to you regarding your position here. Do you recall a few months ago I suggested I might put you under contract?'

'Yes sir.'

'Well, the time has come I think. How do you feel about it?'

'I am overwhelmed sir, I don't know what to say. I thought you meant when I was much older.'

'I want you to realise that this is a very unusual step – it is not often that one as young as you has this privilege but you deserve to be recognised and I believe this is a good way to show your worth, and I do not wish what I am about to say to go to your head, but Justin and I believe you have extraordinary talent – I would like you to stay with us for the foreseeable future.'

'I was not thinking of leaving sir.'

Greg held up his hand for silence

'We feel that you have been and will continue to be a great asset to the Company – you are an attractive talented young man Jed. You will secure offers from other companies which may prove difficult for you to refuse.'

'I assure you sir I have no wish to leave here.'

'At the moment, perhaps not. You still have a great deal to learn and you will not get better training than with us. But later in a few years time, this may not be enough for you.'

'Sir, Dr. Fellini. I like working with you'

'Even so, you will come to me if you should at a later stage feel the need for change – and I will do everything in my power to accommodate you, to assist you.'

'Thank you sir, but as I said, I do not think I shall want to leave.'

'All I ask of you Jed is your loyalty.'

'You have that sir, you always have.'

'That and hard work. And hopefully dedication. I believe you are mature enough to understand your responsibilities. Justin agrees wholeheartedly with me.' Greg passed him an envelope. 'I want you to take this contract, read it through, study it with your Grandfather, then sign it and bring it back to me.'

Jed took the document, stunned at the turn of events – he could not believe his luck.

'Thank you very much sir.'

'Well, good luck boy, off you go. We shall see you later. Do not be late for the performance.'

He looked at his watch - 'Nicole will be home now. I am sure she will be thrilled to hear your news!'

'Dr. Fellini?'

'What is it?'

'You don't mind me spending so much time with Nicole?'
'Good heavens no, she looks forward to your company.'
'Thank you sir.'

Jed's heart was singing as he left the theatre – he had never been quite sure of Greg's feelings regarding the amount of time he spent with Nicole and it was this which pleased him the most. He went straight to the house.

'I asked him if he minded me coming over so much,' he told her. 'He said he didn't.'

Nicole was puzzled, 'Why should he mind?'

'He said you looked forward to seeing me' He put his arm around her 'Is that true Nicki, do you look forward to seeing me?'

'Yes of course I do, I love it when you are here, you know that.'

'Good, I adore you Nicole'

He told her about the contract. 'He seems to think that I will want to leave at some point.'

'But you wouldn't leave Gregoire, Jed.'

'No, besides I wouldn't be able to see you if I did.'

'Its wonderful – Gregoire didn't even give me a contract,' she said.

'He didn't have to did he. He loves you.'

'Let's celebrate – I could dance for you if you like.'

'We haven't much time. We are both dancing tonight aren't we?'

'You'll be too tired.'

'Don't be silly Jed.'

'No, let's go for a walk, maybe get a coke somewhere.'

'Alright.'

It was a sunny day at the end of January. They walked leisurely in Hyde Park.

'We could take a bus back, you look tired Nicki.'

'I'm fine, but we must not be late'

They both ate ice-cream and Jed fetched some coke.

'Are you sure you are okay Nicole?' Jed was concerned, Nicole's face was screwed up with pain.

'It's – I think I have indigestion. It will be better in a minute. I've had it a lot lately.'

'Can I do anything?'

'No, I had it this morning at breakfast. It's probably a bug going around.'

'You'd better tell Greg, perhaps you should not work tonight, see the doctor'

'No, I do not want to worry Gregoire – it's nothing.' She sat up straight.

'There,' she said, 'it's going now but I can't eat the rest of the ice-cream Jed, you finish it',

'Do you want to go back?'

'Yes please Jed, I really don't feel very well. I'm sorry.'

'It's okay. Shall I get a taxi?'

'No, no, I'll be okay.'

'Well, we'd better take the bus.'

'No Jed, by the time we walk back to the bus, we could be almost home. Anyway the pain has gone now.'

When they arrived back Nicole went to the bathroom and splashed cold water on to her face, she felt a little hot and faint.

'I'll make you some tea,' Jed offered

Within minutes she was laughing and back to normal, just as Jed brought in the tea.

'Thank you Jed. I feel better now.'

'Are you sure?'

'Yes, I'm fine.'

Jed looked at his watch 'what time does Greg get in today.'

'I don't know, late this afternoon I expect'

'I'll wait till he gets back,' Jed said

'Jed, please don't tell him he will worry and fuss, and there is no need, look I'm fine', she said as she twirled around the room. She turned on the radio, started dancing to the music.

Jed smiled and joined her. Twisting and turning around the table. They were still dancing and singing when Greg arrived home.

Immediately she left Jed and rushed towards him – he picked her up and kissed her.

'And how is my most beloved this afternoon?' he said

'I missed you' she whispered.

'Nonsense, I am sure Jed has been a very able companion' - he kissed her again.

'I always miss you Gregoire, always. I like it when you are here.'

He gently released her, 'I see you have tea there. Is there any spare?' She poured him a cup.

'Now then Jed, what have you been up to, you certainly look more relaxed this week. How are you feeling?'

'Much better than last week. Thank you.'

'What did you think about Jed's contract my love?'

'It's wonderful Gregoire. You are pleased aren't you Jed.'

'Yes, overwhelmed.' He looked at the time.

'I'd better go now,' he said. 'Gran will be expecting me. She will be really thrilled. I'll see you later.'

Chapter 21

Over the next few weeks Nicole began to feel slightly unwell. When she awoke she felt languid and seemed often to have indigestion after her breakfast but she said nothing to Greg.

Maddie had been watching her for several days.

'I think you should see a doctor Nicole' she said.

'But I will feel better in a little while I always feel better during the day.'

'Nevertheless my dear I strongly advise you to make sure.' She gently manoeuvred her into a chair.

'Nicole, I think you are pregnant my dear. Go to the doctor, just to make sure that's all it is.'

'Oh dear,' Nicole was disturbed. 'Do you think so?'

'Yes Nicole I do – would you like me to go with you?' Maddie offered.

The girl was so young, like a child.

'Would you Maddie? I would be so happy if you would.'

'Get dressed, and I will telephone Dr. Maxwell.'

Dr. Paul Maxwell confirmed that Nicole was indeed pregnant. She was stunned. Maddie made some tea when they returned home.

'Come Nicole,' she said. Don't look so surprised, here is your tea. Would you like me to phone Gregoire?'

'Oh no, I don't want to disturb him. He will be angry.'

'Of course he will not be angry. If I know Gregoire, he will be delighted. Now, shall I contact him?'

'No, oh no, I will wait until later.'

In fact she very much wanted Greg with her.

'You are very young Nicole, you know it is the most natural thing in the world for you to be pregnant. You must not be afraid my dear.'

Nicole ignored the remark, if indeed she even heard Maddie. She looked up at her, her eyes troubled.

'Maddie' she said 'I do want Gregoire, but he is not at the theatre this morning and I do not know where he is.'

'It's alright dear, we can telephone Trudi she will know where he can be contacted.'

'But it is not really necessary is it Maddie,' Nicole said.

Maddie patted her, 'you telephone Trudi dear or would you like me to do it.'

'No, I'll ring her.'

'Is anything wrong Nicole?' Trudi asked

'No, I don't think so I just wanted to talk to him.'

'I'll get him to call you as soon as I contact him – I haven't seen you lately why don't you come round, have some coffee. Rosie would be thrilled to see you'

'Does she miss me?' Nicole asked. 'I expect she loves the new au pair now.'

'She loves you too Nicki. Come and see her she'd love to see you, we both would.'

Nicole wandered through to the lounge and then into the garden. It was not quite so warm now, and she quickly returned to the warmth of the lounge. She stood looking out of the window on this cold February morning. The initial shock and surprise at finding herself pregnant changed into nervousness. She could not imagine having a baby to look after and perhaps Greg would not be pleased. He still got angry with her sometimes at rehearsals when she would not grasp everything he instructed her to do. She began to worry and then he telephoned. He was full of concern

'I understand you wish to talk to me, what is it darling?'

'Gregoire are you coming home soon?'

'Nicole my precious, is something wrong?'

'Gregoire…' she faltered.

'Yes, what is it, are you alright?'

'I am pregnant. I am sorry Gregoire.'

She was on the verge of tears. She knew he would not be pleased. He would have to find a replacement for her in the ballet.

Greg was stunned. 'Look my beloved. I will be home as soon as I can. I love you darling, I won't be long.'

When he arrived back, he found her sitting bolt upright on a chair by the window, her eyes wide and serious. She looked up at him tears forming. He took hold of her, kissed her gently.

'You say you are pregnant. Are you sure?'

'Oui, I am sure. Maddie went with me to see the doctor.'

He gathered her in his arms, 'Why are you crying, are you afraid?'

She shook her head, 'I thought you might be angry.'

'Oh Nicki, Nicki my love, why should you think that. Don't you understand how much I love you?'

She burst into tears.

'Nicole, do you not want this baby?'

'Oui, only, only….'

'Only what, my darling you think I don't, ah Nicole of course I want the baby, I love you, I think it is wonderful, isn't it darling?'

'But the ballet?'

'What about the ballet – when the time comes, we will find a replacement, she will never be as perfect as you, but we shall manage.'

'Come now, smile for me, be happy, there's a good girl.'

Greg was thrilled at the news and as soon as she realised this, Nicole also was ecstatic.

'I will write to Maman – she will be pleased.' She looked at Greg, 'she will be won't she Gregoire?'

'Darling. I would wait a little before you tell them.'

'But, she is my Maman.'

'I know my love, but just wait a little before you tell them.'

'Please, I want to tell them.'

'Alright, but Nicole, please don't be too disappointed if the situation hasn't changed.'

Nicole smiled. 'She will be pleased, I know she will Gregoire.'

He stroked her hair and worried for her. He had no confidence in Belle and Pierre would not go against his wife, however Nicole was happy and he would not spoil her happiness.

'I want to tell Jed. I must tell Jed he will be so happy.'

Greg smiled 'Go along then, tell him the good news. Ask him if he would like to celebrate with us after the show – you would like that wouldn't you.'

Within one month Nicole received her letter from Belle, the first she had written since the marriage. He handed it to her, at the breakfast table.

'Here my love, some letters for you.'

She split open the one from France, and proceeded to read.

'Dear Nicole, I am writing as a duty to you, in place of your Papa. I hope you do not expect me to congratulate you. Or to be pleased that you are carrying that old man's child – I find it obscene. However if you will be prepared to leave England and return to your family, we will help you through the pregnancy and care for you and the child .

The farm and your friends will welcome you. Everything is the same as when you left. Of course your Papa and I miss you. I do not understand how you could have hurt us so – Jacques is still working in the town and misses you also. Let us know when to expect you. Take care of yourself ma cherie. Maman.'

Nicole sat looking at the letter for some minutes, then looked across at Greg. He was engrossed in his own correspondence. She folded the letter and put it back in its envelope – she deliberately took some toast and buttered it.

Greg looked up after a few minutes and smiled. 'Good news I hope darling.'

Nicole could not trust herself to answer him. She passed the letter across the table to him. He spent several minutes reading it.

'Oh dear, I am so sorry Nicole, how could she? She is still angry. How can she stay angry for so long.'

Her eyes clouded, 'What am I to do Gregoire, what am I going to do?'

'Nicole, everyone loves you here, I love you, Jed, Justin and all the cast. I can't pretend to understand your mother's cruel attitude, but darling, I hate to see you unhappy. She is wrong darling.' He paused. 'Listen, perhaps later, when the baby is born, she will relent. After all, how could anyone reject a baby? Especially her own grandchild – try not to be to upset my darling.'

'I think she is too angry to forgive,' she said.

He kissed her.

'How sad,' she said, 'our baby will not know her grandparents.' And although her eyes were moist she did not cry.

Suddenly she squared her shoulders, 'Monsieur, I am going to be a mother. He will be a wonderful baby. Yours and mine Gregoire. I will not cry over the spilling of milk – I must grow up now, be responsible.'

'I will love him and I will not think about Maman. Perhaps as you say she will relent. But if she does not, then it must be so. See I am grown up now – I am no longer a silly child and that is good is it not Gregoire.'

'Oh my love, please don't grow up too much.'

She put her arms around him. 'I have been a child for too long – children believe they can make things come true, don't they? I should have realised long ago that I am not a child, that fantasy is for children alone.'

'No Nicole, that is not true – Darling…'

She put her fingers on his lips. 'Shush Gregoire – I do not mind anymore. I have you and Jed and soon we shall have the baby. You will always love me, won't you?'

'You know that will always be so,' he said picking her up and kissing her.

'Gregoire, I am lucky, you always make things better. I am always happy when you are here. I love you so much Gregoire. It is such a nice feeling to love like this. Will you stay at home with me today?' she asked.

He lit a cigarette 'I should see Jack this morning.'

'Please.'

'Alright my love. Ill telephone him – make another arrangement. Are you alright?'

'Yes, I am very happy.'

'Weren't you going to see Jed today?'

'I want to stay here with you. It's just for today. I feel the need to be with you today.'

'It's alright darling I will stay.'

'Gregoire. I will start to grow up. You'll see how grown up I shall be – this baby, I am a little bit frightened, but I will be more responsible tomorrow.'

'Ah Nicole, I love you the way you are, don't change my love.'

Greg looked at his watch. The appointment with Jack was at 11.30. He would have to cancel.

He kissed his wife. 'Nicole I must phone Jack – he will be expecting me soon.'

'I'm sorry I am being so silly. It is alright Gregoire. You go to see him.'

'No! I said I would stay. Now, I will only be a few moments.'

It took him half an hour to discuss business with Jac and to make another appointment the following day. Then he gave himself up entirely to Nicole for the rest of the morning.

By lunch time he became restless, Greg was not used to being idle. After they had finished lunch, he sat and listened to her chatter, indulging her in her suggestions and plans for the baby.

'Are you really pleased Gregoire?' she asked him for the third time.

'Of course darling – listen, do you mind if I sort out some papers – come with me into the study if you wish. Bring your book or whatever you like. I do need to get some things sorted out.'

'It's alright Gregoire, I'll stay here as long as I know you are here with me.'

'Are you sure you don't mind darling.'

'I will read my book here,' she replied, and Greg retired to his study, relieved to be working again.

At half past three Jed telephoned and Greg answered. 'It's Jed for you darling,' he called.

She picked up the phone and chattered for a few minutes then called to Greg. 'Do you mind if Jed comes to tea?' she asked

'Of course he may come my beloved – he could stay if he wishes and travel to the theatre with us.'

He left his papers, and sat down beside her. 'How do you feel now?'

'A little more settled and happy. I told you Gregoire, I am grown up now I will be alright. This was just a little cough for me.'

Greg smiled at her strange expressions, 'You mean a little 'hiccup' don't you.'

'Yes a little hiccup that's it.'

When Jed arrived she told him about her mother's rejection of the baby.

'I'm so sorry Nicki,' he said

'It's alright now. I told Gregoire, everything will be alright – we do not mind do we Gregoire.'

Greg was a little concerned. The way she was reacting to Belle's cruelty was not usual – she had not cried, not complained much – she was too matter of fact.

'Damn them to hell,' he thought. 'One day I'll make them pay.'

But Nicole was true to her resolution. Over the next few weeks she did mature, and slowly she became more sophisticated. Greg found himself talking to her more seriously of his plans for the company, she made suggestions and he took note of them and their love for each other became stronger than ever. She was still dancing 'Lisa' and the audience loved her.

She also began to revel in her popularity, the male dancers milled around her and she responded flirting a little with them, but she had eyes only for Greg – she worshipped him.

Sometimes he would tease her. 'Do you love me?' he asked

'Yes, I am crazy about you,' she answered.

'Even with all these beautiful young men dancing attendance on you?'

'They are nothing, I love no one but you Gregoire'

'Oh I hope so my precious, I do hope so.'

Even though her figure was still presentable, Greg made her leave the ballet. She was nineteen and a half and felt healthy and energetic.

When her understudy took over, he cosseted and protected her until she felt stifled.

'Please Gregoire,' she said, 'I am not ill. In fact I have never felt so well, please you must not worry so much.'

'I am sorry darling, I love you so much I don't want anything to happen to you.'

'What can possibly happen? I am just pregnant.' She kissed him. 'I love you Gregoire, but you must not treat me like a baby. You are even afraid to make love to me aren't you?'

'I don't want to hurt you my love.'

'But I like you to make love to me Gregoire, you won't hurt me.'

But although he tried not to fuss he found it difficult to let her out of his sight, trying to persuade her to go with him to the theatre and sit in the office waiting for him to finish his classes. In the end she refused to go with him.

'I am bored. There is nothing for me to do. I do not want to go with you there Gregoire. Please let me stay with Maddie.'

Reluctantly he gave in and after a few weeks, he began to treat her normally. Although Jed was still working, still playing Colas, he and Nicole spent a lot of time now together. This pleased her and Jed was beside himself with joy.

They walked a lot and rowed on the lake. Sometimes they spent time in Amy's house and sometimes stayed at Greg's. They also spent some mornings, when Jed was not rehearsing, at the skating rink. Nicole was becoming quite proficient at the sport and she enjoyed the fast movements. Jed had taught her to dance and they made expert use of the dance intervals, dancing almost every dance. When Greg found that she had been skating he was beside himself with anger and forbade her to go again.

'Why?' she asked. 'We have been skating for months. I'm fine. It doesn't matter I am not dancing am I.'

He took her arm, 'Nicole my love, of course it matters – you are pregnant. Suppose you fall or are knocked over, you could be badly hurt as well as the baby inside you.'

'You are being silly Gregoire. I always feel well and happy after skating.'

'Nicole I mean what I say, you will not go again.'

'I like to go skating Gregoire. It will not hurt the baby,' her cheeks were red.

'Nevertheless I forbid you to go, that is final. What has got into you Nicole - try to be sensible. Do you want to injure the baby?'

Nicole's eyes filled and she rushed away from him and into the bedroom. Greg sighed, he was convinced he was right in forbidding her to skate. He poured himself a drink, and sat wondering what he should do.

He finished the whiskey and proceeded to the bedroom where he found his wife sobbing on the bed. He stood looking down at her for a few seconds, then sat beside her on the bed.

'Nicole,' he pleaded. 'Stop your crying now.'

'Leave me alone for a little while,' she said.

He pulled her over to him. 'Listen darling, I do this for your own good you are now five months pregnant. If you fall, it could be serious,'

'I do not fall much,' she sobbed, 'and I like to skate, I am always careful.'

'Stop crying now,' he demanded. 'There must be other activities you could enjoy.'

'No!' she said.

He picked her up, cuddled her. 'Nicole,' he said, 'I love you to pieces darling but you must obey me in this. You will not go to the rink again, until after the baby is born, is that clear.'

'I wish I was not pregnant,' she cried. 'If I am to be treated like this.'

He kissed her. 'You don't mean that Nicole – come now, stop this nonsense.' He stood up. 'Go along now, wash your face and I will take you for a drive before dinner.'

'I do not want to go for a drive.'

'Yes you do. Now come along my beloved, do as I say, we will drive along by the river.'

He smiled as she looked up at him, knowing she had lost the battle, and she brushed the tears from her eyes.

'That's better. I love you my precious you will see that I am right about this.'

'Could I not go just to do ordinary skating.'

'No, it is best now. And I will have a few words to say to Jed on the subject'

'It is not Jed's fault. It is always me who makes him take me. I love it so much,' she said.

'Wash your face darling and then we shall go.'

Greg did not want to discuss the matter further. She came out of the cloakroom and rushed over to him.

'Are you angry with me?'

'Of course not, I am just concerned for your safety and that of the child.'

She put her arms around him. 'I do not really want to go out Gregoire, and I will do as you say. I would like you to make love to me. I need to know that you love me.'

'Of course I love you, of course I do.'

'Please.'

'Come then, I will show you how much I love you, and you will promise me that you will stay away from the rink.'

Jed did not seem surprised that she had been banned from the rink.

'I expect he's worried,' he told Nicole. 'He doesn't realise how expert you have become even Gran told me to be careful, to stop you doing anything dangerous.'

'Oh well, I am disappointed – I really do love skating Jed, but I promised Gregoire that I wouldn't go again until after the baby is born.'

'It won't be that long Nicki.'

'No! Three months I can't wait. Isn't it exciting?'

Jed accompanied her as often as possible and Greg was grateful to see that his wife was contented. He knew Jed would take care of her and he came to rely on him to keep her occupied.

One month before her twentieth birthday Nicole gave birth to a 7lb baby girl. And although she was exhausted after a harrowing labour she and the baby were in excellent health. Both she and Greg were overcome with joy. Congratulations and flowers filled the room. Cards and letters came from different parts of the country and from America - everyone was thrilled for them both.

Greg in his great happiness telephoned Belle to congratulate her on her first grandchild. He received a cool response.

'Is my daughter well?' she asked.

'On top of the world Madame, we all are – you have a very beautiful granddaughter, the image of Nicole.'

'I have nothing to say, Monsieur,' Belle replied.

Greg could not believe this unfriendly approach.

'Will you write to her please Belle,' he pleaded.

'Goodbye Monsieur,' she said and replaced the receiver

'Damn her!' Greg cursed 'Damn her to hell.'

He could not bring himself to tell Nicole that he had spoken to her mother – He had not the courage not the heart to repeat Bella's conversation. Nicole had not mentioned her parents, but that was not because she had not thought about them. She was too nervous to mention them to Greg. Jed went to the hospital every morning. He was fascinated with the tiny doll like little person in the crib beside Nicole's bed. He picked her up, cuddled her and kissed the tiny scrap.

'She is a miracle,' he said.

When Greg arrived he always took the child from whoever held her at the time and Nicole looked more beautiful than ever. Greg could not take his eyes off her.

'You are the most beautiful girl in the world and I sorely miss you when you are not at home with me'

'I miss you too Gregoire,' Nicole replied. 'But we shall be home very soon, only a few more days.'

After much discussion they decided to call the baby Guillese and Nicole adored her. Her room was always crowded with friends from Greg's company and from theatres in London. Nicole had become well known in the profession – the baby was passed from one to another, petted over and kissed over and over until the sister whisked her away.

'The poor child needs rest and space,' she admonished, 'and so do you Mrs Fellini.'

Chapter 22

The moment she arrived home she, sent cards to everyone she could think of. Jed went with her to the post.

'Isn't she wonderful Jed?' Nicole enthused. 'So pretty.'

'She is exactly like you Nicki.'
'She is so good and very friendly – she does not cry at anyone.'

'Well she is very lucky she has you for her Mama'
'And you for her uncle,' she continued.
'Yes, that's right,' Jed replied proudly.
Look how soft her skin is and when she is awake she seems to be laughing already.
'She looks like you Nicki' Jed repeated
'She has Gregoire's eyes' Nicole said.
'I think she is the image of you,' Jed said. 'When she is grown up everyone will fall in love with her, the same as her Mama.'
'Jed you always say such nice things.'
'I mean them,' he said.
Greg was fascinated with his new daughter and for a few days was happy to stay around playing house during the day. But inevitably he grew restless with the inactivity and returned to work with the ballet, immersing himself more than ever with his creative talent, explaining apologetically to his wife for his absence. Nicole understood and was now engrossed with her daughter.
'It's alright Gregoire, I know you need to work.'
He kissed her. 'We will employ a nanny in a few weeks,' he said.

'Then you will be able to join me, and you will be free to do whatever you wish.'

'No Gregoire, I do not want to have a nanny. I am quite able to look after Guillese by myself. I like to do this.'

She was so passionate in her rejection of a nanny that for the moment Greg was disturbed. Soon a nanny would be essential when Nicole returned to work. But Greg said nothing to aggravate the situation.

Nicole was ecstatically happy in her new role of mother. She took the baby everywhere during the day. In the evenings Maddie was always available to baby sit if Greg wanted Nicole with him.

Cards and presents arrived at the house following Nicole's announcement of Guillese's birth. Everyone wrote congratulating them, everyone, except her parents. There was no reply even after ten days. They did not even telephone.

Jed called in one morning and found her crying.

'What is it Nicki?' he said putting his arms around her. She leaned her head on his shoulder and cried afresh.

'I did believe that when Guillese was born, they would forgive me, but they did not write. Why are they being so cruel. I am so miserable Jed.'

'Oh really I am so sorry. Please don't cry – everyone else is happy for you.' he cuddled her. 'They are very silly they don't know what they are missing. Perhaps later they will relent. If you sent a picture of the baby, maybe they will not be able to resist her.'

Nicole dried her eyes and pulled away from him.

'Jed,' she said, 'Jed please do not tell Gregoire. He worries for me. I don't want him to think I am unhappy. I don't want him to worry about me. Anyway, I have cried enough I think, and I will try to forget. It is just that I did think that after all this time they would have forgiven us. You must promise me that you won't tell Gregoire that I was crying today.'

'Okay, if that's what you want, but Greg would want to help you.'

'He can't Jed, it would only upset him. Promise me, please.'

'Oh alright. I won't tell him. Look I've brought Guillese a bear. All children love teddy bears, don't they? I still have mine and I believe Tess does too.'

'Oh thank you Jed she will love it. I never had a teddy bear – none of the children around had even heard of them.'

'You've never had a teddy bear? Who did you tell all your troubles to? I still talk to mine.'

She laughed, 'Don't be silly Jed, I did have a lamb Pascal gave me.'

'Oh well, nearly as good, but not quite. I shall have to find you one. I've brought you some perfume.'

'How kind of you Jed. It smells delicious. Thank you!' She put some on her wrist.

'Where is she then?'

'She's with Maddie'

'I'll go in and see her in a minute. I have to go soon. I only came in to give you the presents.'

With the help of Maddie, Nicole managed to look after the baby perfectly. She was a conscientious mother and both she and Greg never ceased to marvel at their beautiful daughter.

When she was two months old, Greg suggested Nicole should return to work. He wanted her back on stage.

'But what about Guillese. We can't leave her with Maddie all the time. She is so little.'

'Darling I didn't mean immediately, perhaps in another month when she will be three months old and you will be fully recovered. We shall hire a nanny.'

'No, Gregoire, I do not want our baby to have a nanny. I am her Mama.'

They talked and argued incessantly, but Nicole was adamant.

'Do you not want to dance for me my love? Do you wish to give up the ballet? To waste all your talent would be heartbreaking. You know Nicole, you are unique, one of a kind I have missed you on stage all these months.'

'Oh darling Gregoire, of course I do not wish to give up dancing. But I want to be with Guillese – she needs her Mama. She does not want a nanny.'

He drew her towards him, kissed her.

'You will come back won't you Nicole?' he said.

'Of course I will, but I want Guillese with me at the theatre. I do not want to stop feeding her myself yet, and I want her to know me, and love me and you. I do not want some other lady to be her Mama. I could not bear to be away from her Gregoire.'

'Oh dear,' Greg sighed running his fingers through her hair. 'It is not practical my love.'

'She can stay in my dressing room – we could check on her all the time.'

'It would disrupt everything.'

'She is so little, she would be no trouble. Some of the younger students would not mind sitting in with her.'

'I don't know Nicole.'

'Gregoire I would arrange it all, you would not have to worry.'

'Nicole you are not being very realistic.'

'I will not leave my baby. I want to be with her.'

'Well, perhaps something could be arranged, but when she is older, it will not be so easy.'

'We will think of something else then. Please Gregoire, you will not even know she is there, I promise.'

'I don't know how you are going to be able to keep a promise such as that my love. However, we will give it a try.'

'Thank you Gregoire.'

He kissed her. He wanted her back dancing for him. 'When you are ready my beloved let me know and I will see to it. Don't leave it too long. I miss you Darling.'

To make it less difficult for Nicole, he had the basement of the house built into a studio, so that she could rehearse and practise at home instead of the theatre. Also there was enough space for a smaller room to be added, that could be used for the baby's needs and for Nicole to rest and feed her and if necessary to leave her to sleep in the pram or cot which they installed there. This room was also equipped with a small stove where tea or coffee could be made.

Greg supervised the whole venture, making sure that the studio and room were as comfortable as possible. Leading off the studio he added a washroom and toilet making the whole thing complete.

'It is magnifique,' Nicole enthused when it was finally completed.

'Well now, this is yours Nicole, your own little domain, no one will encroach on your privacy.'

'Except you Gregoire'

'Not even me my love.'

'But I want you to come to see us down here sometimes.'

'Well I'm sure I shall not be able to keep away.'

'You are always so good to me,' she said throwing her arms around him.

'I love you,' he said, 'and I want you back dancing my love.'

'Gregoire you will allow me to take Guillese with me to the Theatre won't you.'

'Yes, at least for the moment.'

Nicole made good use of the studio, taking the baby first thing in the morning. She played with her a little, then settled her in her pram for a sleep. At a later stage they installed a playpen which Nicole housed in the studio so that the baby could watch. When Guillese was four months old, Greg talked to his wife about a new ballet he was creating. After one of their special love making sessions he asked her if she was ready to dance for him.

She wound her arms about him. 'If I may bring Guillese to the theatre with me, I would love to dance again.'

'I said so didn't I?' He gave her a playful push. 'I spoil you.'

'I know,' she answered.

But Greg was happy, he had his Nicole back on the stage and he knew that in no time at all she would have the world at her feet. Jed rehearsed occasionally with Nicole in the studio, and partly because Guillese was always there, as well as the fact that the child was so engaging, Jed played a large part in her life.

He often brought his guitar and cassette with him.

'You should let Gregoire hear your songs Jed, they are so good.'

'They are not his 'thing' Nicki. Some day when I am older, I'd like to write for a musical. I'd have to collect some cash first though. I'd love to stage my own musical.'

'You wouldn't leave Gregoire?'

'Of course not. I'm just day dreaming. Just a pipedream – I have a hell of a lot to learn from him. I still watch him, the way he works. His attitude with the students. They worship him you know, even though they are terrified of him. He is fantastic, he gets things done and he is always on top, everyone wants to work with him. I consider I was lucky he accepted me.'

'He knew you were good Jed or he would never have entertained having you. I love him to death but I know he can be cruel and ruthless, and when I start rehearsing I get a bit nervous,' she said.

'He wouldn't have survived if he had been otherwise. I know Justin is softer and more pleasant to work with but, he doesn't get the results that Greg does. He told me he has a part for me in the new ballet. Be nice if I could partner you Nicki. I know I'm not good enough yet. Maybe next year.'

'You are good enough Jed. Maybe Gregoire will give you something big in this ballet.'

'Maybe. I'm only just seventeen.'

'You are old enough to play the lead.'

'Nice of you to say so, but Greg is the one who decides. I guess he still thinks of me as a kid!'

'Would you like me to talk to him.'

'No Nicole don't. He will give me something better when he thinks I am ready. I do trust him.'

'But you think you are ready now don't you.'

Jed shrugged, 'I'm just impatient, Colas is not a bad part I guess. I'm still a bit young. I'll wait.'

'You look so handsome Jed, tall and slim.'

Guillese started to whimper, Nicole went straight to the pram. She picked her up and started to dance with her – she gurgled and shrieked.

'Isn't she wonderful Jed? Look at her she loves to dance – here you take her.'

Jed started to sing to her, she loved it, was fascinated. He continued to sing and dance with her around the studio.

'She really is beautiful Nicki, she looks exactly like you.'

They danced together – the baby between them Nicole propped her up in the pram, so that she could watch.

'Would you like to come upstairs for a drink Jed?' Nicole asked after a while.

'Sure,' he said. 'Shall I bring Guillese.'

'If you like – she seems to like you to hold her.'

'Of course she does, don't you baby?'

They ran up the stairs and into the hall where Maddie appeared, to take the baby. Greg was engrossed for at least another two weeks writing and preparing the new ballet.

'Naturally,' he said to Justin, 'I have written this with Nicole in mind. It will be her first appearance since Guillese was born.

'What about Jed, we should find him something worthwhile. He is seventeen now, and in spite of his youth I believe he is ready for a lead.'

'Yes, well I want to keep either Matthew or Yanni with Nicole. They work so well together. The public will expect that.'

'And Jed?'

'What about him partnering Sadie. Quite a substantial part for him there.'

Justin looked disappointed.

'What is it Justin, Jed has had Colas and other parts quite major for him.'

'I think he deserves better.'

'You know Justin, we must not indulge Jed too much. That boy wants to run before he walks.'

'He has been with us for four years Greg, he needs to know we appreciate him.'

'Is he complaining?'

'Of course not, he wouldn't'

'Well then, at least he is under contract. He will get his chance.' Moving on, he said 'as this is Nicole's fist appearance since Guillese was born, and she is only four months old, Nicole will need longer rest periods whilst rehearsing.'

Justin was silent, because he knew that if and when Greg decided to rehearse them he would work her as hard as the others, he would not think about rest periods – she would become just another dancer.

'Call a rehearsal for next Monday Justin. I must be off now. Do you know where Jed is?'

'No idea, he may be at your studio. He said something earlier about going to your house.'

'Right. I'll telephone you Justin and if you need me I will be at home until seven. I must give Nicole a little attention.'

Greg found both Jed and Nicole and the baby in the studio huddled together at the table in the anti-room.

'What are you two up to then?' he asked

'Gregoire!' Nicole jumped to greet him. He clasped her to him, kissing her fondly.

'Look,' she said, 'Jed is so clever, he has written all these songs. They are really good. Do you want to hear them? We've made up some dances as well. Would you like to see?'

Greg raised his eyebrows, 'Well, well you have been busy – budding little impresario are we?'

He took Guillese from Jed, kissed her then started to throw her into the air. She gurgled with delight. He sat down with her on his knee and turned to Jed.

'Alright, let me hear some of these masterpieces, he said. 'I have some time. Have you recorded them?'

'Some,' Jed said. 'I don't think you would be interested sir. They are not all that good.'

'My wife tells me otherwise. She tells me you have been busy choreographing, so let me see, show me.'

'Come on Jed,' Nicole was pulling Jed's arm. 'Gregoire will like to see them.'

'Alright.' Jed was a little dubious.

They switched on the cassette and began to dance. Greg watched, at first with indulgence but as they progressed, he could not deny that Jed was indeed very talented. Nicole was darting about. She looked sexy and desirable and moved her body sexily with Jed complimenting her movements. Nicole looked excited. A slight pang of jealousy ran through him, watching the two of them. They were so young and she was different with Jed. They seemed to belong together - he shook himself. Jed was still a boy, and he knew Nicole was his. He should be pleased that she was enjoying herself. He smiled when they had finished the dance.

'Excellent Jed,' he said. 'Do you intend to continue to write music?'

'I guess so, it's just something I have always done. I used to write nursery rhymes when I was younger.'

'Really!'

'Gregoire,' Nicole interrupted. 'Have you time to see the one Jed wrote specially for me.'

'No Nicki, you wouldn't be interested sir, it's very jazzy.'

'Please Gregoire. It won't take very long. The music is the best one he's written. Would you like to see?'

'Why not?' Greg said and sat down again, the baby still on his knee.

The dance was an energetic and jazzy number. She seemed to come alive. It was fast, suggestive and very original but Greg did not like it. He had no idea she could or would dance in such a way. She was perfect. When she had finished she ran to him and as though she knew he would not approve. She made a great fuss of both him and the baby. She did not even ask if he had enjoyed it. He kissed her, stroked her hair.

'You enjoy dancing like this,' he said.

'It is so exhilarating Gregoire, but it is just a little fun.'

He turned to Jed. 'You have a great deal of talent my boy, and you dance well with Nicole – perhaps at a later date we might think about partnering you with her.'

'Would you really' Jed said, his eyes wide.

'We'll see and now I need to get upstairs to the office – are you coming with me my love.'

'Of course Gregoire. I'll see you later Jed.'

'Perhaps Jed would care to join us for a drink before he leaves.'
'Thank you sir.'

When Jed had gone Greg asked Nicole if she really enjoyed the dance.

'You are not cross about it are you Gregoire?'

'How could I ever be cross with you my sweet beloved. Of course not, Jed is very talented and you looked absolutely magnificent.'

'Amazing! He sings well too. What about me, do I sing well?'

'You dance much better darling, but you have a very sweet voice. Come here to me – I love you, and I never cease to wonder how I could have got so lucky. You do love me don't you Nicole.'

'Yes Gregoire, I do love you.' She wound her arms around him.

The week before Greg's new ballet was ready for production, Nicole decided once again to write to her Mother. She enclosed a picture of all three of them. Guillese was in Nicole's arms, smiling happily at her father who had his arms around them both.

It was a beautiful picture Jed had taken the previous week.

Surely her mother would forgive them now.

She did not tell Greg that she had written to her parents, he became so agitated and protective.

'You must not be too disappointed if they still reject you darling. I can't bear to see you upset, because of their cruel behaviour. They are not worth it my love.'

But Nicole was sure they would not be able to resist their beautiful grandchild. The day before the new ballet opened she received a curt note from Belle, not even a letter. It read as follows:

'Nicole, you and the baby may come home whenever you are ready, let us know when, and Papa will meet you at the airport. I want nothing to do with him.'

Tucked inside a folded piece of notepaper was half of the photograph Nicole had sent. Belle had cut the photograph in half, she had kept the part with Nicole and the baby and sent back the other half with a wide streak of red pencil slashed through it.

Nicole was shocked she could not believe this of her Mother. To do a dreadful thing like this. 'She must be very angry indeed.'

She left the picture on the table and ran crying to the bedroom.

There was no one about and she lay on the bed sobbing.

Maddie heard and found her. 'What on earth is the matter my dear?' she said.

But Nicole could not answer. She had been crying too long and too hard to be able to speak coherently and her face was swollen with her eyes half closed and red. Maddie tried to calm her.

'Come Nicole, come with me into the lounge by the fire – you are frozen.'

Nicole allowed Maddie to guide her into the chair by the fire. She went to make some tea.

'Now dear, drink this hot tea, what is it, tell Maddie.'

Nicole threw herself on to Maddie and sobbed afresh. Greg walked in to find them there.

'What on earth has happened!' he cried. 'Is she alright?'

'There is nothing physically wrong, but she was hysterical earlier – I can get nothing out of her.'

'Alright Maddie. Thank you for taking care of her.'

He picked his wife up and sat with her on the armchair.

'Now my love, what is it. Why are you so upset?'

She still did not speak. And Greg spoke sharply because he knew no other way to stop her sobbing.

'Come darling Nicole – you must tell me what is wrong. Or I can do nothing to help you.'

Then his eyes alighted on the letter lying on the table. He reached over and read the offending note – glanced at the spoiled photograph of himself. The look on his face was murderous.

'How dare she,' he said

He turned back to his wife. 'It doesn't matter darling it really does not matter. We don't need them. Don't do this my sweet love – it is me they object to. They still love you and that is all that matters. If they can't forgive me, it does not matter. Please beloved, stop crying. I love you so much. We will make a good life. Come now, perhaps one day they will relent.' He was holding her close.

'Gregoire,' she said when she had calmed herself a little, 'I am so ashamed of Maman she should not have done that to your picture it was very cruel. She does not know how good you are, how kind you are nor how much I love you. Gregoire I will not worry about them anymore.'

Greg did not comment just continued stroking her hair and kissing her. But he was angry that they had hurt her. How dare they make her so unhappy. Nicole looked up at Greg. Saw the extent of his anger. She kissed him.

'They will not hurt us again Gregoire. They do not belong anymore in my life. I have you and Guillese and Jed and his grandparents – they can be Guillese's grandparents, no?'

'Yes darling, of course they can. They will be proud.'

She smiled. 'We can be happy without them,' she smiled at her daughter, 'I do not understand. She is so beautiful. How can they not want her?'

'They are very foolish darling. But as you say we do not have to rely on them to be happy, do we? And we will be happy always my love. Soon you will be dancing again for me. Are you looking forward to that?'

She snuggled into his shoulder and nodded her head.

'Are you sure darling, you know you don't have to if you are not ready.'

'I am ready Gregoire, you have given me a long rest – I will dance for you. I always dance for you.'

Greg approached the subject of employing a nanny for Guillese. Nicole jumped off his knee.

'No, no,' she said. 'I do not like that – you promised I could take her to the theatre.'

'I didn't promise that Nicole.'

'Then I will stay at home with her.'

'It's alright my love, we will think of something.'

'She will be alright at the theatre,' she insisted.

And so they took her with them. She slept peacefully in the dressing room. There was always someone around to monitor her. Sophie, Nicole's dresser, was thrilled to act as 'nanny' and between acts either Jed or Nicole checked on her.

The ballet was a success and Jed was given a fairly major part dancing with Natalie, understudy for Nicole. Very occasionally Greg gave Nicole a break leaving Justin to run the company.

'We did not have a honeymoon did we my love. I will arrange something soon.'

'You and I Gregoire, we do not need a honeymoon. It is wonderful just to be married to you. But it is nice to get away from everyone sometimes.'

'Yes it is.'

Even so wherever they went she would never leave Guillese. She could not bear to be away from her for long. Each morning she picked her up from the breakfast table and took her down to the studio. She lay in the pram provided for her until Nicole had finished working. Then she gathered her up and danced with her around the studio.

Greg continued to nurture Jed, weaning him into stronger parts. He did not seem inclined to trust him with too much. Justin tackled Greg about this.

'He is more professional than some of the others.'

'He's still young.'

'He is seventeen Greg.'

'Well, I am a little reluctant in giving him everything he wants.'

There was something about Jed that prevented Greg from giving him the lead role in any of the productions.

'What are you nervous about Greg? He's the best you have. As good as Matthew and probably more dynamic.'

'I think that is what it is. He is too dynamic, almost manic.'

'Rubbish – what on earth is wrong with being too dynamic. Is that possible?'

'I don't know Justin – I've watched him he always seems impatient with the dance. He wants to speed everything up.'

'Come on Greg. You are imagining things.'

'Maybe you are right, but did you notice the other evening he changed the choreography to suit himself. I meant to have spoken to him about that.'

'I did notice, yes' Justin said, 'But I thought he improved the scene – I told him to keep it in.'

'Did you now - don't you think that I should have been consulted.'

'Well frankly I didn't think it was a major problem, however I'm sorry.'

'Did you think I would override you?'

'Greg, as I said I did not think it anything major. You were not around at the time. Also you leave me to cast, rehearse etc. Do you wish me to run to you every time we make changes – I'm supposed to be your partner and you are treating me again like the office boy.'

'Oh I'm sorry Justin, you are right, of course, you obviously have great faith in Jed.'

'Haven't you? There was a time when you could not praise him enough.'

'I know, as I say, you are quite right. I am being unreasonable.' He put a hand on Justin's shoulder, 'I'm sorry Justin I don't know what got into me.'

He left Justin and walked slowly and thoughtfully away. What the hell was the matter with him. Jed was easily one of the best dancers he had.

Was there a slight feeling of resentfulness, rivalry – 'It's madness' he mused 'Absolute madness' and he squared his shoulders and went home.

Nicole was waiting for him. She rushed to him as usual. 'Gregoire, I am so glad you are home so early.'

He kissed her. 'I love you Nicole, I don't know what I would do without you.'

'Me too Gregoire, I love you too'

He hugged her and he knew that she would always belong to him. Jed was a good friend, so necessary to her. He would never deprive her of that.

Chapter 23

At first Greg found the paraphernalia of transporting baby, baby luggage to and from the theatre irritating and showed his displeasure, but after a few days when it all became routine, he reluctantly accepted the situation. It seemed to work extremely well and the baby was never for a moment without willing carers. She was so amenable that when they picked her up from the dressing room to transport her back home, she went straight into her cot without any trouble and slept through the night. She was truly a theatre baby and everyone adored her.

With his wife's agreement, Greg started to allow the more mature students, those who did not need supervision to use the studio with Nicole for private sessions.

'It will be better for you my love,' he said, 'to work sometimes with the other dancers.'

'I would like that Gregoire. It will be nice to have company sometimes.'

She looked up at him.

'What is it?' he asked.

'Jed, could Jed come as well?'

'Jed.'

'Yes, Gregoire, would you mind if he came with them?'

Greg looked puzzled. 'I thought Jed was always here, isn't he?'

'No, not when I am practising, but I would like him to be here.'

'It is entirely up to you my dear. But Jed should not play around with the tapes, whilst the others are working.'

'No, of course not.'

He smiled at her. 'If you wish Jed to be here of course he may come. I have told you, my beloved that this studio was built for you. It is your own special retreat. I want you to be happy and contented here.'

'I am very happy and I love it, so does Guillese.'

'And you do not mind sharing it a little with the other dancers.'

'Of course not, Gregoire.'

The studio became a haven for Nicole, a place where she could fantasize, pretend her parents shared her happiness, that they had not rejected her, where she could dream and where, if she felt low as she sometimes did because of them, she could cry. But in the main she was happy. Her husband and child gave her a feeling of purpose, much more so than her great talent in the dance world. She loved them both with a fierce passion as well as the close, loving friendship she had with Jed. Her world was almost complete.

Jed came upon her one afternoon sitting motionless, tears streaming down her face.

'Nicki? Nicki, what's up?'

'Oh, Jed,' she brushed away the tears. 'I'm so glad to see you.'

'What's wrong?'

'Oh, I am just being silly again. I was just thinking if only Maman would forgive me, the whole world would be beautiful' she smiled, 'it is very silly of me to keep thinking about it – she will never forgive.'

'I'm sorry Nicole, I'm so sorry.'

'Never mind, I cannot have everything set on a plate for me. I should be satisfied with half the cup.'

Jed laughed. 'Oh Nicki, you are absolutely priceless.'

'I say it wrong?'

'No Nicki, you say it absolutely perfectly. Cheer up, I have a new tape for you. Hello baby,' he held his arms out to Guillese and she went to him immediately.

'She loves you as much as Gregoire and me,' Nicole observed.

Nicole always enjoyed the excitement of the fast exciting dances that Jed choreographed for her.

'Where did you learn to choreograph, Jed?'

'Books from the library and watching Greg at work. He's a great artist, fascinating to watch.'

She proceeded to move across the dance floor, her beautiful body swaying provocatively. Jed's heart missed several beats. He could not take his eyes off her. Whenever she came to the end of a dance, she ran laughing, her arms around him impulsively.

'Jed,' she cried, 'I love dancing like this, you are such a clever boy.'

'Oh Nicole, I love you,' he murmured into her hair. He lifted her chin and kissed her on the lips.

Previously, she would have laughed, probably held her face up to kiss him back, but something in his earnestness warned her and she drew away.

He pulled her gently back to him. 'Will you let me kiss you again, Nicki?'

'Jed,' she said, 'you know I love you, you are so very dear to me, but I love Gregoire, you must know that. You are my friend, Jed, my brother. Jed, don't spoil it please.'

He turned from her, ashamed of his indiscretion.

'Forgive me Nicole, I am truly sorry. It won't happen again. I am such a bloody fool. I must be mad. Is this going to make a difference to our relationship?'

'Of course not, silly. I understand, and Jed you will find someone you can love soon, you will always be my true friend and I yours. We are family you and I Jed, aren't we?'

He nodded, but he didn't want to be her family.

'Come here.' She put her arm around his shoulder realising his discomfort, wanting to put him at ease, to make him feel more comfortable with her. 'Will you take me skating this afternoon? I don't have to work tonight. We can have a hamburger afterwards. Greg will be at the theatre.'

He smiled. 'I do have to work tonight' he said, 'but we can still go. I will just have to forego the hamburger.'

'We can do something else.'

'No, we'll go to the rink. You do still trust me Nicki?'

'I know you will not do anything to hurt Gregoire or me. I know that, and I am very flattered you think you feel so much for me, but you are still young and very handsome. You will find someone to love soon. You will, Jed, believe me and whoever she is, she will be a very lucky girl.'

Jed did not answer for he was convinced that he would never love anyone else the way he loved her.

On her twenty-first birthday, Greg took her to the 'Inn on the Park'. Just the two of them.

'I intend to give you a better celebration as soon as the production has finished my angel.'

'You don't have to do that Gregoire.'

'Oh yes, my love. I certainly do.'

He had given her a beautiful ruby pendant on a very unusual gold chain and with the pure white velvet dress she looked exquisite. She had the perfect figure, not the paper thin anorexic look that many young girls have. People turned to look at her as she entered the restaurant.

* * *

Greg was so enchanted with his beautiful daughter, he wrote and choreographed a fairytale ballet for her. It was purely for children and he staged it to coincide with the summer school holiday. It was about a sickly girl who travelled on a white swan to exotic places, based on a Russian tale.

Guillese was enthralled and just before her third birthday she and Justin's two children were taken to see the ballet.

'Will Maman be dancing?' she asked.

'Yes, she is the girl who becomes a beautiful princess.'

'And Jed?'

'Yes Jed and Natalie, all your friends.'

'And Matthew?'

'Of course Matthew. He will be the king of all Russia who falls in love with the princess.'

Guillese put her arms around her father. 'I do love you Papa,' she sighed.

'And I love you, sweetheart.'

Their eyes sparkled with wonder at the fairy scenes, the music and dancing and when the performance ended, Justin gathered the 3 of them backstage. Jocelyn and Daniela, Justin's children were thrilled as the white swan in all his feathered glory opened its beak and produced a box of chocolate for each of them. When Guillese approached, the wide open beak terrified her and she ran screaming to her father. Nicole tried to pacify her to no avail, until she removed her headdress and the swan retreated from the stage. Even then she was not completely comforted. The tiara Nicole handed to her snapped as the child clutched it, making her cry afresh. Greg took her, kissed her and cuddled her crooning until she fell asleep in his arms.

'I think we had better get the children home,' he said. 'Did you enjoy it girls?'

Jocelyn and Daniela were tired but excited and talked incessantly about the tale until Justin decided to leave.

'They want us to go for a meal,' Nicole came running to Greg.

"Who, who want us to go.'

'Matthew, Jonathan and the others.'

'Well darling, I don't think we can. We have to get Guillese to bed. She is exhausted.'

'Can't she come with us?'

'Darling you know that is not possible.'

'Oh!' Nicole looked disappointed.

'Nicole my love, you go with them. I'll take Guilly home.'

'No Gregoire. I will come with you.'

'Go on darling,' he looked around for Jed.

'Did you want me sir?' Jed called. 'Oh, Jed, Nicole is going with you all for a meal. Can I rely on you to look after her?'

'Of course.' Jed was more than willing.

'You will make sure she gets home safely won't you Jed.'

'Of course I will. Come on Nicki. I'll make sure she is safe, sir.'

'Have a good evening darling,' Greg said. He kissed her and left.

'I should have gone with Gregoire.' Nicole said.

Don't be silly. It will do you good to have some fun.'

They settled in one of the restaurants in Covent Garden. At first Nicole was a little subdued but after a few glasses of wine she began to relax and enjoy herself, and the rest of the artists found her charming company.

'You should come out with us more often Nicole,' they told her. 'We are going on to a night club. Why don't you join us?'

'No, I don't think that I will thank you.'

'Oh come on. Dr. Fellini won't mind will he?'

'No but, well we'll see.'

She left with Jed at half past one, having established that Jed would not be going.

'You could get Gregoire to take you next time,' Jed said. 'It's not really a lot of fun though except when you are with a crowd.'

'I hope they didn't think I was being unfriendly,' she said.

'Don't worry about that. They won't think about it.'

When Jed left her at the door, Greg was waiting for her. 'Did you enjoy yourself my beloved?' he asked.

'I would rather you had been with me. I don't like going anywhere like that without you.'

'You had Jed.'

'I know, and I love Jed, but it is not the same as being with you.'

He took her to bed, put his arms around her and kissed her.

'You should mix more with your contemporaries,' he said, 'people the same age as yourself.'

'Gregoire, I don't want anyone else but you.'

'Alright darling, I will try to take you out myself more often, spend more time with you. I do not want you to get bored my love. I don't ever want you to get tired of being married to me.'

'Gregoire, I am never bored and you are all I want. You and Guilly.'

'You are a truly wonderful girl. Are you truly happy with me?'

'Yes, I am very happy.'

Most of the time she was but occasionally Greg noticed the sadness clouding her eyes and he knew she was thinking of her parents. It was a great tragedy to her. He was always aware of her distress.

'We have each other and the baby, please don't be sad my beautiful one.'

'I am not sad Gregoire, truly I am not.'

Their love was a legend throughout the theatre and indeed the theatre world. They were obsessed with each other and their child.

Chapter 24

They continued to take Guilly to the dressing room at night.
'She is 3 years old now,' Greg said. 'She is getting tall.'
'Yes, and she grows more beautiful every day doesn't she Gregoire.'
'Just like you my angel.'
But Greg knew that he was going to have to persuade Nicole to leave her at home at night. It was time to talk to his wife. He drew her onto his knee.
'I want to talk to you darling.'
'What is the matter? You look so serious.'
'I am serious Nicole. Guillese is getting too big to sleep all night at the theatre. She should be sleeping in her own cot here at home.'
'No Gregoire. She won't like that.'
'She will get used to it.'
'No Gregiore….' Nicole attempted to jump off his knee, but he held onto her.
'Nicole darling, she will be perfectly alright. We can put her to bed before we leave or at least get her ready for bed. Maddie will be here, she will look after her.'
'No Gregoire.'
'Yes darling, it has to be.'
'Gregoire, she is used to being with me, with us. I want her to be with me.'
'Nicole, the dressing room isn't a place for a child of Guilly's age. She does not sleep properly and she has already wandered into other dressing rooms, and she is getting very spoiled.'
'She is just a baby.'

'She is nearly 3 years old Nicole. Her health will soon start to suffer.'

'I will make sure she sleeps properly.'

'Tell me darling, how are you going to ensure that? It isn't fair to her.'

Nicole wrenched herself away from Greg.

'It isn't fair to make her sleep at home. You are being cruel.'

'Rubbish, come here my love.'

'No I don't want to. I will stay at home with her then.'

She rushed into the bedroom. Greg had expected protests, a few tears, but he also expected her to give in without much protest. Slowly he made his way to the bedroom and saw that she was crying on the bed.

'Oh come now Nicole, don't cry my love. I hate to see you cry.'

'Why are you being so cruel?'

'Listen darling, you must do as I say regarding this matter. I am sorry, it is best for Guillese.'

'Then I will stay here with her.'

'No Nicole, you will not. You will carry on with the ballet, at least until the end of the season. You know I can't replace you at such short notice. If you feel this way at the end of it, then we will talk.'

'Why don't you want her with us?'

'I have told you.'

'You don't love her.'

'Don't be ridiculous. Of course I love her. Now please stop this stupidity and dry your tears. Come give me a cuddle.'

'No, I will not. I don't love you just now.'

He grabbed her arm. 'Oh Nicki, don't fight with me. I love you.'

'No! No you don't love me, go away.'

She ran away from him, grabbed her coat and ran out of the house. He sighed. He had never seen or believed that his sweet tempered wife could be so stubborn. He sat and waited for her to return. He looked at his watch, it was three thirty. He sauntered along to the nursery where his daughter was playing and knelt down beside her.

'Hello shrimp,' he smiled at her.

She looked up and smiled back. He picked her up, cuddled her and kissed her.

'I want a drink,' she commanded.

'What else?'

'I want a drink of orange.'

'Please Papa,' he prompted.

'Please Papa,' she echoed.

'Alright.'

He went to the kitchen and poured some orange. He took her into the study, opened a drawer and took out the book he had printed for her.

'Guilly,' he said. 'Listen darling, you remember I promised you a book just for you alone.'

'Yes, is that the one?'

'This is the one. Shall we look at it together?'

'Yes!'

He started reading, flipping the pages, each one was colourfully illustrated, beautifully presented.

'Is it really just for me?'

'It really is, and you may have it just before you go to bed, because tonight you are going to be a very big girl and sleep here at home in your own bed as all grown up girls do.'

'But I sleep at the theatre.'

'Not tonight shrimp, you sleep in your own bed.'

'Is Mama going to be here too?'

'No, Mama will be dancing. Maddie will stay with you.'

'I want to go with Mama.'

'I know you do, but it is better for you to sleep at home now.'

'I want to go with Mama.'

'Oh god, don't lets have trouble with you too shrimp. Now listen, this book is only for little grown-up girls, so if you are going to be a baby I don't think we can give it to you.'

'But you said it was only for me.'

'I did – but babies don't read books do they?'

'I am not a baby.'

'Of course you are not. You are a very good girl aren't you, and you are going to do as Papa asks you aren't you.'

He kissed her again.

'Why can't I go with Mama?'

'I have told you shrimp. You are a big girl now. You will be more comfortable in your own bed.'

'I am comfortable in the theatre.'

He looked at her – saw tears starting.

'I don't want to be a big girl,' she said, 'I want to sleep in the theatre.'

'Guillese, I am sorry. You must stay here and sleep in your bed. Now come darling, don't cry.'

'Why do I have to stay here?'

Greg stayed silent for a while. He opened the book again. 'Come, let us read the book again.'

Half way through she turned her face up to him. 'Papa.'

'What is it?'

'May I sleep with the book in my bed?'

'Of course you may, and you will be a good girl and not cry.'

'Yes, will you read the book when I am in bed?'

'Yes of course.'

'And will it be my book?'

'I have said so haven't I? And listen shrimp – in the morning you may come into our bed and wake Mama.'

She pointed to the corner of the book. 'That says my name!'

'That's right, because it belongs to you.'

He finished reading the book and sat down.

'I want you to read it again Papa,' she cried.

'In a minute. You just look at the pictures shrimp. I will be back in a minute.'

He was concerned about Nicole. She had been out for more than half an hour. He telephoned Jed.

'Is Nicole with you?' he enquired.

'Yes she is. She is a little upset.'

'I know. She had told you what a brute I am I suppose.'

'It came as a bit of a shock to her sir.'

'Is she still making a fuss?'

'Not really, Gran is with her. She is drinking some tea.'

'Do you think she will come to the phone?'

'I'll get her.'

'Just a minute Jed. Maybe it is better to leave her to your grandmother. I hope she is drumming some sense into her.'

'Gran is pretty sensible, but Nicole still wants Guilly with her.'

'I suppose you think I am being harsh.'

'Not at all.'

'Try to persuade her Jed. She listens to you. It really is best that Guillese sleeps in her own bed. You know I found her wandering about the dressing rooms yesterday.'

'What about Guilly? How will she react?' Jed asked.

'So far she is being more sensible than her mother. She has agreed to stay here. I have never known Nicole so stubborn before.'

'Well I'll try to calm her.'

'Jed, I'm sorry to bother you, would you bring her back.'

'If she'll let me.'

'Jed, insist on it. I don't want her to come back on her own. I am worried about her. Can I rely on you Jed?'

'Sure, don't worry. I'll see she is okay. I'll try to be with you in half an hour.'

'Greg went back to the nursery, picked up the book proceeded to read.

Phyllis, who Greg had hired to help Nicole with Guilly, brought the girl some tea and asked Greg if he wanted a cup.

'No,' he said. 'I'll get myself another whiskey later. I'll see to Guillese – you may go.'

'Are you sure sir,' Phyllis said; as far as she knew, he had never given his daughter her tea. It was always Nicole. She lingered uncertainly.

'Of course – off you go now.'

He watched his daughter for a few minutes then he said, 'Don't put so much in your mouth shrimp, look at the mess you are making.'

He wiped her face and fixed her near the table. 'Eat your food nicely now,' he said.

He was not used to sitting with her at tea time. Usually Nicole either sat with her or took her out.

'I guess your Mama isn't too fussy about the mess you make.'

At a quarter to five Jed and Nicole walked into the nursery. Greg went to her and clasped her in his arms.

'I was worried about you darling.'

He turned to Jed. 'Thank you for looking after her,' he said. 'Would you like some tea, or something stronger?' He ushered them into the lounge.

It was the first time he had offered Jed an alcoholic drink.

'No thanks sir. I'll get back if you don't mind.'

Guilly came running into the lounge.

'Are you going to play with me,' she cried, clasping Jed round the knees.

'Not today baby.'

'But I want you to. Come and see my book Papa made me – It is just for me.'

'Alright just for a minute.'

Guilly dragged Jed into the nursery. Nicoles eyes were red with weeping. Greg brought her a drink.

'Here darling.'

She took it and looked up at him. 'I'm sorry Gregoire I should not have run off. I was so upset.'

'It alright my love you know I love you don't you?' She nodded.

When Jed had departed Greg put his arms around her.

'Come here my darling, I have just talked to Guillese – she will stay here, she does not mind.'

Her eyes filled, 'I thought you will let her come, you know how I feel.'

'It is all fixed, she will stay here. Now come along my love, don't be a silly girl. Give me a kiss now.'

She did as he asked. 'But you are making me unhappy.' She really believd Greg would allow her to bring Guillese.

'Look darling. Let us see how Guilly deals with the change. I think you will be surprised. It really is best for her.'

'We are abandoning her.'

'Nonsense, don't be silly. Now come along, no more arguments, or I am likely to get angry.'

'Gregoire you are not the same any more.'

She started to cry again. 'Poor baby.'

Greg's face hardened. 'Nicole, I think you have done enough arguing and weeping. Guillese will sleep here tonight and you had better accept that. I'm sorry darling, she is not a baby any longer. She is quite happy to sleep in her own bed so you had better stop feeling sorry for yourself and think positively about the situation.'

'Now you are cross with me.'

'No! I am not cross, but I am loosing patience with you.'

'Please Gregoire, just a few days more.'

'No Nicole, I don't want to argue any more. Go and see her, and don't say anything to her about this. She has accepted the situation.' He then left her to go into his study.

After they had bathed her Greg picked Guilly up. 'Let us clean your teeth and then we can read your new book to your Mama.'

Nicole was very quiet while Greg was attending to their daughter.

'Now shrimp, I am going to carry you to your bed and Mama is going early to the theatre.'

'I want to go with Mama.'

'You promised me you would be a good girl and sleep in your own bed.'

'But I don't want to now, I want to go with Mama.' Greg ignored her and took her to the nursery.

'Now you stay here for a minute. I am going to get you a drink.' He took the book off the table and gave it to her.

'I'll fetch your Mama and then we can read it to her, alright.' She nodded.

He found Nicole weeping again. He sighed and spoke sharply to her. 'Nicole for god's sake stop this. It will do you no good. Guilly is sleeping here, and that is the end of it. Come now, Guillese is waiting for you, and put a smile on your face.'

'I can't.'

'Yes you can. Now do as I say and come along to the nursery and Nicole, you are going early to the theatre. I will see Guillese into bed.'

'No Gregoire. I won't do that!'

'Nicole. Your daughter seems to have more sense than you at the moment. She is not making a fuss.'

'Because you have bullied her.'

'Nonsense.'

They read the book together a couple of times. Nicole cuddling her daughter. Then Greg took the book and placed it on the table. 'Say goodnight to Mama. She has to go early to the theatre tonight.'

Guilly hugged her. 'Good night Mama. Papa says I may come to wake you in the morning.'

'Of course you may ma cherie.'

She kissed her and looked pleadingly at Greg. Greg shepherded his wife out of the room, ordered a taxi and waited with her for it to arrive.

'I'll see you a little later my love,' he said.

It would never have occurred to her to go against him.

Greg returned to the nursery. 'I think it is time to sleep now shrimp,' he said. 'Shall I read the book once more, or would you like to read one of the others.'

'Are you going to stay with me Papa.'

'For a little while, then Maddie will be here to look after you. So you will be fine.'

'I wish I could come with you, why can't I?'

'I've told you shrimp, because it is better for you to stay here. Now you are going to be a good girl aren't you?'

'Yes!' Her eyes filled. 'I really can't come with you?'

He smiled at her and lay her down. 'Would you like your book?'

She nodded and looked up at her father, 'I want my Teddy that Jed brought me.'

'Here he is ready to be cuddled. Good night my little one, sleep well.'

'Papa, may I have the light on.'

'Of course – go to sleep now.'

Once outside the door he heaved a sight of relief. He lingered for a few minutes to make sure she had settled. He yawned, exhausted with the trauma of the last few hours. He spoke to Maddie, then drove to the theatre.

Chapter 25

The show was halfway through the first act and Greg stood at the back of the auditorium.

'My God,' he thought. 'She is incredibly beautiful.'

She was exquisite, perfect, like an angel. There was no one even remotely like her. The audience screamed for her and Matthew when the curtain came down.

He moved backstage towards her. She was laughing and joking with Jonathan. As soon as she saw Greg her smiled faded and she turned, walked away from him. He let her go. She would get over her anger. Halfway through the final act he telephoned Maddie.

'Is Guillese alright,' he asked.

'Of course she is fast asleep, quite happy.'

'Thanks Maddie.' He put the receiver down relieved. He had not been too sure that Guilly would not wake.

At the end of the show he made his way to Nicole's dressing room.

'You were absolutely superb my love,' he said putting his arms around her.

She looked at him with hostility. 'Justin is going to take me home.'

'Why?'

'It is what I want.'

'Well it is not what I want. You will come home with me, Nicole. Don't pull away – you are being childish. Guilly is fine - has not woken up at all. She is sleeping peacefully, much better than she would here. Now get changed. I will wait for you outside.'

He was being harsh with her but he knew of no other way to deal with her. She cried all the way home. Greg said nothing to her. When he opened the door she rushed inside and through to the bedroom without speaking. He sat down, demolished a whiskey and lit a cigarette. He was not sure how he was going to deal with the situation. She had never before behaved in such a manner.

He looked in at Guilly and found her sleeping. He made his way to their bedroom, undressed and slipped into bed beside her. She turned her back to him. He touched her and she shrugged away from him.

'Nicole darling,' he pleaded but she stayed as she was.

'Turn over darling – I love you.'

She drew further away.

'How long are you going to keep this up Nicole – is your love for me so shaken that you would reject me simply because you are angry with me because I would not give you what you wanted – don't you love me Nicki?'

He started caressing her gently. 'I watched you dancing this evening you were so beautiful my angel.'

He kissed her shoulder, 'I didn't know you had a temper my little love.'

He manoeuvred his arm under her shoulder and tried to force her round to face him but she resisted. He found her breasts and caressed them.

'Don't let's quarrel my darling. We have never quarrelled have we – I can't bear it.'

Within a few seconds she relented, turned towards him and flung her arms around his neck.

'Gregoire, I love you. I am so sorry. I do love you.'

He held her close and caressed her. 'I can not bear to see you unhappy. Don't cry anymore my love.'

He reached for some tissues and wiped her face, kissed her eyes, nose and mouth. He buried his face in her hair, 'Oh Nicki, Nicki, how I love you.'

He stroked her body, whispering his love for her, his hands touching every part of her, caressing her for a long time, before he made love to her. Her anger and disappointment disappeared and she lay contentedly in his arms until she slept. However for the first few evenings, after they had put Guillese to bed she crept back into the room, knowing how her daughter was feeling – comforting her, promising to bring her back little treats when she returned from the theatre. Greg was completely unaware of these little instances. As an extra treat Nicole took her with her on Matinee days and Greg drove her home after her tea – leaving Nicole with Jed and the others to grab a quick snack and rest before the evening performance. For a few weeks Greg left the theatre early so that he could check on Guilly. She never woke and seemed contented with her new routine. Jed or Justin brought Nicole home at the end of the show. She was a popular member of the Company and although male dancers made a great play for Nicole it was light-hearted and innocent, they all knew that she belonged entirely to Greg. Except for Daniel, a newcomer. He was determined to establish himself in her affections.

At first Nicole smiled and bantered with him until one evening he grabbed her and kissed her, holding her close to him.

'Daniel' she said, 'please let me go.'

'Why? Come on Nicki, you are not that averse to my charms are you. You know how beautiful you are, you send me crazy just looking at you.' He kissed her again.

'Don't,' she raised her voice, becoming a little disturbed. 'Please Daniel, be a good boy. Please.'

He laughed. 'You must be joking,' he said, 'who could be good with you around?'

He still had hold of her. She tried to push him away. When she started to cry he let her go.

'Come on Nicki. I didn't hurt you.' He tried to put his arms around her shoulder. 'Sorry Nicki, look get dressed, I'll take you across the road for a drink.'

'No Daniel. I want to go home.' She shrugged away from him.

'I'm only asking you to come for a drink with me.' He took her arm, 'come on get dressed.'

'You should not be in here, please go away,' she said.

'What's up Nicki?' Jed looked in as he was passing.

'She's okay,' Daniel assured him. Again he attempted to embrace Nicole.

She threw him off. 'Don't, leave me alone Daniel,' she said.

'Back off Daniel,' Jed told him. 'Lay off her.'

Daniel looked at Jed, 'Oooh, want her for yourself do you – everyone knows what you'd like to do with her.'

'Shut your filthy mouth,' Jed retorted.

Daniel laughed and walked off.

'Get dressed Nicki,' I'll take you home.

'I guess I ought not to be such a baby, but I couldn't stop him.'

'You are not a baby. He is a shark. He tries it with all the girls. He is a menace. Justin should get rid of him. Trouble is he is a bloody good dancer.'

Daniel tried to inveigle himself a few more times into Nicole's affections but eventually gave up.

Chapter 26

When she was not working she Greg and Guilly would drive out to the country for the weekend – Nicole would still not entertain leaving her daughter behind and so Greg would take one of the older students with them to baby sit for them.

'May be it would be much better if we employed a nanny. This arrangement is not very satisfactory, is it darling?'

'Why?' she asked. 'The girls are quite happy to come along with us.'

'Even so, I think it would be better. There are times when I would like to be alone with my wife for more than a few hours.'

'No Gregoire, please don't go on. You know I do not want her to have a nanny.'

'Alright, just for now. But you are going to have to think about it.'

'I don't want to think about it. I will not feel any different.'

'Wouldn't it be nice if we could go away for more than a weekend just the two of us?'

'She is never any trouble.'

'Oh my God. Why can't I get through to you Nicole. There is nothing wrong with employing a nanny.'

'I don't want one.'

'I don't want one,' he mimicked.

'You are making me unhappy Gregoire.'

'Well of course,' he said with irritation, 'we must never do that must we. What about me Nicole?'

He lifted her face up to his. Her eyes started to water.

'Now you are angry.'

'No, no of course I am not angry, but Nicki, you are becoming obsessed with her. You rehearse with her and afterwards you look after her until she goes to bed. You never rest unless I take over and insist. It is too much darling.'

'Jed helps me with her a bit.'

Jed is a young man, he needs to have time to himself. You treat him as though he is her nanny.'

'But she is happy and Jed doesn't mind.'

'Of course she is happy. She is getting everything she wants and she is becoming spoiled. She is quite naughty sometimes with Maddie.'

'Maddie understands. She is only little.'

'She is three years old Nicole.'

'I want to go home,' she said.

'Oh for god sake don't be so childish. I will instruct Maddie to arrange something when we get back.'

Nicole stood still stunned, he had never spoken to her so harshly before.

'Gregoire,' she pleased. 'Please don't be so angry.' She stood looking up at him like a distressed child, her eyes glistening with tears.

Greg could not bear it. 'Nicole, come here, it is not all that bad. Listen darling. It is like when you thought Guilly would be unhappy sleeping in her own bed. She was fine wasn't she. Hiring a nanny would be the same.'

'She wasn't fine at first.'

'When was that?'

'She cried to me. She didn't like it at first, I had to comfort her after you'd gone.'

'Oh dear, what can I say to you,' he sighed. 'You went against me on that did you?'

Suddenly she knelt in front of him clasped his knees. 'Please Gregoire please don't do it. I implore you. Please.'

'For god sake Nicole – get up at once' He jerked her to her feet. 'What the hell are you doing?'

By this time she was sobbing.

'Now now, that's enough.' He picked her up and cuddled her.

'Nicole,' he said when she had calmed down. 'Alright. I give in. We will manage without a nanny. I do understand your objections but you may have your own way, at least for now. But sometimes Guillese stays with Maddie. Is that understood? She can't always travel with us.'

Nicole nodded, she had not expected him to give in to her.

'And Nicole. Don't you ever do that to me again.'

She looked enquiringly up at him.

'I am referring to you kneeling before me to get your own way. It is demeaning.'

'I'm sorry Gregoire but promise me. Please you will never make me have a nanny for her.'

'I will promise no such thing. However as it distresses you so much we will leave it for a while. But there have to be some changes. You need to rest more and Guillese has to have more discipline. We shall have to work something out and whatever I decide you will agree with.

She nodded, 'You still love me don't you.'

'You are such a silly girl. Do you think there is anything in the world that could ever stop me from loving you?'

'But you were very angry. You shouted at me - you were horrid.'

'I did not shout at you, and if I hadn't loved you the way I do I would never have given into you. You know, you can do exactly as you like with me, can't you my little witch. You enslave me with those beautiful eyes. I can refuse you nothing.'

'But you did,' she teased.

'When was that?'

'You wouldn't let me take Guilly to the theatre to sleep.'

'Oh Nicki even that was touch and go. You know I was right about that.'

'Yes.'

'But you have not forgiven me?'

'Of course I have. I love you Gregoire.'

'So, can we be happy again now?' He said.

'Yes. I know you will not break your promise.'

'And what promise was that.'

'About the nanny.'

He pulled her against him. 'You know very well that I promised nothing. You are a devious little minx. I ought to beat you. Instead we shall go into the hotel and I shall take you to bed. I assume you will not object to that.'

He kissed her and carried her inside. Although Greg had made the stipulation that Guillese stayed with Maddie when they took breaks, he never insisted, consequently they continued to use the students as baby sitters. He made a point of making sure that Nicole rested at least 2 afternoons during the week when he often took charge of Guilly. He was strict with her, so there were occasional battles between them, but even at her tender age she learned quickly that Greg meant what he said so that she was usually well behaved when he was in charge in contrast to Nicole's benevolent easy way when they were together.

She was a very strong-willed child and fought much of the time to get her own way.

'You are too harsh with her,' Nicole complained.

'Somebody has to control her. Anyway we get along famously, don't we shrimp. We understand each other.' He picked her up and cuddled her, 'She loves her daddy don't you shrimp?'

Despite the spectacular costume and scenery Greg's ballet flagged soon after the children went back to school. It was after all a children's story and when the schools started the theatre was half empty. He decided to bring the show to a close and in its place put on the 'Firebird' – always a favourite especially with Nicole and Matthew. Unfortunately when dancing Matthew twisted his ankle quite badly. Greg instructed Daniel to take his place. He was an excellent dancer.

'Couldn't Jed do it Gregoire?' she asked.

'Not this time my love. I have other plans for Jed. Daniel is very experienced. He will be perfect for you.'

Daniel was ten years older than Matthew and was more energetic and gave the part more zest, but he took advantage of Nicole, held her unnecessarily close during some of the scenes. Nicole begun to dread each night with Daniel getting bolder as the ballet went on.

She approached Greg and asked him how long they would be performing the 'Firebird.'

'You are tired my love, I am working you too hard. I am sorry.'

Within 2 weeks he brought the ballet to a close. He left the running of the theatre to Justin for a month and took Nicole away for a rest.

Naturally Nicole protested when she discovered Guillese would not be going with them.

'Now Nicole, please do not oppose me. I want you to have a complete rest so Guillese will stay with Maddie.'

'Oh no Gregoire – she will be no trouble.'

'I insist darling. Jed will call in on her and Maddie says she can manage with the help of Phyllis and Lydia. I can assure you she will have a wonderful time between them all. She will be completely spoiled when we return. Come now my love, you are not going to give me a hard time now are you?'

'I shall miss her.'

'Oh dear, we are not going to resort to more tears are we.'

'I'm sorry Gregoire.'

'It will be just for one month.'

'A month is a long time. She will forget me.'

'We have not spent one moment alone together. I would like to spoil my beautiful wife for a change.'

He lifted her chin. 'Nicki you have not tired of my company have you?'

She reached up, threw her arm around him and kissed him.

'I love you Gregoire. I will never tire of you. I will always love you.'

'Good. Then you will be a good girl and be happy for me won't you.'

'Yes I will. I am happy. Where are we going?'

'Ah. First I thought we should go to Italy – to Florence and Venice – then we shall travel back perhaps visit Holland and Belgium.'

'You do not wish to go to France.'

'Oh my darling. I do not think it is wise. I want nothing to spoil our time together. I doubt if your Mama has changed. Perhaps next year we will make the time and try to see them, but this time I think not.'

'You are right Gregoire,' she said, 'I am so excited, so lucky.'

'No darling, I am the lucky one, but let's go to bed now. It is getting late.'

Chapter 27

A week before the trip he took her to buy some new clothes.

'You have already given me so much, I do not need any more,' she protested.

'For this trip you do my precious. We are staying in some famous places. When we visit Venice I have booked us into the Cipriani - the most beautiful hotel of all in Venice. You will need something extra special.'

Greg enjoyed the shopping trip as much as his wife. He was stunned by her beauty when she tried on the elegant gowns.

'You will outshine every lady wherever you go my love. You are so very beautiful Nicole.'

'So are you Gregoire,' she countered. He smiled

'Every man on the continent will be envious of me. They will wonder what on earth such a treasure is doing with an old man like me.'

'Nonsense Gregoire, but I do love the dresses – they are all so exciting.'

'Gregoire!'

'Yes darling, what is it?'

'Could we buy something for Guillese, a pretty dress or an outfit, to make up for us leaving her here.'

'Nicole, you know Guillese will have the time of her life, you must not worry.'

'But could we?'

'Of course we could. Why don't you take her tomorrow and choose something for her.'

'Yes I will, she will like that. Will you come with us?'

'I shall be extremely busy. I am sure you will manage. If Jed is not working the two of you could take her out for lunch that would be a great treat for her.'

'Alright, I will ask Jed later. You won't go to the theatre tonight Gregoire, you will stay home with me.'

'Of course I will. We will drive to Luigi's and then we can come home together.'

She contacted Jed later in the day.

'I'll miss you Nicole,' he said. 'A month is a long time.'

'I know, you will look after Guilly while I am away – call and see her, the same as always.'

'Yes, I will be glad to. She'll miss you too.'

'I know, I can't bear the thought of not seeing her every day, but Gregoire says it will be too difficult to take her. She is always very good when we take her with us.'

'You need a rest Nicole – She'll be okay. I'll take her out for lunch or tea if I'm allowed.'

'She'll love that Jed, and Maddie won't mind you taking her, but I know I am going to miss her.'

'Don't worry, she'll be fine, and you will have a wonderful time.'

'Yes, I know, I am very lucky.'

They took Guillese the next day and the three of them enjoyed going from shop to shop looking for dresses for the child. Once or twice having to dissuade her from the bizarre designs she chose. They bought her some pretty shoes in addition to a velvet cape which she had set her heart on. She was delighted with the purchases and was ready for lunch as soon as they were packed into shining designer carrier bags.

'I'm going to have to tell her,' Nicole said. 'She is so happy isn't she. She has never done this before. She loves that velvet cloak – I hope she won't be too upset when I tell her.'

'Don't do it now Nicki, it might spoil her day.'

'I don't want to tell her at all, but I must.'

'Leave it until tomorrow – if you like I'll be there with you. We'll make it sound like fun.'

'Oh thanks Jed. Gregoire doesn't really understand. We've always been here with her every day.'

'We'll think of something. Don't worry Nicki.'

'I know let's take her to the skating rink.'

'What a wonderful idea – she's never been. You can teach her to skate.'

'We can try,' Jed laughed. 'We'll take her on the bus.'

He looked down at Guilly, skipping along between them. 'Come on then baby, we'll find somewhere to eat. I'm starving. Are you hungry?'

'Yes I am,' she said, 'are we going now?'

'Yes,' Nicole said. 'We are all starving.'

'Do you think Papa will like my new dress and the cape?'

'I'm sure he'll adore them. You can put them on when we get home.'

'Lovely,' Guilly said. 'Can Jed come back with us?'

'Maybe.' Nicole looked over to Jed

'Yeah, that's okay. As long as your father doesn't mind.'

'Good. We can all have tea together, with you in all your beautiful clothes poppet,' Nicole said.

Guilly modelled her new dress, cloak and shoes in front of her father – who was as enthused as was expected of him – before sitting on his knee for a while relating the exciting morning she'd had.

'And Mama and Jed bought me this pretty bracelet – look it really sparkles.'

'It's beautiful shrimp and you look as pretty as your Mama.'

He kissed her sat her on a chair and they proceeded with the tea, and Greg thanked Jed for accompanying Nicole.

'It's ok sir, I enjoyed it. We had a lot of fun didn't we baby.'

'All the same it was good of you to give up your time.'

During the next few days Nicole braced herself to tell her daughter about the separation she was about to experience.

'I thought you would have told her by now,' Greg said. 'I thought that was why she was being indulged with new clothes which she did not really need.'

'I know, but she will be upset.'

'You should have told her at the time.'

'Jed suggests we take her with us to the skating rink. We can tell her then.'

'My God Nicole. It is not as if we are leaving her for good. Bring her to me, I will tell her.'

'No, no please Gregoire. I'll tell her.'

'Very well but please do not invoke a tragedy of it. It will not be the last time. There will be many more. She will have to get used to it.'

'I'll tell her tomorrow. When we take her to the ice rink.'

'Such a fuss. Good heavens you would think we were going for a year.'

'Would you like to accompany me to the theatre this evening?'

'Do you mind if I stay here. I have some things to do.'

'Alright, but don't moon around Guilly, she'll be absolutely fine.'

They told her together, half way through the first session at the rink.

'But I don't want you to go away Mama,' she whimpered.

'The time will soon pass ma cherie, and I will bring you something very special back.' She started to cry.

Jed picked her up. 'Let's get a coke for her and some coffee for us,' he said to Nicole.

'There baby,' Jed said. 'When you are finished I'll take you on the ice and teach you the right way to skate.'

'I don't want Mama to go,' she cried.

'Listen, ma cherie - Maddie and Phyllis will be looking after you and Jed says he'll come by and take you out.'

'Yes! – to a grown up restaurant.'

'Just like Mama and Papa go to?'

'Yes, you'd like that.'

'Come on baby – let's go on the ice.'

Nicole watched as Jed gently guided Guilly through her first steps. After ten minutes he took her and sat her in one of the seats. Nicole saw them both laughing together and then they returned to the rink café and finished their drinks.

'She learns fast,' Jed said, 'a few more sessions and she'll skate by herself.'

Nicole laughed. 'How clever,' she said.

'Jed said he will take me to skate every week you are away,' Guilly told her.

'Really, that will be good, because when I come back we can all go skating together sometimes can't we.'

'Yes.'

'And I will be back as soon as I can ma cherie. I shall miss you, but Jed will come by often won't you Jed.'

'You bet, we'll have lots of fun.'

'Okay,' Guilly said.

'And you will be very good won't you baby – for Maddie and me.'

'Yes I will be good, can we go back on the ice again now.'

'Of course.'

'Thanks Jed.' Nicole threw her arms around him. 'You have really put my mind at rest. Thanks for offering to look in on her.'

'Forget it – it will be a pleasure.'

Chapter 28

On the way back from the airport Nicole lay her head on Greg's shoulder.

'It was the most wonderful holiday Gregoire,' she said, 'all those beautiful places. I loved Italy, especially Venice – I have never seen anything so beautiful.'

'But now we are back and I have to share you with the world. You will capture their hearts my beloved, as you dance for them.'

'Gregoire, I dance only for you. I do not see them. I dance for you, always for you.'

'Ah my sweet love, you know exactly the right things to say to me.'

'But, I mean it Gregoire.'

'I know my love, and that is what makes it so special to me.'

As they neared the house, she turned to him a little nervously. 'You won't mind,' she said, 'if I go straight to see Guilly when we get home. I am so excited about seeing her.'

He drew her towards him, 'Do you think I am not. We shall go to her together Nicole darling. Don't think I want to keep you from her. That is the last thing I want. Is that what you thought?'

'No, of course not. We will go together as you say. You are her Papa – she loves you.'

Maddie had kept her up late so that she could greet them. Nicole could not wait, she broke away from Greg and rushed towards the lounge.

'Guilly, Guilly,' she called. 'We are home.'

She turned back and dragged Greg with her, pulling him towards Maddie's room where she could see her daughter sitting on her knee.

'Hello ma cherie.' Nicole hugged her close. 'I have missed you so much.'

She picked her up and carried her over to Greg.

'Well,' he remarked solemnly, 'you have grown while I have been away. My goodness you are quite heavy.'

She wriggled free and ran back to Maddie.

'I drawed you a picture!' She exclaimed.

'Have you had a lovely time ma cherie?' Nicole came over to her again. She was as excited as a puppy.

'Yes. Jed took me skating and he bought me some skating boots, I can skate by myself now.'

'That's wonderful ma cherie,' Nicole was surprised.

'He took me to a grown up restaurant.'

'Did he now' Greg said.

'Yes and Maddie brought me to a theatre with dollies dancing.'

'You mean Puppets.'

'Yes puppets – and Jed took me to see Justin at the theatre. I like it at the theatre Papa.'

'I hope you have been a good girl.'

'I have, haven't I Maddie?'

'Yes she has been perfect.'

'Maddie read my book and it made me sad.'

'Why was that?' Greg said.

'Because you weren't here Papa, not for a long time.'

'Oh my poor Baby,' Nicole said. 'Never mind we are here now.'

'Papa,' Guilly ran to Greg, 'will you make me another book, just for me like the other one?'

'Perhaps, we shall have to see.'

Greg then left her with Nicole. He could see she was overcome with excitement at being reunited with her daughter. He knew she had missed her.

'Any problems Maddie?' Greg asked.

'Not after the first morning, fortunately Jed arrived and took her out for lunch . He has been in nearly every day at some point and it is true apparently he has taught her to skate. I wanted to reimburse him when I realised he had bought the ice-skates for her, but he would not hear of it. He has been very good, he really loves that child and she worships him.'

'I know Maddie. And how have you survived? I know my daughter can be quite a handful.'

'Oh I'm fine I have enjoyed looking after her. But I am afraid my other duties have suffered a little.'

'I want to thank you Maddie – Nicole really enjoyed the break and

Guilly looks very happy. Nicole would never have entertained leaving her with anyone but you. I am afraid that now we are going to have to think about getting back to work. It's quite late, perhaps we should be putting Guilly to bed?'

'Would you like me to do that tonight?'

Greg laughed. 'I think, Maddie, that matter has been dealt with.' They looked across the room to see Nicole, Guilly in her arms, dancing up the stairs.

'Thank you once again Maddie. I know Nicole has missed Guilly, but she had a good rest and we both really enjoyed the break. I do wish she was not so dead set against employing a nanny.'

He walked up the stairs to find Nicole still playing with Guilly.

'I think my love it is time Guilly was in her bed.'

'Yes I know, come along ma cherie it is very late now. Come with us Gregoire.'

'I will come in later. I can see how happy you are to be back with her darling.'

'But I really did enjoy the holiday Gregoire, we had a wonderful time didn't we.'

'We certainly did my love, and you have another whole week before I ask you to work, a week darling in which to spend time with Guillese - a reward for making me feel so good, for loving me!' He kissed her. 'And in a few days I might have a surprise for you.'

'What, what surprise Gregoire, please tell me now.'

He touched her nose affectionately. 'You must be patient. I will tell you when I am ready.'

'You will come with us, I mean to put Guilly to bed.'

'I will be there in a few minutes.'

'Will you read my book Papa,' Guilly called.

'Not tonight shrimp. It is very late, perhaps tomorrow.'

'I will read some of it to you ma cherie,' Nicole whispered 'When Papa comes to say goodnight.'

She was nine tenths asleep when her father eventually returned to the bedroom.

'Look at her Gregoire,' Nicole whispered, 'isn't she beautiful.'

'Yes she is – and she can twist you around her little finger.'

'You did not mind me reading to her.'

'Of course not, come, I have a drink for you downstairs.'

Chapter 29

The next morning Greg called Justin into the office.

'Good morning Greg,' Justin said. 'How did the holiday go?'

'Very well. I think Nicole enjoyed the break. After the first few days when she was worrying about Guillese, I had to get a little tough with her, but she soon rallied and started to enjoy herself. However she cannot tear herself away from Guillese at the moment. How have you fared? No problems.'

'No, we have had full house last week and this. I decided to put on Prevosto Manon.'

'That was ambitious wasn't it?'

'I suppose so but the audience loved it. And the dancers were really fantastic. They seemed to enjoy it as much as their audience. I promised them another week.'

'Ah good, well I will sit in one evening. Who are the lead dancers?'

'Matthew as De Griene and Natalie as Manon. Jed was perfect as the Beggar chief.'

'Hmn - Justin what do you think about staging a treat for the public.'

'What do you mean?'

'I mean casting Jed and Nicole in the greatest love story of all time.'

'You mean Romeo and Juliet?'

'Exactly.'

'I think that would be terrific.'

'I agree, especially as the lad is in love with her. It would shine through.'

Justin never ceased to be amazed by this man. Most of the company were aware of Jed's feelings towards Greg's wife but for Greg to actually come out with it so casually – didn't he care - didn't he feel vulnerable.

'Well…' Justin began, 'I…….'

'You are wondering at my wisdom in view of this close friendship. Well Justin, I have no illusions – Nicole is half my age, she needs young company. She needs Jed, he is like a brother to her. She will never betray me.'

'How can you be so sure?'

'I am sure Justin.'

'And Jed?'

'Jed, I am not so sure about. As I said Nicole regards him as her brother, whatever he feels. And if we put them together, it will be sensational.'

'Have you discussed this with Nicole?'

'Not yet, but I am certain she will be delighted. You think about it Justin. We will discuss it in the morning.'

'I can't tomorrow – I have a rehearsal'

'Well when you are free let me know. I am serous about this.'

Justin watched Greg walk from the theatre. He must be mad. He seemed oblivious to any sort of danger. Justin had observed Nicole and Jed together. They were too often together but it was Jed for whom he was more concerned. Greg was probably right. Nicole loved her husband, there was probably no chance of her directing her affections elsewhere – But Jed, Well!

He shrugged. Greg was right though about partnering them in Romeo and Juliet – they would be truly sensational.

Nothing was said of the proposed production and Justin began to think that either he had forgotten about it or that he had changed his mind. However one morning he called Justin

'Have you thought any more about my suggestion Justin?' he asked.

'You mean the ballet with Jed and Nicole, yes. I have thought about it, but I presumed, you had changed your mind.'

'Why on earth would I do that? What is Jed doing at the moment?'

'The Three Cornered Hat on Tuesdays and Thursdays.'

'Good we can talk to him during the week. Let me see he is nineteen is he not?'

'I think so.'

'Right, and Nicole is twenty-three. Perfect.'

'By the way,' Justin said, 'I hope you don't mind. I've had Jed sitting in with me on some of the classes. He seemed interested. He has a good eye for talent.'

'I have no objection, providing it does not interfere with his performance. Do you think he would be interested in learning how to teach?'

Justin shrugged. 'Probably not – he likes to perform.'

'Well, I must get back,' Greg said. 'I really must give Nicole some time. I have neglected her these last few days. I have promised her she may have an extra week free. So that she can spend time with Guillese. When they start rehearsing there will be little time for that.'

'By the way Greg, I'd like you to see a young girl as soon as you are free, she seems very anxious to join the company.'

'Another stage struck youngster.'

'I doubt that, she seems genuinely interested.'

'What is she like? How old?'

'Young attractive, good figure – about fifteen I suppose. She is very keen.'

'Is she good? Have you seen her dance?'

'Briefly. She moves well and has a pleasing personality.'

'Is she not at school?'

'Private school. I'd like you to see her Greg.' Justin refrained from telling him that it was Jed who thought she had talent.

'Alright, I'll see her one Saturday morning. Later in the month.'

Nicole had her week free as Greg had promised and Greg started work on the new production. He shut himself away in his office. Seeing no one, until he had finished working out the dances and music. He gave the first scene to Justin to study. Nicole had not expected to have so much time with Guilly. She was overjoyed. Taking Guilly to the studio each morning after breakfast, where she proceeded to practise.

She picked her daughter up, and danced around the studio with her. 'We have another whole week, isn't that good my poppet.'

Guilly laughed and patted Nicole's head.

Greg always tried to join them before lunch taking the child on his knee to watch his wife at the barre, giving her advice, sometimes taking her in his arms, gliding around the floor with her. He was an expert dancer. Lithe and romantic.

'You should be dancing in the show mon cheri,' she told him.

'My dancing days are over beloved, but with you I could dance forever.'

'Why don't you choreograph a sketch for you and me Gregoire. I would love that.'

'Hmm, I am not good enough to partner you my love. Not any more. But listen darling. How would you like to have Jed partner you in Romeo & Juliet?'

'Do you mean it?' Nicole's eyes widened.

'I do, would you feel confident dancing with Jed in such a major role.'

'Jed is very good, of course I would. Does Jed know?'

'I believe Justin is talking to him right now. He will be rehearsing with you soon.'

When Nicole started to work again, Guillese became tearful after having her mother dancing attendance on her for so long, angling to stay at the theatre again. Nicole pleaded with Greg to let her stay.

'Just as a treat Gregoire.'

'That would be fatal. No Nicole she will stay here.'

'But Gregoire....'

'No Nicole, I will go to her, you sit here and relax. You are only dancing two nights during the week. She will stay.'

'Its alright I will put her to bed,' she protested.

But Greg insisted. He bathed her, then brought her down to say goodnight to Maddie and Nicole - and although she knew better than to make a fuss while Greg was around, her spirit fell when she realised she was not going to be allowed to sleep in the dressing room.

Nicole tried to reverse Greg's decision. 'You are so hard,' she told him. 'You can see she is lonely.'

'Nevertheless she is staying home, and Nicole do not make an issue out of this or I will make you sort her out if she cries.'

'You have a cold heart,' Nicole reproached him.

Greg picked his daughter up, cuddled her and whispered comfort in her ear.

'You are a very big girl, now let us not have any bother with you. Maddie is always here. Now tell your Mama how good you are going to be.'

When she failed to answer him he kissed her and said, 'You will be good Guillese or I shall be angry.'

And realising that there was no possible hope of her father indulging her she nodded and lay her head on his shoulder.

'Will you read my special book?' she said.

'Of course I will shrimp.'

He tucked her in, kissed her and quickly and went back to his wife.

'Are you coming to the theatre with me darling?'

'Yes,' she murmured.

'No more tears.'

She shook her head.

'Alright let's go then. I need to see Justin this evening. We have to arrange when to stage Romeo and Juliet.'

Greg had arranged it so that Nicole would only be dancing two evenings a week. The rest of the time she was able to spend with her daughter. She enjoyed the free time. She loved taking her out and looking after her, sometimes she took her to the Theatre to see Justin and the rest of the dancers. They always made a great fuss of her.

'Gregoire, it is so nice when I don't have to work every evening.'

'I know darling and for the moment we can keep it that way. But soon I must ask you to rehearse again.'

'How long have I got?' she asked.

'I don't know, but I thought you would be happy to know that you are dancing with Jed. Justin and I are not quite ready, but when you start you will be very busy most mornings and part of the afternoons. This ballet has to be perfect. You understand. You may take Guillese sometimes with you during the day. Providing there is some one responsible to supervise her.'

'Jed will be very happy.'

'What about you my love? It will be a beautiful ballet.'

'Yes.'

He pulled her close, 'Nicole, what is wrong – are you tired of the ballet. You are not happy to dance for me.'

She put her arms around him. 'Of course I will dance for you. It is just that I shall miss Guilly.'

'Come now darling, you must not let her rule your life. You will have her all day once the rehearsals are over, and think how thrilled Jed will be to partner you. He will be beside himself with joy.'

'You are right Gregoire, I am happy, but it won't be ready for a little while yet will it.'

'No, you have at least a month.'

She smiled – her despondency gone. Greg was troubled at Nicole's attitude but assured himself that once she was back into a proper routine she would be fine. He kissed her.

'I love you Nicole – you are the most beautiful thing in my life. I would do anything for you. You will be perfect as Juliet and Jed is so young you will both be absolutely right together.'

'Have you seen him since Justin told him.'

'Not yet. I will discuss details with Justin and the two of you tomorrow.'

'And may I take Guilly with me?'

'I suppose so. But Nicole I will need your full attention, you will have to make sure she is looked after and kept out of the way.'

'Of course I'd rather she stayed at home with Maddie.'

'She will be no trouble, I promise Gregoire.'

Nicole telephoned Jed – he was excited about partnering her.

'May I come over?' he asked.

'Yes, I'll see you in a few minutes.'

When he arrived, he picked her up and twirled her around. 'God, Nicole - I never in a million years thought he'd let me do this.'

'Why not! You are better than all the others, except perhaps Matthew.'

'You don't think I am as good as him'

'You are different, Matthew is older, more experienced and is very expert at holding me.'

'Nicole, I can be just as safe as Matthew.'

'I'm just teasing.'

'No, you're not.'

'Yes! I didn't mean anything. It's just that I am used to Matthew.'

'Would you rather he partnered you then?'

'Jed, I'm really looking forward to dancing with you. And Gregoire is very excited.'

'Aren't you?'

'Of course I am, but you know Jed, I'm going to miss Guilly. I won't be able to be with her as much while we are rehearsing.'

'She'll be okay Nicki. There will be times when we can take her out for tea.'

'I suppose so. Anyway I have had such a nice long time since we came back from holiday. I'll get used to it.'

'Oh Nicole, it's going to be absolutely wonderful.'

Greg collected her for rehearsal the next day and began to lecture his wife.

'Who is going to look after Guillese?' he asked.

'A girl called Gina.'

'Gina! Where is she from I have never heard of her.'

'Jed says you were going to interview her. She didn't mind sitting in the dressing room with her.'

'You should not arrange these things without my knowledge Nicole, everything will be disrupted. We do not know this girl.'

'Jed does.'

'Well, I hope your daughter behaves or this whole exercise will prove useless!'

Nicole wisely did not answer, but Greg was further irritated when Nicole had to return Guilly to the dressing room. When she returned to the stage he reprimanded her again.

'This obsession with your daughter Nicole is becoming ridiculous,' he told her. 'Now, I hope you are going to concentrate on what we are about to discuss.'

He went through the technicalities of the new ballet, the dance and the drama.

'And the music must be exactly right – comfortable with both dance and drama. And you Jed, are you happy and confident that you can put the necessary emotion across.'

'Yes sir, I am positive – it's fantastic. What about Matthew though?'

'Matthew understands. This ballet is for the very young. You and Nicole will be perfectly cast. So both of you make sure you are fit, ready to start rehearsal properly next month. I want this production to have a lasting effect on audiences. I want them to be spellbound, to remember this performance for the rest of their lives. I want it to be phenomenal.'

He turned to Jed and Nicole. 'You have to *be* Romeo and Juliet, to feel the way *they* would feel. That is all, you may go. Justin and I have a lot of work to do.'

'Aren't you coming home Gregoire?'

'No my love. I won't be very long this afternoon at the latest.'

'But then you will be out again in the evening.'

'Ah please now Nicole, do not whinge. You have Jed for company. I will be home as soon as possible. Now take your daughter home. As I say I will be home soon.'

He kissed her and watched them leave then turned to Justin.

'Before we discuss anything else Greg. I did ask you to take a look at Gina, the fifteen year old. She came in especially to look after Guilly. It won't take long to talk to her. Please.'

'I said Saturday, but I suppose as she is here – call her in.'

'Greg please don't be savage with her.'

'What words you do use Justin, you make me sound like a monster.'

'You can be terrifying. You know that Gina is only a kid. She's pretty and has a good style. I only ask you to be gentle.'

Gina appeared and was introduced to Greg. He asked her about her dancing experience, her school and her parents.

'Let me see what you can do,' he said.

She proceeded to obey his instructions although she was slightly nervous. As she went she quietly apologised for her mistakes.

'Come along now girl. I am not going to chew you up. Think about what you are doing and listen to what I tell you to do. In other words concentrate on the dance instead of yourself. If you are to become a dancer you will need to be less concerned with your vanity.'

He rasped out some more instructions with which she complied, still apologising for her nervous mistakes.

'Alright my dear I am willing to give you a trial. Justin will give you all the details about times of the classes. Off you go now. See Justin in the morning. Leave your telephone number.'

She thanked him smiled and left the stage.

'Well,' Greg looked at Justin. 'Was that to your liking – did it meet with your approval?'

'Not too bad. You were a little strong but what did you think.'

'She seems a pleasant young girl. Hopefully we shall make her into a dancer.'

'I thought she was better than average, considering she has hardly any training.'

'Well, we shall see Justin, we shall see.'

Chapter 30

When rehearsals for Romeo & Juliet started six weeks later, neither Guillese nor Nicole were ready for the separation and so Nicole took her daughter with her. The new girl Gina was prepared to look after her, but this time Guilly was not prepared to be parted from her mother.

Nicole pleaded and tried to bribe her but she started to cry as soon as Nicole was about to leave so that it took time to settle her. However, as soon as Nicole left the room she started to yell quite loudly.

Nicole went back once again and tried to talk to her. Consequently she was not on stage when Greg was ready to rehearse. He became irritated and strode into the dressing room.

'Nicole you are late. What is the problem?'

'It's Guilly. She's not happy.'

'Go on through to the stage,' he commanded. He shut the dressing room door and took Guilly on his knee.

'Now then shrimp, what is the matter?'

'She doesn't want to stay with me.' Gina said.

'Is that right shrimp. You don't want to stay with Gina?'

'I want Mama.'

'Mama is working. She can't be with you this morning.'

'But I want to go with her.'

'Listen to me. You can't be with your Mama. Either you stay here with Gina and be a good girl, or you will be taken home to Maddie. Which is it?'

Tears ran down Guilly's cheeks, but after a few seconds she established the fact that her father would do exactly what he threatened, unlike her

Mother who would always try to bribe her with treats and giving in to her. Greg stayed for a moment looking at his daughter.

'Stop crying now. We will come to see you in a little while. Now do you want to stay here or go home?'

'I want to stay.'

'Right, you will be a good girl.'

He turned to Gina. 'If you have any problems with her, send Danny to the stage.'

And looking sternly at Guilly he said, 'I will come along myself and take you straight back home. Do you understand?'

She nodded and Greg left the room. Guilly turned and stared at Gina

'Play with me,' she demanded in a voice uncannily like Greg's.

When Greg finally reached the stage he reprimanded Nicole.

'Now,' he said. 'I hope the two of you are in good form. We have already wasted fifteen minutes through the tantrums of your daughter Nicole, you should have left her at home. Let us not waste any more time.'

He proceeded to instruct them, guiding and criticising for an hour then looked at his watch.

'You had better have a break. Ten minutes.'

Nicole put on her wrap. 'I'll go and see if Guilly is okay,' she said.

As she went past Greg caught her arm. 'No, Nicole, I will go. Stay with Jed get a drink. You need a rest. I am sure Guilly is fine. I do not want to waste any more of my time waiting for you while you spoil her. I can envisage you bringing her up here on stage.'

'Are you angry with me,' she said.

'No of course not, but Guillese knows exactly how to twist you around her finger.'

'I would like to see her. I have worked very hard.'

'I know, but she will be quite happy, I am sure. Go with Jed – get a drink and sit down.' He kissed her, stroked her hair. 'I'll be back in a minute,' he said.

Greg found both Gina and Guilly playing with grease paint and costumes.

'I see you are winning with her Gina – another half an hour and we will release you.'

'I don't mind looking after her,' Gina said

'Nevertheless I am sure you have had enough. You may bring her on stage in half an hour.'

Greg worked Nicole and Jed without mercy until Nicole was exhausted. Then he glimpsed Gina and Guilly advancing towards the stage.

He swooped the child in his arms, kissed her and hugged her. 'Well now shrimp have you been a good girl for Gina – you may stay now.'

'Go and get changed Nicole we shall go home.' He turned to Gina. 'Are you happy to stay with Guilly during some of the rehearsals?'

'Yes Dr. Fellini,' she smiled. 'I enjoyed looking after her.'

'Good, then you had better be here at ten each morning. Perhaps Jed will see you home.'

'Yes of course,' Jed said. 'I'll get changed, come on Gina.'

Nicole emerged fully dressed and took Guilly from Greg. 'Hello ma cherie, did you like playing with Gina? I love you. We are going home now and I will play with you.'

'You will rest first Nicole.' Greg said.

Jed came back with Gina to say goodbye. 'Where do you live Gina?' He asked as they walked towards the door.

Nicole turned to watch them. 'Is Jed going with Gina?' she asked.

'He is taking her home, it is the least we can do. She has been stuck in that dressing room all morning.'

'I suppose so.' Nicole was looking forward to Jed's company.

Greg glanced at her. 'Are you objecting?'

'Of course not Gregoire, I just thought he was staying with us for lunch.'

'I'm sorry,' he said a little peeved, 'if you do not find my company sufficient for your needs.'

She put Guilly down, full of concern. 'Gregoire you know that is not true. How could you think it? It is just that after lunch you will shut yourself away in your study.'

She put her arms around him but he was not placated.

'Come, I think we should get Guillese home for her lunch, she is getting tired.'

When they arrived home Nicole wrapped her arms around him again. 'Gregoire please don't be upset or angry.'

'Why on earth should I be either?'

'But you are upset aren't you.' She pulled his face down to hers. 'You should not be thinking that I want anyone else, I just want you. I love you Gregoire.'

'Are you sure you are not getting tired of me.'

'No, oh no, I am not. Please believe me.'

He relented smiled and kissed her passionately and possessively – 'I do get a little worried sometimes my angel.'

'Gregoire, I have never, nor will I ever cause you to feel that way I wish you would believe that.'

'I do my precious. You must forgive me if sometimes I feel unsure. You are so young and very beautiful. There are so many gentlemen out there wishing they were in my shoes.'

'Nonsense Gregoire. In any case it doesn't matter – you know there will never be anyone else but you.'

Guilly was tugging at Nicole's skirt. 'Play with me Mama,' she cried.

'Alright darling in a minute.'

'I said you were to rest Nicole,' Greg said.

'Just ten minutes Gregoire please. Then we can have lunch – I will rest this afternoon and you can amuse her.'

'Alright, but you must not overdo it darling.'

When they were at lunch Nicole asked Greg, 'Does Gina have promise Gregoire?'

'She is only fifteen years old. She says she has been dancing since she was three. She has good basic knowledge but that is all. She is really keen to work with us, and works hard according to Justin.'

'Do you think you will be able to use her in the company?'

'As I said she seems keen, she could do well if she so wishes and if she wants to join the company I will be happy to take her, providing her enthusiasm doesn't wane. However at the moment I do not think she will make a ballerina. I hope I'm wrong, we shall have to wait and see. It is early days yet.'

The fact was that Greg had taken quite a benevolent attitude to Gina. She did not cringe from him like most of them and she was pretty with a pleasing nature. She was intelligent. He liked her.

'Guilly was good with her wasn't she, she must like her.'

'Guillese knew she had to behave or she would have been taken home, I would really rather you did not bring her but as I promised I will not go back on my word.'

'When the ballet starts will I be dancing all the time?'

'Nicole my love, do I detect a little reluctance here.'

'I am thinking about Guilly.'

'You will have plenty of time for Guilly, most mornings and afternoons. Ah, Nicole darling, please don't loose your enthusiasm for dancing. You were born to dance my precious.' He stoked her hair. 'There is no one remotely like you darling. You are unique. I have always known it and in this particular ballet with you and Jed so perfectly matched. Well, you will take London by storm. You will be famous worldwide. The audience already idolise you but this will be different.'

'I'm sorry darling, I did not mean that I wanted to give up the ballet. I love to dance for you. As you say it will be wonderful and I know Jed is really looking forward to it.'

'And you my love, what about you?'

'Yes. I am too.'

Justin took rehearsals most mornings. Greg interjecting his own suggestions. The dancers worked hard, even so Greg sometimes became irritated if one or other of them faltered.

Jed tended to hold back especially in the close love scenes. When Greg took rehearsals this caused him to yell at Jed.

'For God's sake boy, hold her – you are supposed to be lovers. Come on now wake up. You are going to die for each other. Let me see some evidence of that. That's better. Now we will go through that from the beginning, and remember your whole lives depend on your love for each other. And you Nicole, help him. You look as though you are going for a dental appointment. Here I'll show you. Look carefully Jed'

He took Nicole in his arms, his eyes expressing only desperate love for her. Releasing her he pushed Jed nearer.

'Try harder,' he told him.

They rehearsed until eventually Greg seemed satisfied. 'Right that's good we'll take a break now for 15 minutes.'

He went through to his office, whilst Jed and Nicole bought themselves a coffee. They were both emotionally, and physically exhausted.

'Are you okay, Nicki?' Jed asked.

'Just tired,' she sighed.

'This is difficult for me you know.' He draped his arm around her shoulder. 'You know I am in love with you. I found it hard to let myself go especially in front of Greg.'

'I think that is what he wants from you Jed, it is just a ballet.'

'Not to me it isn't . It's real.'

'Come on Jed, we are just very close that is all. I belong to Gregoire. I love him.'

'I know.' He kissed her shoulder. 'It doesn't change the fact that I also love you. But I'll give him what he wants. It will be the easiest thing in the world. So be prepared my love.'

For the whole of the following week Justin took rehearsals. Jed found it less inhibiting. He let himself go and Justin was stunned. He had never seen anything more beautiful. He praised them both.

'That is absolutely perfect, both of you. I don't think Greg will have any more complaints, now lets go through this last scene from the beginning,'

He watched them closely. This was no act on the part of the youth – he could sense it. Like the rest of the crew he had his own thoughts on Jed's feelings towards Nicole. She also was responding to Romeo's love making. He had never seen anything more realistic than this. It began to disturb him.

God, he thought – Greg must be bloody sure of his wife. If ever I saw a love sick pup it is Jed. By the time the rehearsal neared the end they were dancing with perfection, oblivious to anything or anybody.

'It's incredible. They are fantastic.'

'Yes,' Greg enthused, 'I believe this is going to be a masterpiece Justin.'

He went to the dancers. 'I am overwhelmed, extremely pleased with you both. Now we shall be able to concentrate on the rest of the ballet.'

He stood between them his arms around each of their shoulders.

'You have achieved a miracle. I really do not think we can improve on it. You may both take a couple of days off whilst Justin and I prime the rest of the dancers, and on Wednesday, I will expect the same output you produced today. You may go now.'

'When are you coming home Gregoire?' Nicole asked.

'After lunch darling. Why don't you and Jed enjoy yourselves today? And later I will take you to dinner. Justin can look after things here.'

'Please don't be too long before you come home,' she pleaded.

He smiled, hugged and kissed her. 'Run along, get changed and go home. I will be as quick as I can.'

It took Justin and Greg a whole week of bullying and nurturing to get the rest of the cast dancing to their satisfaction and another week of rigorous rehearsals before the dress rehearsal. Nicole was completely exhausted and Greg made her take more time off. He took Guilly and played with her so that Nicole was not disturbed. She amused him, acting out the simple dances Jed had taught her.

'Look Papa, I can do little Miss Muffet,' and she proceeded to act out the Nursery Rhyme.

'Very good shrimp,' he said. 'Do you know anything else?'

'Yes I can dance the fairy song.'

'Which one is that?'

She started dancing, falling over occasionally and trying to sing. Nicole came into the Nursery while she was performing. She sidled up behind Greg and threw her arms around his neck.

'Isn't she clever Gregoire? She looks so sweet doesn't she?'

'She does very well for her age. We shall have to make sure she does not become too precocious.'

'She won't. She is cute and so pretty.'

'She is the image of you my love.'

Guilly stopped her performance and ran to Nicole. 'Mama are you going to play with me?'

Greg picked her up. 'I have been playing with you for nearly two hours. I think we should take a rest now. Leave Mama alone.'

'I want her to play with me.'

'Alright darling I will play with you until tea time.'

She took her from Greg and started to run with her playing hide and seek and tag. Greg watched for a while then wandered off to his study.

Nicole and Jed needed little perfecting. Their performance was riveting, encouraging the rest of the cast to give their best. Greg took Jed and Nicole out of the evening shows for the last week of rehearsals and Nicole was very happy to be able to spend more of her time with her daughter. She loved being with her especially at bedtime. She stayed in the room with her long after time and Guilly became more and more reluctant for her to leave.

'You know darling, you should not stay so long with Guillese at bedtime. She will get too used to you indulging her.'

'Gregoire, please let me stay with her. Next week, I won't even be able to put her to bed.'

'I know my love, but you are spoiling her. Making it difficult for her and yourself. Try to leave her a little earlier each evening from tomorrow. I know it is hard for you, but we don't want her to be difficult when you are not here do we.'

'I do miss her Gregoire.'

'I know darling, but next week when the ballet opens, you will have her all day won't you. There will be no rehearsals.'

'Yes!' Nicole cheered up a little. 'Are you pleased with the ballet Gregoire?'

'It is wonderful and you and Jed are absolutely perfect. The audience will go wild - and Nicole, I worship you darling, you know that don't you. Come give me a kiss and as we are not working tonight I will take you out to dinner. So leave your daughter to Maddie and get changed in good time.'

Chapter 31

Greg's Romeo and Juliet was an immediate success. There never was a more devoted Romeo – the poignant love scenes captivated the audience, and Jed lived the part at every performance. The two young lovers stirred the emotions of the audience. Many patrons were in tears even before the tragic end.

They were so enthralled that when the last scene came to its conclusion there was a hushed silence before the applause started. Then they clapped, stamped their feet and stood up calling for the artistes over and over until the safety curtain descended. Even then they were reluctant to leave their seats. Night after night the spectacle was repeated and night after night Jed became more obsessed with his love for Nicole.

Justin watched as the ballet continued, each night witnessing the pain and sensual joy mirrored in Jed's face, and wondered whether he would be strong enough to cope with these emotions. Was Nicole aware of Jed's anguish? On stage she appeared as much in love with him as he with her. And Greg - did he realise what sort of hornet's nest he had created? Did he even care? For whenever he attended the performance he observed his hard work with extreme satisfaction. He had achieved the results he had aimed for.

At first the show ran every night for three weeks then Greg noticed Nicole wavering. Both she and Jed were exhausted, the tension never leaving them. Jed especially showed his fatigue with short bouts of temper. Nicole occasionally burst into tears.

'They need a rest Greg,' Justin told him.

'But the box office is busier than ever before. We are sold out every night and the bookings are still pouring in.'

'Both those kids need a respite. Let Matthew and Natalie take over for a couple of nights.'

'No, it would be an anti-climax. The patrons would never permit it.'

'You have to do something Greg'

'I'll close the show for a week.'

'What about the bookings'

'Cancel any after next week, we will reimburse them.'

'It will be difficult.'

'Just do it Justin.'

'You should take Nicole away for a few days.'

'I'll talk to them both, see how they feel.'

And although Greg was reluctant to see any great problem, he had to admit that Nicole was pale and listless away from the theatre and Jed was tense and short tempered. He decided to close the Theatre for a week.

Justin appealed to him. 'Greg, put something else on, or ask Matthew to take over. They are both experienced and popular dancers.'

'Alright do as you please. There will be complaints. If some want reimbursing then oblige them, it is the least we can do.'

He insisted that Jed stay with Jenny to recuperate.

'You need rest and fresh air,' he said. As Jed started to refuse he countered, 'It is an order Jed. Jenny is a good soul. You will be looked after and the sea air will do you the world of good. I want no arguments you leave in two days time.'

'Where does she live?' Jed asked.

'Bournemouth, her house is only minutes from the sea, now be a good lad and do as I say.'

But Nicole refused to leave Guilly. 'I will rest just as much as if I were away. I promise I will rest Gregoire'

'You stay in bed in the mornings and rest all day. Guilly will be looked after by Maddie and me.'

'But I need to see her, play with her sometimes, please Gregoire.'

'We'll see, but for the first day you will rest and maybe the second. Nicole you are exhausted. I want you to be recovered by next Monday. I insist I take you away at the weekend. We shall leave Guilly with Maddie.'

By the end of the week Nicole looked more rested. The fact that she was able to organise Guilly's tea and bedtimes did more for her than anything else. And on Friday Greg took her to Devon for the weekend where she was cosseted and spoiled and Greg never left her side. They returned on Sunday afternoon.

'We shall have a rehearsal tomorrow morning my love. Just to get back into the swing of things. You won't mind will you?'

'When is Jed coming back?' she asked.

'He should be back now. I'll ring him later.'

Greg could not wait to get his prodigy on stage again. He telephoned Jed and told him to be at rehearsal at ten o'clock on Monday morning.

'I hope you are rested boy. Did you have a pleasant stay with Jenny?'

'She was fantastic – like an old mother hen. I had to stop her from feeding me too much or I would have come back twice my size.'

'That would never do. But you feel better, stronger?'

'Yes. I feel fine, can't wait to start.'

'Good! You get a good night's sleep and we will see you in the morning.'

Jed would have liked to have seen Nicole before that. He had missed her. But Greg was firm in his advice of an early night. When they saw each other back stage they were a little shy, but Jed could not resist putting his arms around her.

'Oh Nicki I missed you. I wish I'd stayed with Gran instead of going to Bournemouth. I could have at least telephoned you.'

'I missed you too.' She put her arm around him, 'but you had a nice time didn't you?' she said, 'Jenny is lovely.'

'It was okay – did you miss me Nicki?'

'Of course, but we start again this evening,' she said

After rehearsal Greg insisted on taking Nicole home. 'To rest,' he said.

'But I have had a lot of rest Gregoire, I'm honestly not any more tired.'

'Nevertheless, you have a performance this evening and I want you at your best.'

The theatre was full, some standing at the back of the stalls. And as soon as the music started the audience settled themselves, a few coughs and seat adjustments and then absolute silence. As the ballet proceeded one could feel the tension in the audience. Jed was on a high – he lived, ate and slept Romeo and his performance increased in perfection. The balcony scene was a masterpiece.

Within one month Greg's ballet was the talk of the town and the theatre was booked for weeks ahead. The rest of the company became fascinated with the intensity that projected from the stage, especially when the two lovers were together.

During the day Nicole spent time with Guilly, and if Greg was around they played with the child together. Greg adored his small daughter.

The ballet was now firmly established as the most popular in London.

Greg put his arm around his wife. 'Do you feel rested my love?' he said kissing her neck several times.

'I am fine Gregoire,' she answered him.

'The ballet is a great success is it not my darling? You and Jed are superb together, absolutely perfect.'

It was still a great wrench for Nicole to leave Guilly at night so that most evenings she was a little unsettled when she reached the theatre. Jed comforted her knowing how she felt.

'Guilly is okay Nicki,' he assured her.

'I know, it is just me, the way I feel.'

Greg was reluctantly persuaded to rest Nicole and Jed for at least one performance a week.

'It will be a long run Greg.'

'They'll get tired - they won't be able to take it. Matthew and Natalie performed excellently the week they took over.'

'Very well, I suppose you are right.'

Jed would have carried on non stop but Nicole was grateful for the extra time she was able to spend with Guilly. The ballet had been running for two months, bookings were still coming in for two or three weeks ahead. The two young people were thrown together often eating out with Greg who decided more often than not to go home to monitor Guilly, relieving Maddie from the responsibility. Either Justin or Jed brought Nicole home. Greg was usually unwilling to involve himself with the small talk of the dancers. Occasionally he would collect his wife and take her out to a restaurant of his choice and Nicole was always happiest at these times. Sometimes she would look at him pleadingly, ask him to take her home with him directly after the show.

'I miss you when you are not with me,' she said 'I prefer to come back with you.'

'You are young darling,' he would say, 'you need to mix with young people sometimes, and you have Jed.'

'Yes, I suppose, but I never see you during the day – you are always either busy or out.'

'I will try to be with you more my love and I am gratified that you miss me, and still love me.'

'Of course I love you, always I will love you. I never want to be without you.'

They made love most nights and Nicole took comfort from that.

Jed became more and more preoccupied with the ballet. The audience idolized both Jed and Nicole. He began to fantasize, to see them as real life lovers. They were photographed together and often seen together, and Jed ate his heart out, for he knew that for Nicole there was no one except Greg in her world.

But she clung to him, and one matinee she drew him aside. 'Jed, may I talk to you.'

'Of course let us go into your dressing room. We have a few minutes before your call. What's up Nicki?'

He sat down next to her and looked at her, waiting for her to speak. God how he worshipped her. He knew something was bothering her, he knew everything about her. Each performance was a joy and torment for him, when he held her during the love scenes it was sheer heaven. She was his for those few hours on stage. His alone – He loved every minute and hated it when the show came to a close. She looked up at him.

'Jed,' she said tears in her eyes. 'Jed, I am pregnant again, I am so afraid.'

'Are you sure Nicki?'

'Yes, I am sure, how am I going to tell Gregoire. Oh God Jed what am I to do?'

'Nicole, you aren't afraid of Greg, surely?' She didn't answer. 'Nicki?'

'I don't know how to tell him.'

Jed knelt in front of her. Clasped her hands between his.

'He loves you Nicki, you know that. He would die for you. What are you afraid of?'

'I should have been more careful.'

'Nicki, tell him. He will be thrilled to bits.'

'I don't know'

'I'm sure of it.'

'He will be disappointed and angry. I will have to leave the ballet.' She started to cry.

'Not yet, you wouldn't have to leave for ages. And then you will come back after the baby is born, like you did with Guilly.'

He held her away from him, stared anxiously into her eyes. 'You will, won't you Nicole, you will come back?'

'I don't know.'

She cried and she thought even Jed did not understand her desire to be with her children, so how would Gregoire?

'Nicki, my sweet, Gregoire is a kind man, he loves you and he will do whatever you want. Talk to him later tonight.'

'Yes, this I must do. You must not tell him that I want to stay home – you must promise never to tell him.'

'Of course not, I won't say a word.' He dried her tears. 'He loves you,' he said again.

'But I am afraid you see. That he will not like me as much if I do not dance,' she said.

'That's nonsense, how could he not love you. That's your call, you'll have to go. Talk to me afterwards or better still, tell Gregoire'

The performance that night was more riveting than before. With Nicole unable to subdue her private emotions and Jed's compassion and love shining through. At the end a truly distraught Juliet had tears streaming down her cheeks as she realised her Romeo was dead. She knelt, and facing the audience raised the sword and stabbed herself, falling across her lover. It was the most moving scene since the ballet had commenced and the spellbound audience was crying with her as the curtain descended.

Jed was concerned for Nicole. He led her out to face the audience as they clapped their appreciation, calling for them long after they had left the stage, after several curtain calls. They had loved every moment and were reluctant to let them go.

Jed escorted Nicole back to her dressing room. 'I am going to fetch Greg,' he said.

'No, Jed, it is best not to. I am okay now, see I have stopped crying – I will wait for him as usual out front. Thank you for being so kind!'

'Oh Nicki don't you know I would do anything for you. I love you as much him.'

'Please Jed.'

'It's okay. I would never do anything to hurt either of you. I love him too - shall I wait with you?'

'No Jed. You need to change, I'll be fine.'

He kissed her forehead. 'Goodnight Nicki.'

Within minutes Greg was in the dressing room smiling and elated.

'What a performance, my beautiful one. You were absolutely brilliant. Where is Jed? I must congratulate him. I have never seen such a performance.'

He drew her in his arms kissing and hugging her. 'They adored you my darling.'

She put her arms around him, holding back her tears. She was exhausted. When he released her, she stroked his face, and wondered how he would receive her news.

'I will get dressed, could we go home tonight Gregoire, I am so tired.'

'Of course my love. You finish dressing while I talk to Jed.'

He knocked at Jed's door and went in. 'I've just come from Nicole,' he said, 'How marvellous, the performance was this evening Jed. Congratulations – you and she excelled yourselves. I'm very pleased with you both.'

'Thanks, she's tired tonight.'

'I know my boy. I'm taking her home, we shall dine there. Would you like a lift?'

'I'm going with the others but thanks.'

'Alright I'll see you tomorrow.'

She was waiting for him.

'Are you alright darling?' he said putting a protective arm around her.'

'Yes, I'm fine. I would like to go home instead of the restaurant. Do you mind Gregoire.'

'Of course not we shall eat at home, and then we shall get you into bed my precious.' He kissed her and they made their way home.

He went into the kitchen to look for some food when Maddie appeared, 'Is there anything I can do Gregoire?'

'Oh Maddie, could I impose on your good nature.'

'You want me to cook something for you. I will find something and bring it to you in the lounge. Nicole looks very pale.'

'Something very light Maddie, thank you so much. Nicole is very tired this evening.'

He stood at the lounge door watching Nicole – she was stretched out in the armchair. 'Am I working you too hard Nicole my love?'

'Oh no Gregoire. Sometimes it is a little hard, but I am alright. Gregoire you do love me don't you?'

'How can you ask me such a question? You make life worth living for me. I could not survive without you – oh yes I love you.' He pulled her on his knee, stroking her hair and kissing her.

They stayed quietly – Greg whispering words of love to her until Maddie brought in some risotto and put it on the table.

'Thank you Maddie my dear. Come darling. You must be hungry, let us eat.'

She was quiet through the meal knowing that she would have to break the news to Greg carefully. The production of Romeo & Juliet was running beyond his expectations. He would not want her to leave. She put down her fork; she could not finish the meal.

'What is it Nicole you have hardly touched the risotto – try to eat a little more.'

She toyed with the food a little longer. Then pushed her plate away. 'I can't eat any more.'

'Very well, I daresay you are overtired.'

'No, I am, I mean, I'd like to talk Gregoire.'

'Alright – I have to sort something out in the study. You sit in here ma cherie and wait for me. I will not be long. When he did not appear again in half an hour, she went to the office.'

'Gregoire, I am sorry, I have to talk to you. I am sorry to disturb you.'

Immediately he put the paper aside and was beside her, his arms encircling her. 'What is it my love? Is something bothering you?'

'Yes Gregoire there is.'

'Oh darling you have such a serious expression, surely it can't be that bad.'

'It is, Gregoire. I am pregnant again. I am so sorry.'

He was silent for only a couple of seconds. 'Do you not want to be pregnant Nicole?'

She did not answer this.

'Am I to understand darling, that you do not want this baby?'

'I do, but….'

'But what Nicole?'

'I thought you might be upset or angry with me.'

'Ah Nicki, Nicki, when have I ever been angry with you. How could you think I would be anything but pleased – are you sure?'

'Yes I am sure.'

'Well then. I shall leave these tiresome papers and you and I will celebrate. I love you darling.'

'What about the ballet?'

'What about the ballet!'

'I mean, it will be a trouble to you training someone else.'

'You must not worry your pretty head about that my love. In any case you will not have to give up yet. We have a little time before that happens. Of course it will be impossible to continue this production with anyone else – it would be impossible to replace you. You know darling you've made history these last few weeks. The public have been mesmerised, absolutely, spellbound by your performance. We shall honour the present bookings then finish'

'Couldn't Natalie take over?'

'There could never be anyone to emulate my beautiful Juliet. No we shall finish. Perhaps at a later stage, when you are ready, we could repeat it. We shall have to see.' He picked her up, and hugged her. 'I am so delighted my beloved – how could you have thought otherwise?'

'Jed said you would be pleased.'

He held her away from him.

'You told Jed, before me.' He was consumed with jealousy.

'I didn't mean to. But he was there and I was worried.'

'You could have waited for me could you not!'

'I am sorry, please don't be upset Gregoire.'

'I am not upset a little disappointed that is all, still never mind.'

'I'm sorry – I didn't want you to be hurt.'

'He kissed her. I am not hurt,' he lied. 'Why shouldn't you tell him? Come my beloved - he opened a bottle of champagne and filled two glasses. 'I am very happy, Nicole, very happy.'

She smiled, 'You really do not mind about the baby?'

'Mind, I am thrilled. It's wonderful and she will be company for Guillese.'

'Would you not like a boy?'

'Whatever comes is fine with me, especially if they all look like you my love. Now let us drink to our good fortune and then we must get a little rest. I expect Jed was pleased wasn't he?'

'Yes he was, but I didn't say much to him. I'm so sorry.'

He stroked her hair. 'It's alright Nicole Jed is family – you love him don't you?'

'I love you Gregoire, but Jed, yes I love Jed too. He is always my friend.' She hugged his arm. 'You are truly pleased Gregoire. I am sorry I told Jed first – tell me again that you are happy.'

'Nicole, I am absolutely ecstatic. Go to bed now. I love you so much.'

It was not often now that Nicole mentioned her parents, but she could not help thinking about them especially now.

'I wish Mama could see Guilly, and I could tell her about the baby.'

'Do you want to write to them?'

'Perhaps I will a little later. Gregoire would you take me to France with Guilly? Maybe when they see her they will be happy for us.'

'Is that what you really would like?'

'I would.'

'You know they would not want me there.'

'Guilly is three years old, surely they would forgive and accept us if they actually saw her.'

'Alright my love, we can but try. As soon as the ballet concludes, we shall go to France. We shall try once again. However if they have not changed their attitude you must promise me that you will not be too upset. I couldn't bear to see you hurt again.'

'I'd like to go Gregoire.'

'Very well. We shall try.'

'Thank you. I do love you. I will always love you.'

She looked up at him, her beautiful eyes full of adoration and his heart turned over at the sight of this beautiful girl who loved him so completely.

Greg and Justin set about bringing Romeo & Juliet to a close.

'You don't want to continue with Natalie?'

'No I think it would not work.'

'They are so perfect together – so young. It could never be the same. Perhaps much later we could do it again. I don't know. But not now. We should stage something light for a few nights. Something completely different.'

'I am taking Nicole and Guillese to France as soon as the ballet is finished,' Greg informed Justin.

'Is that wise? What with her mother's attitude still…'

'It is what she wishes. I shall take her.'

Chapter 32

Since Jed had warned Daniel off he had not troubled Nicole too much except for the odd wink or a quick pat in her rear as she passed.

However as the weeks went by, he started grabbing her, putting his arm round her. She suffered his advances until one evening before the performance he placed his hand on her breast, holding her.

'Please Daniel let me go,' she pleaded struggling in his arms.

He kissed her passionately before he released her. 'Christ Nicki, you are really something,' he said.

She pushed him away, but he set out planning his approach to win her over. He knew she could not be as easy as some of them, but he was confident of his success in the long run. Not many resisted him for long.

He left her alone for a while until one evening he approached her, 'Hi Nicki, come and have coffee with me after the show or I'll buy you dinner.'

'I have to wait for Gregoire,' she replied. She smiled at him and continued to the stage.

'Oh come on please.'

'I'm sorry Daniel – I have to be on stage now.'

He stood aside for her. 'I'll have a snack ready for you during break.'

'No. I am with Jed then.'

He shrugged then walked away. But he was not about to give up. The following night he watched as she left Jed to go to her dressing room, before the evening performance. He knocked on the door.

'Come in,' she called thinking it was one of the girls come to borrow something.

He went in and shut the door. 'Hi Nicki,' he said smiling.

'Daniel, what are you doing here? I have to get ready.'

He went to put his arms around her. 'Com on Nicki, you know I'm crazy about you.'

'Please Daniel go away. You should not be here. I am already late.'

He bent to kiss her. 'Just a kiss Nicki.'

'Please go Daniel.' She started to panic.

'Okay,' he said. 'Have dinner with me. Give me a time.'

'I can't. I do like you Daniel but I can't do what you are asking.'

'Why not, come on don't be such a prude. The other girls don't mind. Honestly, you are such an innocent. You are stuck with that old guy. You haven't tasted life at all. You and I could have a great time. You don't know what you are missing.'

'Let me go Daniel,' she cried. 'Please.'

'You must like me a bit, don't you?'

She didn't answer, but her eyes filled. She pulled away from him and rushed to the door. She heard Jed calling.

She straightened up. 'Go now please Daniel. Jed is calling – I am late.'

He stole a long kiss before he swept out of the room. She washed her face and proceeded to the stage. Jed joined her.

'There are omelettes, if you'd like some we'll have to go to the canteen now or they will be gone. Good God what's wrong. Are you okay,' he said.

'Yes.'

'Is it the baby?'

'No I just feel a bit faint,' she lied. 'It's hot in here. I'm alright, come on let's get something before all the best stuff disappears.

Jed settled for the special omelettes and found a lone table.

'I'm not hungry,' she said.

He put his arms around her. 'Tell me what's wrong Nicole. I can read you like a book. Tell me.'

'Nothing is wrong. Jed I am going to ask Greg if I can leave the ballet soon.'

'Why, why Nicki?'

'I want to stay home with Guilly. I don't think that he will mind. He was thrilled about the baby.'

'But he won't want you to leave yet, not until the end of the month. The ballet is closing then isn't it.'

'Oh god I don't know. You think he will make me carry on?'

'No, I don't think that. He won't make you do anything. He'll do whatever you want'

'You mean I will disappoint him.'

'Oh Nicki, you are putting words in my mouth. Talk to Greg. He worships you. He will do what you want I think.'

But when Greg took her home she had not the courage to speak to him. When she undressed she touched her stomach. The baby was growing. Soon she would have to stop, she would start to show. Her costume would be too tight. Another few weeks would not be so bad. She could cope for another few weeks.

Greg took to staying with Nicole most evenings. Leaving Maddie to deal with Guilly, and Daniel became bolder during the show. She always managed to ward him off but she was disturbed by him. Maybe I should tell Jed she thought. She didn't want to tell Greg. He would kill Daniel. However, she had witnessed the other girls, they seemed to manage him, and I ought to be able to do the same she determined. She decided not to be so feeble. Sometimes she was so nervous when Greg picked her up from the dressing room that he was concerned and asked her if she was unwell. But she assured him everything was fine. Then one night as they lay in bed she said, 'Gregoire, I am getting very big now. I will be too big soon for Juliet.'

He bent his head to kiss her stomach. 'Yes I know – I will speak to Justin. We will terminate the production and then you must stay at home and rest.'

'You will take the ballet off?'

'Yes my love. I do not think that the public will take kindly to another Juliet just yet. It would be best to terminate. It is best to replace the ballet rather than you.'

'I am sorry to have to do this Gregoire.'

'Don't be silly. You have worked very hard. It's time you had a rest.'

'What about Jed?'

'Oh yes, Jed. Well I think it would be better for Jed to keep working. Take his mind off Romeo or rather Juliet.'

'You know?'

'Know what my precious.' He kissed her possessively. 'That he is in love with you. I have known that from the beginning. But you are mine aren't you darling?'

She was stunned and stayed silent.

'Nicole,' he whispered, 'you have not tired of me.'

'Nicki!' He switched on the light, leaned over and looked into her eyes. 'You still love me?'

'I will always love you Gregoire.'

'What about Jed?'

'No! I love you.'

'I hope so Nicki, because I would die without you.'

She wound her arms about him. 'I will never love anyone else – you do believe me?'

'Yes I believe you, but half the world is in love with you.'

'You are my world Gregoire. Make love to me. No one will ever touch me but you. There could never be anyone else.'

He closed his eyes trying not to doubt her and drew her close. Had he taken a risk throwing them together for so long and in such an intense situation. A moment of terror invaded his subconscious. 'What if she was beginning to have feeling for Jed? She had been very nervy of late.'

He took her face in his hands. 'You are still mine are you not my love?' He kissed her eyes, cheeks and neck, his lips searing over her then he made love to her possessively violently, his hands entangling her hair.

'You will never stop loving me my precious one will you,' he murmured caressing her roughly.

Then he realised he might have hurt her, kissed her tenderly once again. 'I am sorry Nicole, I am so sorry. I did not mean to hurt you.' He brushed her bruised lips with kisses.

She understood. 'It's alright Gregoire you did not hurt me. You must never worry, you are my only love – I have always loved you.'

'Nicki my love, what would I do without you and he gathered her in his arms his peace of mind slowly but surely returning.'

The next day he took her aside.

'Listen my love, do you think you can carry on a little longer. At the end of the month we are closing this show. Could you do that for me darling. There are only two and a half weeks more and then you will have your well earned rest.'

'Of course Gregoire.'

'Are you sure?'

'Yes I am sure.'

'Alright then, but you must promise me that if you feel it is too much then you will tell me. Promise me.'

'Yes I promise.'

'You are so good, so beautiful. I am the luckiest man alive.'

Nicole continued and her confidence in herself returned. She was happy and her Juliet was more poignant with Jed's Romeo becoming more dramatic with the knowledge that his fantasy was coming to an end.

Daniel still harassed Nicole, but with the knowledge that soon she would be safe at home with Guilly away from his attentions she managed to cope, even took his attentions with good humour, laughing as she had seen the other girls do at his suggestive comments. It was the worst thing she could have done, her change of mood encouraged him, spurred him on. Jed watched with concern.

'It's okay Jed. He doesn't matter, not now.'

'Be careful Nicole. Keep clear of him if possible. I don't trust him.'

'Jed, I am more worried about Guilly. Gregoire telephoned earlier. She isn't well, Dr. Maxwell says she might have tonsillitis.'

'I'm sorry.'

Greg was a little late meeting her this evening. She was waiting in the foyer with Jed.

'I am sorry I'm late darling. Thanks Jed.'

'How is she?'

'Now Nicole. You are not to worry. Guilly has a slight fever. Dr. Maxwell says it is nothing serious. Just a heavy cold and sore throat. She will be fine in a few days. He left some medicine for her.'

'She hasn't got tonsillitis.'

'Apparently not.'

'You have to tell me Gregoire.'

'Paul is coming to see her tomorrow. He says it is not serious.'

'I should be with her.'

'You can be soon. We do not want to wake her now do we? And listen darling, I am just as capable of looking after her while you are at the theatre. Soon you will be home for good.'

'Yes only one more week.

She could not resist peeking into the room as soon as they arrived home.

'She doesn't look very well,' she said.

'She is just a little flushed. She will be better in the morning. I am sure.'

'Poor baby.'

When they were in bed she kissed her husband. 'Gregoire I want to ask you something.'

'What my love.'

'When the baby is here, would you mind if I stayed home and looked after both of them myself.'

'Of course you will. You will want to feed the baby yourself so you will be home for quite a long time.'

'I mean, I mean…'

'What my precious one.'

'Gregoire, I mean. I want to stay like a proper Maman.'

'You mean you wish to give up the ballet?' Greg was dumfounded.

'She did not answer.

'Nicole, my darling. Let us take one step at a time. You will be having a very long rest. I'm sure that you will want to dance again. You love to dance. When the baby is a little bigger, three or four months old, then we can see. Surely you can't mean that you wish to give up forever.'

She looked at him and smiled, saw the consternation in his eyes and she could not disappoint him.

'No, of course not forever.'

Nicole as soon as you are ready to dance again I will choreograph something very special for you, a solo maybe if you wish. He took her face between his hands.

'You will dance for me again Nicki won't you?' He pleaded.

'Of course I will Gregoire.' She put her arms around him, and dismissed all thoughts of leaving the ballet. 'It will be nice to have two babies won't it Gregoire.'

'Wonderful.'

He would have liked to broach the subject of employing a nanny for them, but remembered his promise and refrained. However a nanny would have to be discussed at some point. They could not expect Maddie to be responsible for a small baby as well as Guilly. He hoped Nicole would agree to come back as soon after the child was born. Her attitude disturbed him. He wanted her back on stage, but not against her will and he did not want her to dwell on the desire to stay home. He could not envisage his productions without her. He started to talk about other things encouraging her to talk about her childhood on the farm in France hoping it would take her mind off the problem.

Far into the night she talked delighting him with her chatter.

She tried to talk to him about the happy times she had spent as a child. 'I used to help feed the animals with Pascal and sometimes Grand-père would take me to market, but I always felt sad when they took the calves from their mothers. Guillese would love to go there. You will take us Gregoire?'

'I said I would darling. When the ballet has concluded. You can have a short rest. Perhaps a week at home and then we shall go. There, you have something to look forward to.'

'Yes, it will be wonderful.'

'And you will dance for me again Nicole?'

'Yes I will when the baby is bigger.'

'Thank you my darling – but please try not to be too upset if they still feel the same.'

'It is a long time now, I think they must have forgiven us by now.'

Greg had his doubts. 'Maybe,' he said. 'You are not sorry you married me.'

'Oh no Gregoire I love you. I would never be sorry about that, but I wish Mama had not been so horrid. I thought she loved me.'

'Of course she loves you Nicole. It is me with whom she is angry.'

'She does not know how good you are, how wonderful you are.'

'Perhaps later, if you wish we could buy a place in France. We could take some time away from the theatre and London some times.'

'I would like that.'

'Then that is what we shall do.'

'I'd love that Gregoire,' she said kissing him, winding her arms around him, but she knew he was concerned.

She knew he wanted her to dance again as soon as possible after the baby was born, and she vowed never to disappoint him. Guilly had recovered very well from her chest infection and Nicole spent the days playing with her daughter, always reluctant to leave when it was time for her to go to the theatre, but she was happy and excited that she would soon be home for a long while.

When she left for the last night of the show she clasped Guilly to her.

'Mama is going to stay home with you ma cherie, we shall play games. Go to the park, perhaps with Jed and I will be here to put you to bed, won't that be nice?'

'Will you put me to bed tonight?' Guilly pleaded.

'Tomorrow darling. Tonight Papa will stay and bathe you.'

'I want you to.'

I know darling but tomorrow. I will be here all day and night and the next day and the next.'

'And lots of nexes.'

'Yes ma cherie – lots and lots.'

She kissed and hugged her daughter until Maddie came to fetch her, while Greg drove his wife to the theatre.

'I'll pick you up later darling,' he said. 'It is the last performance. Would you like to go out for dinner, or would you prefer to dine at home?'

'Do you want to go out Gregoire?'

'I want to do whatever you want.'

'Then I would prefer to come home. I can cook something.'

Greg smiled, 'No need for that my love. Maddie will prepare something tonight if you want it.'

'That would be nice,' she said.

Chapter 33

The theatre was overflowing, patrons were standing at the back of the stalls spilling down the sides into the isles.

There was an atmosphere of love and affection from the audience for their idols. The hubbub and coughing ceased as soon as the curtain went up and the whole of the auditorium was still as they watched the dancers. There was absolute silence through the palace scenes and the fighting between the Montagues and the Capulets right through to the climax with the sad poignant deaths of the star crossed lovers, danced so realistically, so exquisitely by the two artists.

There was the usual hush for a few seconds before the applause, but what an applause.

The whole audience was hyped up knowing that it was the last performance. After six curtain calls they were still applauding and calling for them to appear again and again.

Eventually the exhausted dancers left for the dressing rooms. Still they called, stamping and clapping. As Jed and Nicole came through, Justin turned them back.

'One more time,' he said.

Elated and exhausted the two 'lovers' faced the audience once again. The roar that came from the audience was deafening but they were satisfied. Tears were streaming down their cheeks as the safety curtain was lowered.

Chapter 34

Nicole had found the last scene with Jed, intense, disturbing and emotional. She removed her costume and slipped on a white satin robe, sat in the dressing room and proceeded to massage her legs.

She was pleased the ballet had come to a close. Slowly she walked to the wardrobe. She took out her street clothes ready to put on after she had removed her make up. She stood looking in the mirror when the door opened and Daniel stood inside.

Nicole turned, 'Daniel, what are you doing here? I am undressed.'

'And very charming you look,' her replied as his eyes gloated over her.

He moved towards her and quickly clasped her in his arms.

'Oh Nicki you are the most beautiful creature on gods earth. Why are you married to that old man?' He started to kiss her.

'No, please no Daniel, please go back to your dressing room.'

'Come on Nicki, you don't really want me to do that do you?'

She struggled in his grasp. 'Please go,' she cried.

'This is the last chance we'll get Nicki. You won't be back for a while, will you?'

'I'm pregnant Daniel,' she pleaded. 'Please go back.'

'Oh yes I know, makes you all the more desirable, hasn't he told you that?'

'Please, please let me go.'

She tried to turn away, but he was too strong for her. He pushed her against the wall.

'Nicki,' he whispered, nibbling her ear, forcing her lips apart. 'I bet you've never been with anyone else but him have you.

He pushed the gown off her shoulders kissing her neck and breasts. Then he lifted her on to the little sofa tearing the rest of the gown from her.

'Oh Nicki, you are beautiful. He doesn't deserve such a jewel.'

He kissed her body her arms, his hands probing her stroking her thighs. When he began to prize her legs apart that was when she screamed.

He covered her mouth with his hand. He crashed his mouth on to hers prying her lips apart.

'Don't be daft Nicki,' he pleaded between kisses, 'all the other girls find me a very satisfactory lover, you will too.'

'No,' she cried, 'Gregoire will kill you.'

'Oh! But you are not likely to tell him are you.'

She kicked and screamed afresh.

'My! What a firebrand you are. I didn't know you had it in you.'

He held her more firmly, his lips again on her, and in seconds he was on top of her. Then with one last desperate attempt she bit his lips at the same time tried to push him away, kicking him hard. He fell off her, cursing her and dabbing his lips – then she screamed for Jed.

Jed heard the commotion and came running. He could not believe his eyes. He rushed over to Nicole draping her gown around her shivering body.

'Are you okay Nicole?' He turned to Daniel, 'What the hell are you doing here? What have you done to her?'

"Nothing – she was enjoying it.'

Jed was aghast. 'You filthy pig,' he yelled and lashed out at him, knocking him on the floor.

'What the hell.' Daniel was genuinely surprised.

Jed bent over him and grabbed him. 'If I ever see you near Nicole again or any of the other girls I'll kill you. Now get out of here.'

'Want her for yourself do you. Everyone knows you have the hots for her. You just don't have the guts.'

'Shut your foul mouth,' Jed retorted. 'You heard what I said – get out. We'll deal with you later.'

'Okay, okay I'm going,' Daniel said holding up his hands to ward of any future blows. 'She's not worth bothering over.'

'Keep thinking that way,' Jed warned.

'Are you okay Nicole. I'm sorry I didn't hear you earlier.'

'It's not your fault. Thank god you came when you did. It's my own fault.'

'No it isn't. It's entirely his. I'll ask Justin to get rid of him.'

'No no, please Jed. Don't tell anyone else what happened. If Gregoire got to know it would be dreadful.'

'Did he touch you, did he hurt you Nicki?'

She shuddered, shook her head. 'I feel ashamed, contaminated. I do not want Gregoire to hear about it please Jed.'

'But he should know Nicole. He should be chucked out.'

'No I'm okay. I encouraged Daniel. I was nice to him, but only because I knew I was leaving.'

'What do you mean? You let him come in here.'

'No of course not. He just appeared but I let him flirt with me so you see it was my own fault.'

'Nicki of course it wasn't – don't be so silly.'

'You must promise me that Gregoire will never know, promise me. You must never tell Gregoire or Justin.'

When Jed stared at her and did not answer she became hysterical.

'Alright, alright I promise,' Jed said. 'Don't worry – I won't say a thing. Get dressed love. I'll wait with you until Greg gets here.'

'You will keep your promise won't you Jed?' she pleaded.

'I swear.' Jed puts his arm around her. 'I'll wait for you outside.'

She was trembling, what would she have done if Jed had not heard her? She shuddered. She had never wanted anyone else but Greg. No one had ever touched her but Greg and now Daniel had put his hands all over her and would have raped her, she was sure. She could not get the thought out of her head. He had ruined the climax of her last performance and she felt as though she had been violated.

'Oh God, I can't bear to think of what might have happened. I should never have indulged Daniel.'

When she was dressed, she packed her things away. Tomorrow she would be home with Guilly. Home for a long time. She tried to feel happy about that but she could not. The thought of Greg even accidentally hearing about it made her tremble again.

Slowly she came out of the dressing room and Jed led her to the foyer – to wait for Greg. Suddenly she felt sick, she could not breathe. Her stomach was heaving, her head spinning. She darted forward, away from Jed and ran through the crowds, out into the street.

Jed ran after her, 'Hey Nicki wait. Where are you going?'

She did not hear him. She ran blindly, she felt stifled, she needed air. The theatre was so hot. Her heart was racing, at the thought of her parents' rejections of her, of Guilly being unwell without her, of the new baby and worst of all the feeling of Daniel's lips on her and his hands and body all over her.

It was raining. She was grateful for the cool water on her face. Then she heard Jed calling. She leaned against the lamppost, her mind slowly beginning to clear. As she turned to retrace her steps she stumbled, her foot slipping.

She gasped as she saw the huge truck looming towards her. Too shocked to move she put up her hands to shield herself, then she screamed.

Jed saw it hit her, crashing her head against the curb. She lay still and bleeding.

Chapter 35

The truck screeched to a halt. The driver saw the look of terror on the girl's face as she fell, arms outstretched, against the front of the vehicle then scream as she bounced back, hitting the lamp post.

'God almighty,' he said, 'What on earth was she doing? I didn't stand a chance; she keeled over straight in front of me.'

Someone took his arm and sat him on the step of his truck.

'It's ok mate, it wasn't your fault.'

The rain beat down on the girl's face; she looked up for a second.

'I'm sorry Jed,' she said, 'Do not tell Gregoire about Daniel.'

She pulled his sleeve, 'Please Jed, he must not know.'

'Don't worry Nicki, you'll be fine, the ambulance will be here soon.'

'Promise me Jed.'

'Okay, I promise - keep still now.'

She was shivering; her face ashen - Jed removed his jacket and gently, reverently covered her.

She tried to rouse herself, clutching at Jed's shirt sleeve 'Look after her Jed, look after Guilly.'

'Of course I will, but you are going to be fine, Nicki.'

'And Gregoire.'

'Of course I will.'

She was staring him - why was she talking like this, she had just cut her head. But as he looked down at her, he saw the blood gushing from her head and seeping from her mouth. He began to be afraid. People were rushing from the theatre, some crossing the road to join the crowd at the scene of the accident.

The rain continued relentlessly - Jed took Nicki's hand, raised it to his lips.

'Don't die, Nicki,' he whispered. 'Please don't die.' But Nicki had already lost consciousness, blood still trickling from her mouth, mingling with the rain in the pavement.

Justin appeared amidst the sounds of police and ambulance sirens. He looked with compassion at Jed, crouched beside Nicole.

'Come, Jed.' He helped him up from the ground. 'Let the paramedics take over – there's nothing we can do now.'

END OF PART 1

About the Author

Peta has been writing since she was quite young. Born in Teddington, one of five siblings, she was educated at a tiny private church school in Putney [fees three shillings per week] and then a technical college in Wandsworth. Unlike her siblings she was never interested in higher education and could not wait until the end of the day when she could indulge in "childish scribblings" as her parents called it. Later she dabbled in a course with the London school of Art, then worked for Vogue Fashions selling dress patterns in a strange little office in a London back street. She married when she was twenty one and they produced four children who, between them, presented them with twelve fantastic grandchildren. There has been tragedy but also much love and happiness over the years. Peta would like to thank her eldest son Clive for taking the time to promote both parts of Heaven Promises No Favours, which together make up the first of a trilogy of stories set amongst the richly drawn characters of the ballet world.